A THOUSAND SMALL WISHES

Most of **Sandra Hall**'s career has been spent as a feature writer and critic contributing to newspapers, magazines and radio. She has worked as *The Australian*'s television critic and its literary editor and, for more than 20 years, has been *The Bulletin*'s film critic. In 1994, Hall was the recipient of The Pascall Prize for Film and Television Criticism. *A Thousand Small Wishes* is her first novel.

A THOUSAND SMALL WISHES

Sandra Hall

ALLEN & UNWIN

© Sandra Hall, 1995

This book is copyright under the Berne Convention.
No reproduction without permission.

First published in 1995 by
Allen & Unwin Australia Pty Ltd
9 Atchison Street, St Leonards NSW 2065 Australia

Publication of this title was assisted by The Australia Council,
the Federal Government's arts funding and advisory body.

National Library of Australia
Cataloguing-in-Publication entry:

Hall, Sandra, 1942– .
  A thousand small wishes.

ISBN 1 86373 997 1.

I. Title.

A823.3

Set in 10/12 pt Palatino by DOCUPRO, Sydney
Printed by Australian Print Group, Maryborough, Victoria

10 9 8 7 6 5 4 3 2 1

'Hollywood is the mass unconscious—scooped up as crudely as a steam shovel scoops up the depths of a hill, and served on a helplessly empty screen. A thousand small wishes are symbolically satisfied . . .'

Parker Tyler, *The Hollywood Hallucination*

JUHU BEACH

The young Indian in the seat next to hers had a knobbly linen jacket, a caramel-smooth voice and wraparound glasses with opaque lenses in cobalt blue, which he wore for most of the flight. He was in the video business and was returning to Bombay after a visit to Los Angeles to see what was what. He was telling her about it when he broke off to say what nice eyes she had.

She guessed instantly that he was not making a pass and she was right.

'Do you wear lenses?' he asked, peering into her irises.

She shook her head. His own eyes were the friendly brown of English teapots. He removed the glasses to show her—very slowly—like someone in a film preparing to reveal to the audience some dreadful disfigurement.

'All Indians have such eyes,' he said, his voice deepening. 'I wish so much that they were clear like yours.'

He told her how much he disapproved of the casual way she was approaching her arrival in India. 'Did you not think to make a booking?'

Without waiting for an answer, he took out his wallet and produced a business card, on the back of which he wrote a name and address—the Oasis Hotel at Juhu Beach—saying gravely: 'You will like it there, Katharine. It has a pool and a disco and it attracts a very nice crowd. The film stars go to Juhu Beach.'

So Juhu Beach it was. Because of the film stars.

She was given a room on the seventh floor with a balcony and a sidelong view of the beach and its merry-go-round with painted horses. Directly across from her window was a Holiday Inn perched above an expanse of dusty ground, home to a nest of shanties roofed with thatch, rusty iron and some mud-caked palm fronds weighted down with bricks. There were two goats, three boys washing at a well, a midden studded with banana skins and eggshells, and a shiny blue motor bike. There was also a strange four-legged creature lying belly up in the dust. Without wishing to, Kate stared uneasily at this mystery. Only when it waved a languorous paw was she able to look away.

The room had tide marks of mould and a gritty carpet, and the hall was permeated by a rich and complex odour. When she went downstairs, instead of film stars she found Russian conference delegates and American missionaries, and the pool was empty for its annual clean-up—ten men were crouched on its floor, scraping off patches of green muck with chisels. None of this mattered when she saw the garden.

It ran on to the beach and was bordered by a stone retaining wall where people drew up chairs, as if at the circus. A camel loped along the shore, a snake-charmer performed nearby and the fires of the food vendors' stalls flared in the soft light. She stayed until the sky darkened and the strolling figures turned into silhouettes and all that was left of the sun was a smoky orange band above the horizon.

She spent the next morning in the garden, reading. The Russians were there, too, pink and fleshy in tiny swimsuits, tossing a volleyball inscribed 'He-man'. Becoming bored with that, they decided to go swimming, disobeying the guidebooks' warnings about the undesirable things to be caught in Bombay waters. As a uniformed guard unlocked a gate in the retaining wall, they bounded on to the sand like blond labradors.

Kate went through too, lured by the sight of a boy swimming with his horse, its dark neck arching above the pewter sea. Before she could focus her camera, she heard the voice.

'Hello, Madame.'

The tone was singsong and knowing. It took Kate back to

childhood and made her feel as if caught in an unauthorised act. Its owner was a small boy. 'Lovely picture, Madame.' He pointed at the horse, waiting while she took the photograph, and fell into step with her as she walked along the sand. 'Bombay that way,' he said pleasantly. 'Chowpatty Beach.'

'I know.' She smiled and gazed out to sea.

'Look, Madame. Look.' He was smiling up at her, the fingers of one hand pressing the middle finger of the other backwards so that it lay improbably flat against the knuckles.

She did as she was meant to and gave him a rupee. 'Thank you, Madame.' He flashed another white-toothed smile. Already more boys were converging, as well as a gaunt old man and a snake-charmer. Up the beach, the unencumbered Russians were returning to base. Reluctantly, she headed after them, magisterially handing out the last of her money as she went. The old man was still following, rubbing papery fingers together and murmuring 'Baksheesh', when the gate clanged shut behind her. A loud, sharp, reverberating clang, shaming in its finality.

For the rest of the day she sat and read in the garden. The next morning was the same. After lunch she decided to go into the city.

The desk clerk, friendly and well-meaning, had said: 'You must take the train. The taxi is charging you too much. Take the slow train and travel in the ladies' compartment.'

In the street, her nerve failed and she hailed a taxi.

It was different on the way back. The crowds buoyed her up and she went with the tide to Churchgate Station.

The ladies' compartment was not hard to find. She followed three plump matrons in silks and chiffon. There were plenty of seats, and at first the multi-coloured saris and kurtas and the food vendors swaying through the aisles made her feel as if she were sitting in a field of butterflies.

The sensation was short-lived. As the compartment began to fill, all that was delicate and feminine about the scene vanished, replaced by the hoydenish spirit of a schoolyard of uncontrollables. There was a raucous race for the last few empty seats, the boisterous winners' buttocks smoothly sliding into place to leave the losers tottering back to trample all over their neighbours' feet. And at the third station, the beggar woman got on.

Like the old man on the beach she was thin and dusty, but this time there was no sidling, no whispering, no humbleness at all. She was all jutting angles, a swooping figure with long, sinewy arm outstretched. She had with her a small boy whose head was bald and scabby. Kate gave him a few crumpled one-rupee notes, wishing she hadn't when the woman advanced on her with a glint in her eye and a wolfish smile. The smile was eloquent. There was no disputing it. It said: 'You owe me.'

Kate got out her wallet and passed over a note, which was instantly snatched up and waved in a parody of a victory salute.

The compartment was now so crowded that she couldn't see through the windows. Shamefully, she started to panic. A woman nursing a sack of oranges was gazing at her with clinical interest. 'Santa Cruz,' the woman said as the train started to slow. 'The next stop is Santa Cruz.'

Rising to her feet, Kate found herself wedged in a solid block made up of what may well have been every woman in India. She tried to push forward. Later she might feel shocked by the malice with which she used her elbows. Now she was just determined. Useless to tell herself that if she missed this station there would be another. In her head, the train was going on forever and she with it, destined to face at every stop the same fearful scramble for air.

The train slowed to a crawl, then stopped. The doors opened and a surge of bodies forced her forward. Still short of the opening, she was stalled by a competing crowd trying to get on. Rushing by her right shoulder was the hawk-nosed profile of a young girl, wild-eyed, mouth wide open in a rebel yell. The girl swept by as the wave took Kate up and dumped her, staggering, on to the platform.

She swung upright and in the movement her bag was dislodged from her shoulder and lost from sight. At the same moment her voice returned. 'Stop,' it shouted into the air for the crowd had evaporated. It was no longer a force, inhuman and all enveloping. There were only individuals, moving routinely about their business. She scanned the platform desperately.

'Madame.'

The intonation reminded her of the boy on the beach, inducing the same unspecified guilt. Turning, she saw the woman of the oranges.

The woman was still curious, still intent. Kate might have been the latest case of some increasingly common, though as yet unnamed, disease. 'In India,' the woman whispered, handing over the lost bag, 'you must be holding on very tight.'

By the time she reached her hotel room again, she was exhausted and fell asleep with her clothes on. She woke in the dark from a dream of piercing sweetness so thoroughly infused with memories of good times gone by that she lay stunned by it. Shakily, she sat up, turning to the window.

The Holiday Inn's neon sign cast a lunar light on the wasteland of dust and corrugated iron, making it seem so alien and abandoned that the thought of no one knowing where she was, so intoxicating only hours before, now made her sweat with panic. She switched on the room's two lamps which were no help at all, surrounding her with unfriendly shadows.

The bathroom was at least brighter but the news from the spotty mirror was not encouraging. She looked more or less as she had expected to. Her eyes were dull, her face was pasty and infinitely depressing in its inability to surprise.

Back in the bedroom, she found the scissors beneath a pile of underwear in her bag. At first she hacked away carelessly, taking hanks of the straight, shoulder-length hair in one hand and sawing with the other, but as it fell around her feet, forming a tufty mat on the cracked tiles, she slowed down, shaping it carefully at neck and forehead into . . . what? A cap? A helmet? Helmet. That was it. Staring blearily into the mirror, she took comfort from the word.

By the time she was finished it was ten o'clock. She swallowed two Valium and lay back on the bed, still in her clothes.

When she stirred again it was to a rhythmic thud, which sounded in her sleep as drumbeats.

'Madame, Madame!'

She staggered to the door and opened it to the desk clerk of the night before. He gazed open-mouthed at her hair.

'Miss Conroy . . . we are telephoning your room for a long time. Such a long time that we are becoming worried.' She looked at her watch.

'Damn.'

To his distress, she banged her head very hard and very deliberately against the door.

PART ONE

CHAPTER ONE

1

As Matt emerged from the Taj Mahal Hotel's lift, he was greeted by the sight of Hunter peering over the banisters of the grand staircase. Hunter heard him coming and flicked him a glance, calling him over. It was the most economical of gestures. A smile may have been included. Then again it may not. Matt was prepared to extend the benefit of the doubt.

A buzz of voices wafted up from below. Matt looked down to see a dozen people trying to manoeuvre a forty-foot length of carpet around a bend. A handsome gilt mirror was in danger of being wrenched from the wall and the shouting, tugging carriers darted back and forth, redistributing the weight. Finally, mysteriously, something gave and the great sausage moved around as smoothly and majestically as a liner at sea. The shouting stopped; there was a moment of profoundly self-conscious silence succeeded by a belated outburst of shushing, its sibilance pursuing Matt and Hunter along the hall.

Matt was apprehensive. He already knew enough about Hunter's working methods to suspect that he was thinking of a way to incorporate the carpet into the script. India was a constant temptation to Hunter. He seemed to be trying to get it all up on the screen. The whole teeming landscape.

But he was wrong. Hunter had something more important on his mind.

'Crisis,' he snapped as he loped ahead with the key to his room. 'Our star's gone missing.'

'Which one?'

Hunter didn't answer. After letting them into the room, he opened the connecting door to the next suite and disappeared inside. Matt could hear him shouting. 'Charlie. Where the hell are you?' A moment later he was back. 'Charlie's in the shower. He's always in the shower. To hell with him.'

A lunch tray was laid under the window. Hunter poured coffee for Matt and himself and sat for a moment staring distractedly at the television set in the corner where a Hindi-speaking compere in a dove-grey tuxedo was exuberantly giving away prizes in a quiz show. The set was tuned so that even in the morning light the colours were A-grade Technicolour. The real world outside the window was in monochrome. Beyond the pock-marked stone of the Gateway of India, kites and crows floated like torn paper against a sky of battleship grey, matchstick boats forced a course through leaden waters and on the streets, young men in dun-coloured body shirts and flared trousers heckled passing tourists.

While Matt had many misgivings about what lay ahead, none of them spoilt his rejoicing in this view and in being in Bombay doing what he was doing.

'Come on, Hunter. Tell me. What's happened?'

Hunter's attention switched abruptly from the television. He regarded Matt apologetically. When he remembered them, he had disconcertingly good manners. 'Kate Conroy. She wasn't on the flight she was supposed to be on. No message, no nothing.'

To Matt this seemed a small thing. Hunter shook his head. 'A fragile character. Good. Or rather, can be good. But fragile. Charlie will tell you that you can't have one without the other, but Charlie's not the director.'

The telephone rang and Hunter went into his bedroom to answer it. Matt could see his back hunched over the bedside table. His tone had softened so much that only the odd word was audible. He seemed to be coaxing someone—or perhaps comforting them. His outstretched foot frantically described wide arcs in the carpet.

PART ONE

Returning, he shook his head at Matt's unspoken question. 'No, not Kate. My son. The ten-year-old. He's being bullied at school.' He sank back into the chair. 'Jess thinks we shouldn't panic yet and take him away from the place. I suppose she's right . . .' His face registered pain and puzzlement. 'But I don't know what to tell him.'

Matt could understand his helplessness. It seemed inconceivable that Hunter himself had ever been bullied at school or anywhere else. Everything about him denied the possibility.

Despite his tallness, the word lanky, with its implication of knobbly disjointedness and lack of co-ordination, did not apply. Smooth-skinned and smooth-haired, he seemed to slip through life with the sleekness of a seal. Looking at him, Matt, who was three inches shorter, felt physically outclassed—ashamed of his barrel-chested footballer's frame, long gone slack at diaphragm and abdomen for lack of exercise. Thrusting through the Bombay crowds with Hunter gliding beside him, head and shoulders above everyone else, he had felt heavy and graceless.

Yet Hunter seemed shaken by the phone call, at a loss. His foot had resumed its aimless, circular motion.

Matt tried to reassure him—'Kids are resilient . . .'—then stalled. What did he know? His sole knowledge of kids was drawn from increasingly faint memories of once having been one. He tried again—'He'll find his feet.'

Hunter wasn't listening. He wandered back to the television, staring at it, as a shaft of pale Bombay sunlight silvered his floppy hair. 'By the way, the new stuff you've written for Jake is good. Of course there are one or two points.'

'What points?' asked Matt much too quickly. Take it easy, he told himself. The honeymoon is over and the show is about to begin. Hunter is a film person. Film people are rarely satisfied. You knew that before you knew any.

Hunter had read his mind. He gave him a slow smile. 'I'll wait till you've actually met Jake. It'll be easier.'

'Come on, give me a hint. After all, I've seen him in things . . .' Matt ran on, unable to stop. 'Not lately, of course. There hasn't been anything lately.'

Hunter's smile faded.

Just in time the connecting door opened and Charlie Wells burst into the room, wearing only a towel. Stocky and pink-faced, his hair standing moistly away from his scalp, he beamed at Matt.

'Get some sleep?'

'A bit.'

'Good. You won't get much in the next few weeks.' Charlie's brash pinkness was disarming. He filled the room in a doggy way, disturbing the air. But Hunter was not disarmed.

'So?'

'So everything's okay. She's on her way.'

'And what's her explanation?'

'Some last-minute thing came up to do with the picture she's just finished.'

They wrangled for a while about Kate Conroy's failure to telephone. Charlie spoke of her fondly, eager to convince, then turning back to Matt. 'I read the new scenes. They're great.'

Before Matt could reply, Hunter spoke for him. 'I don't think we've quite sold Matt on Jake.' The remark was tossed into the conversation and abandoned provocatively.

Matt made a late try for nonchalance. 'I just said he hadn't made a film in a while.'

'Absolutely right,' said Charlie. He lit a cigarette and coughed. He was giving up smoking. 'I'll bet you four beers for title, year, co-star and director of his last film.'

Matt got the first three easily, then stalled.

Charlie responded with the glee of the competitive film buff. 'Not good enough. You should have remembered him. He did a nice job. It wasn't a bad little thriller. Anyway, it doesn't matter. What matters is that the big boys have heard of Jake. It's a silly bloody business, I know. But it pays better than writing books.'

Silently Matt conceded this, although for a first novel *The Indian Summer* had done very well, something he put down to it having been written unselfconsciously and from the heart. In those days the idea of becoming a real novelist had seemed ridiculous.

Hunter was pursuing his own line of thought. 'I suppose

we are expecting a bit too much of you, Matt. To want you to take to Jake straightaway. After all, we're talking alter egos here, aren't we? Deep down, you probably want to play Fletcher yourself.'

Matt ignored the tightness in Hunter's smile. 'I'm too young. And healthy. And much, much easier to get along with. No, Fletcher is what we novelists call an amalgam.'

Charlie laughed. 'Next thing, you'll be trying to tell us that Susie's another one.'

'Too late for that.' One night, after too many drinks, he had been rash enough to confess to the bruising affair he'd had with the model for Susie, Fletcher's much younger girlfriend. Writing the novel had been part of his cure.

Charlie went to get dressed. A moment later, his telephone rang.

'Sweetheart,' he cried jubilantly, 'you're here.' He poked his head around the door. 'That was Kate. She's coming straight round.'

2

Charlie had replaced his towel with shorts and a pink polo shirt. At Kate Conroy's knock he flung open the door and she walked into his embrace. All Matt could see were slim, pale arms clasped around Charlie's neck.

Hunter was not embraced. He offered his hand in a formal, straight-armed handshake and smiled faintly, hair falling into his eyes.

She had sleek fair hair cut short, a fine-boned oval face, straight nose and wide mouth. Waiting to be introduced, Matt checked off each of these features against their filmed images. Starstruck since childhood, he had diffidently begun to join in Charlie's and Matt's businesslike dissections of screen glamour, but doubted that his coolly constructed insights fooled anybody. At heart he was still a fan.

Charlie introduced them. 'Kate Conroy, Harold Matthews.'

Matt disliked his full name. Even his big, working-class

family had had to admit that Harold's bank managerish connotations didn't suit him. At home they had called him 'Harry', but in high school his peers had rightly decided that its heartiness wasn't right for him either. Nor was the gallant, princely fellow conjured up by 'Hal'. So he became 'Matt', an ordinary, dependable syllable, defined and limited by the plosive 't' which brought it to a quiet full stop after its deceptively smooth start.

'How do you do.' He took her hand, ducking his head politely, as if he had never heard of her.

She smiled back, not quite at him, an off-centre smile directed at the room at large, and apologised for missing her flight.

'What happened?' Hunter's tone was stern—schoolmasterly.

The off-centre smile vanished and Kate Conroy considered Hunter gravely. 'I thought Charlie told you.'

'Not really.'

Charlie ranged restlessly in the background. 'Come on, Hunter, lighten up. She was delayed, for Christ's sake. They called you in to do some last-minute dubbing, didn't they?'

Hunter ignored him. 'Heard of the telephone?'

'I thought my agent phoned you. He was meant to.'

Charlie inserted himself between them. 'Hunter,' he chided.

Like Matt, Hunter was never called by his first name, which was Tom. His surname suited him too well. With his smooth, graceful ways, he might not have seemed particularly tenacious, but the beaky nose gave him away and the manner with which he moved when in a hurry, striding along with one shoulder thrust forward. Unstoppable.

'Let the girl sit down,' said Charlie.

Kate sank obediently into a chair. Matt noticed the smudges of tiredness in the pale skin under her eyes as she turned her face towards him.

She told him how much she liked the script. She didn't mention the novel. He had discovered that film people didn't read books. They had others do it for them. He had hoped that she might be different.

PART ONE

She wanted to know the latest on the casting of Rajiv, another key character. 'Did you decide on Girish?'

Charlie shrugged. 'The test he did with you and Jake was great, but we've promised the Indians we'll look at a guy called Sunny Kumar. A big star here. All go well in North Carolina?'

She explained to Matt that she had been filming in an old town in the American south. 'Lovely place. Too bad about the picture we were making.'

Charlie patted her arm. 'You're being too tough on the bloke. Could be a genius in the editing room. You never know.'

'Yes, you do.'

Matt was seized with a desire to cheer her up. He told her how pleased he was that she was playing Susie and was rewarded with a diffident hint of a smile.

'I know I'm not exactly type-casting but I like her.'

Hunter said that she didn't have much choice. Liking went with the job. 'If you want to stay sane. By the way, why did you cut your hair?'

Immediately the atmosphere chilled. Matt was fascinated. The hair was obviously a big thing here.

'It's the way I see her.' Kate turned to him. 'Don't you?'

Did he? For a mortifying moment he didn't know. What was the alternative? He tried to think. His own creation, with whom he had lived for years, stubbornly refused to show him her hair. Lips, nose, eyes, walk. All present and correct. But the hair was a blur. His continued to be transfixed by Kate. He had seen all her pictures. Hair. Think hair. Weakly and belatedly he said: 'Yes, yes, I do.'

The conversation had already moved on without him. Kate and Hunter were now on to Susie's wardrobe. Kate thought that as the action progressed, she should be seen more often in Indian dress. Hunter said that Western women looked terrible in saris. 'Especially blondes.'

'That's the point. Susie wouldn't see that. She'd think what the hell.'

Of course, thought Matt, why didn't I think of that? Before

he could say so, Kate and Hunter had moved on again and were arranging times for make-up and wardrobe tests.

'Now I'm going to unpack.' She rose from her chair.

On her way out, Matt got another fleeting smile. 'Bye for now,' she said in a cool, distant voice.

3

Charlie's eyes were slightly bloodshot and infinitely kind. Yet the news they conveyed was much worse than anything she'd had from Hunter's pale blue hostility. Charlie's eyes crinkled round the edges with concern on her behalf. In their warm, hazel irises she saw a waif-like image. The pathetic wail she heard turned out to be her own.

'Oh, Charlie. It's so long since I've been any good.'

He took both her hands and bounced them on his knee. 'Come on, it can't have been that bad in North Carolina.'

'It was.'

He let go of her hands and became brisk. 'You shouldn't have damn well done it then. The bloke's got no track record and the money was nothing to write home about. Either get a new agent or learn to read a script.'

The briskness was infectious. She managed to summon up a bit to throw back at him. The script had been all right, so had the part. A few scenes had been better than all right. Then, pausing for thought, she was lost. 'The shoot went wrong from the start,' she said lamely. 'It just . . . slipped away.'

'Slipped away?' He chewed on the words in disbelief. 'Slipped away?'

She had done the film for the usual reason and was unwise enough to say so. 'I wanted to work.'

'You shouldn't work with fuckwits.'

He was right but how could you recognise them? So often they were the ones with the luck.

'What does your agent say?'

Her agent was strong on the importance of getting together

'a body of work'. Her agent tried to make his clients feel like artists. He was very popular. She was lucky to have him.

Charlie took her hand again as if calming a mad person. After this picture, she should relax for a while, wait for something really good. She could afford to. 'Enjoy yourself . . .'

He had missed the point. Work was the only place she came anywhere near to feeling human.

Resourcefully changing tack, he began jollying her along with talk about his own problems. He had spent the past three months in India, spinning the web of connections which was going to carry them from Bombay to Calcutta, through Rajasthan, and south to Tamil Nadu. He had persevered through a stunning array of setbacks; solving the puzzles posed by Indian bureaucracy, charming, cajoling and sorting out those who could help the production with props and locations from all the would-be patrons with nothing more tangible to offer than a desperate desire to get into the act somehow. He had hired an army of stagehands, carpenters, painters, electricians, grips and gofers to join the Australian production people they had brought with them. He had conferred with travel agents to make special deals for transport and accommodation and with accountants to establish a working relationship with Indian banks.

She was a responsive audience. His greatest fan. He was heroic. He was also her friend, the reason she was on the picture. He had got her the part and was ready, she knew, to defend her against anything.

He wound up the account of his adventures and was instantly overcome with embarrassment. They had arrived at the moment. She made it easy for him.

'You want to know the truth,' she said. 'Why I was late getting here?'

She did her best to turn it into a funny story with emphasis on the Russian tourists and the gritty carpet. He wasn't fooled.

'And the hair. Why did you do that?'

She told him about not being able to sleep. 'I thought I made quite a good job of it really. In the end.'

'You did it *yourself*?'

She knew what he was imagining, and it wasn't so far from the truth. A dawn attack of self-loathing. Lucky to have escaped alive.

She smiled, anxious to reassure. He didn't deserve any of this. 'I thought it would make me feel better.'

The hazel eyes narrowed. Though he didn't believe her, he made an effort to pretend. 'You should have told *him* first.'

'He would have talked me out of it.'

'You've got to start talking to him. He's not God.' He paused, fleetingly amused. 'He only comes on that way.'

They giggled like children delighted to have Teacher out of the room. Buoyed up on laughter, she at last felt ready to ask a question of her own.

'The insurance. Was that his idea?'

'No, of course it wasn't.'

He looked stricken. She didn't care. 'Charlie, it's a year since I was sick. I've made two pictures since then. They didn't need to insure me.'

He made soothing sounds. 'I know, I know, but it wasn't his idea. Believe me.'

'Are you sure?'

'Absolutely.'

They sat looking at one another. She took a deep breath. 'But he's got someone else, hasn't he? Someone waiting in the wings, just in case.'

Charlie's moon face, with its cheerful curves, recomposed itself into doleful verticals and diagonals. 'Oh, hell. Bloody hell.'

She sadly contemplated his bowed head.

4

Charlie was racing Jake Ward the length of the hotel pool, churning the water with choppy, straight-armed strokes. Beside the pool, Kate and Hunter sat, watching.

The race was Ward's idea. He had wanted her and Hunter to be in it but Charlie had been the only one to say yes.

PART ONE

Already people were slipping into the roles they would inhabit for the next three months, both at work and at play. Charlie would do his best to keep everybody happy because he was the producer and prime organiser and because he was a genuinely sociable person. If Ward needed a playmate and fellow wild man, Charlie, within reason, would do his best to oblige.

She stole a glance at Hunter, who was sipping a lime juice, marking a copy of the script and giving very little away except a wish to be taken seriously.

They had gathered by the pool to talk over the next day's plans. She had arrived last, and as she walked across the grass towards them had observed him studying her in theoretical long shot, his expression unreadable behind his sunglasses.

Paradoxically, the garden—green and pleasant—reminded her of her first day at school when she had been driven by claustrophobia to put up her hand and ask if Miss would please leave the door open. There were no closed doors here but it made no difference. Just outside was India, the India of the hawk-faced beggar woman with the look that said, you owe me. Confronted with that look, Kate's own troubles shrank to nothing and she with them. She and they were one now. Indivisible.

Had it always been this way? Her mind returned to the closed door. With a maternal chuckle, Miss had obliged and left it open. Which was more than she could expect from Hunter. No room to move with him. No reminders of Miss in his face.

She risked another glance. He looked both frightening and desirable. A familiar combination, that. She knew it well.

She sought to comfort herself. After all, Charlie liked him. For years the two of them had been making small, personal, good-looking films and had attracted several Hollywood offers which they had refused. Or rather, Hunter had refused them. 'He wants to find his own path into the big time,' Charlie had said doubtfully. But he was doubtful no longer. Now he said Hunter had been right all along. 'This is it,' he said. 'The big one.'

She wanted desperately to believe him. Acting was her

lifeline. It had happened by accident, years ago. Her school had been doing *Twelfth Night*, 'Olivia' got sick and, because she and Kate were alike, someone thought of her. She had had to be talked into it. But when she learned the lines, it happened—a sudden, glorious lightening of the spirits. A new dimension of self, together with a new sense of her own femininity. Make-up brought her pale features and sandy eyebrows into focus and the costume gave her a licence to change, to play, to be anything she wanted. The painfully inhibited teenager whose grave stare made her mother squirm could be banished for hours at a time. Oh, yes, acting had been good to her.

She glanced enviously at Ward, who was hoisting himself out of the pool, stomach sucked in, arms taut. He was in his mid-fifties, short and compact with a square jaw and a leonine head. Classic screen actor's looks and all the signs of the convinced extrovert.

Hunter was looking at him, too—coolly computing features and flaws as he had earlier with her.

'Jake's in good shape,' she murmured.

Hunter smiled at her faintly. 'He is, isn't he? And why not? If this picture works, he'll have a new career.' His voice dropped. 'And so will you. Remember that.'

Her anger was a nice change. 'Tell me. Why did you cast me?'

He turned to her and paused a moment. 'Not now.' He raised his dark glasses, flashing her a tantalising glance of complicity. 'Not in front of Tarzan.' He returned to his contemplation of Ward and Charlie, now padding towards them, wiping the water from their eyes. Charlie was puffing, Ward was not.

'Great hotel,' Ward said, flopping into a banana-chair beside Kate. 'Great country. Should have come here before. Been everywhere else.'

He lit a cigarette and settled back in the chair, sensuously working his shoulders to the point of maximum comfort. For an uneasy moment she was reminded of her father, who gave off a similar air of being in constant and delighted communion with his own body.

'I've done a lot of parts because I liked the sound of the location. Big mistake. But fun at the time. And without fun you might as well be dead.'

Hunter seemed amused. Had he taken the part only to see India?

'Yeah, that's right.' He winked at Kate. 'Hell, I might as well say it again. I know you like to hear it. I wanted to work with you ... and you.' He clasped her hand briefly, managing this gesture without looking at her or altering his position in the chair.

5

As she dressed for dinner, she thought wistfully of years ago when clothes had been fun instead of defensive weapons. Tonight she was bringing out the heavy artillery. She had slicked back her hair, put on antique gold earrings, a close-fitting black dress and a necklace that had been her grandmother's. The effect was somewhere between socialite and dominatrix. She spent a long time before the mirror trying to find the right expression to go with it.

Her father would approve. As she made up her face, sprayed on perfume and checked that her nails were clean, she continued to dwell on the similarities between him and Ward.

Her father was wealthy. Having inherited a great deal of money, he had added even more to the pile during his long career as a merchant banker, although making money had never been as important to him as spending it. Spending wisely took style. This was one of his many precepts and he stated it often, tanned cheeks glowing in the candlelight over a good dinner, silver hair brushed back from his temples, wife or girlfriend at his elbow.

There had been three wives. Kate's mother was the first. The marriage had lasted until Kate was twelve when she and her mother—but not the dog—were moved out of the Bellevue Hill house into an apartment at Darling Point. It was not exactly a hard-luck story. Since her father's convictions about the relationship between style and spending extended even to ex-wives and children, the apartment was large and elegant with a wide-angle view of Sydney Harbour but the message was clear, especially to a twelve-year-old. She and her mother had been superseded.

Downstairs in the classiest of the Taj's restaurants, Charlie bustled about making sure of the right table and a diplomatic seating plan. Kate was placed between Ward and Matt who helped Charlie do the ordering.

After organising a gin and tonic for her and a double Scotch for himself, Ward took charge of the conversation. 'Know what I like about Fletcher? He's a survivor. Keeps on punching. Is that you, Matt? Are you a Fletcher?'

She couldn't make up her mind about Harold Matthews. She had an actor's prejudice against writers on sets. In her experience, they mooned about, fussing about any changes made to their precious scripts, or retreated to the nearest bar to avoid actors wanting to improve their lines. The fact that this one was an ex-journalist with Irish looks did not bode well.

Matt said that Fletcher was the way he wished he could be. 'I'm in training.'

Ward's laugh was a hearty baritone. 'You got the theory right, anyway. So tell me, what is it you like about this country?'

Matt told them about his first visit as an ABC correspondent in the seventies. He had stayed three years and had been coming back ever since. After the years spent in Asian postings, he was finding it hard to settle in Sydney again.

'We're his salvation,' said Hunter.

Matt seemed mildly embarrassed. 'Salvation? If only.'

Ward was still preoccupied with survival techniques. 'They're both survivors. Susie, too. You know who she reminds me of?' He looked expectantly at Charlie and Hunter. Both shook their heads. 'Tina, that's who. The same way of taking the knocks and bouncing right back.'

PART ONE

Hunter nodded in agreement; Charlie looked stunned.

Kate had yet to meet Tina Epstein, whose name peppered everybody's conversation. As the film's American co-producer, she had sold North American rights to the unmade film for a sum so large that Charlie whistled whenever he named the figure. She was also Jake Ward's lover.

'A package deal,' Charlie had said. 'No Jake, no Tina. And no Tina, no Acorn.'

Acorn Pictures, known in the trade as a 'mini-major' was big and powerful enough to ensure that the film would open in a respectable number of American theatres with plenty of publicity. It was Acorn's idea that Kate be insured. At least Charlie had led her to assume so. Now she wondered if Tina had been responsible.

Ward's thin-lipped cragginess seemed to soften as he dwelt on Tina's street wisdom. Nobody knew the industry better than she did. 'Nobody. I let myself get out of touch there for a while. Gave up. Christ, it's a foreign country now. New people, new rules.'

He was interrupted by the arrival of the food. As Charlie briefed them all on the composition and flavour of every dish, he smiled indulgently, not listening. He ordered another double Scotch then turned to Hunter. 'So how did you and Charlie here get together?'

Hunter laughed. 'We were born joined at the hip.'

'Huh?'

Hunter flashed a glance at Kate. She observed him carefully, looking for clues. A basis for hope.

'We were at school together,' said Hunter. 'A good Catholic boys' school. Taught by the Jesuits, we were.'

Ward had already lost interest. He was moving about restlessly and sending out smoke rings. Hunter didn't care. He wasn't talking to Ward.

Charlie broke in. 'I hated the place.'

'I didn't. I loved it. I sang in the choir.'

'He did, too.' Charlie still seemed bemused.

'And I won the Latin prize.' Hunter picked up his wineglass.

'Come on,' said Charlie, 'don't stop now. Tell them all about it. Stroke of the eight, big wheel in the debating team, cricketing bloody star. For the first four years, I couldn't stand the prick.'

'So?' prompted Matt.

'We lapsed,' said Hunter, 'at the same time. It bonded us forever.'

'For different reasons, though,' said Charlie. 'Mine was simple. I discovered girls. Lust and the church didn't go together. I had to make a choice, didn't I? There was no contest.'

'What do you mean, different reasons?' Hunter seemed put out.

'Okay, the same basic reason. But you made more of a big deal out of it. You had to bring bloody philosophy into it. With you it took longer.'

'Of course it did. I liked the whole thing. The ceremony, the paraphernalia. I missed it.' He stared at Kate. 'Still do.'

Ward was thoroughly bored. Sizing his chance he moved the conversation back to business. They got round to agents, the new Hollywood ruling class. Ward asked the name of Hunter's agent, nodding sagely at his reply. 'So now you're in the big time. At last. How's it feel?'

Hunter surprised Kate by taking the question seriously. 'I'm scared.' He made it sound as if he'd achieved something. The required state of mind.

Ward approved. 'The only way to be.' Restless again, he pushed his plate away, having eaten very little.

'Want me to order you something else?' asked Charlie.

He shook his head and lit a cigarette, blowing smoke across the table, then he tucked the cigarette into the side of his mouth, squinting at Kate through the smoke. 'What was the name of that young guy, the British director you used to work with?' He leaned towards her, putting his arm along the back of her chair. Charlie winked at her encouragingly.

'Dermott . . . Dermott Mills.'

'Yeah, that's the guy. You two had it made when you first came to LA. Then you dropped right out of sight. Now why was that?'

She took her time, managed a smile. 'No mystery. We'd

been living together, we split up and working with one another didn't seem such a good idea anymore.'

She had to clear her throat and he grinned. 'Pity,' he said. 'For you, anyway. He's doing okay. The girl he's got now wasn't so hot when he first started using her but she's got better.' The blue eyes twinkled maliciously through the smokescreen. 'You haven't been so lucky, have you?'

She searched for words; none came. She could think of nothing but Hunter, whom she could see out of the corner of her eye, watching her with ominous interest. For a moment, in the flickering of the candlelight, she thought she saw sympathy in his face. When she looked again, it was gone.

At last the silence was broken by Charlie. 'Until now,' he said. 'Now her luck's about to change.'

6

Mr Shankar, manager of the Bombay's Film Factory, the pride of 'Bollywood', was small, smiling and friendly. He was also soft and smooth, as if planed down by years of wry resignation. 'They are not actors. They are stars,' he said with a slight shrug of his flexible shoulders, 'and stars keep their own time. There is actually not very much we can be doing about this.'

Matt was sitting with Charlie on the edge of the Factory's largest sound stage watching a musical in rehearsal. It was a brash, Westernised musical being filmed against a midnight-blue sky with tinsel stars, but despite the denim jackets and the Benetton T-shirts of the chorus line, it was not quite modern. The girls had ponytails and bouffants and the musicians had teamed their gold satin shirts with string ties and lacquered kiss curls, making them resemble leftover Comets from the days of Bill Haley. Like everyone else on the set, they were waiting for Sunny Kumar and had been for some time. Sunny was the star.

Matt and Charlie, with the rest of *The Indian Summer* party, had already toured the three hundred and fifty rolling acres of the Film Factory, with its gardens, its temple and the lake enabling it to double for Kashmir when required. And on the edge of the lake they had visited another set where a director who might have been Mr Shankar's twin was waiting for his own star, whose name was Bobby.

There, plump extras wearing lipstick and pancake and pretending to be villagers lounged against the walls of specially built thatched huts, while nearby their real-life counterparts—the shanty dwellers of the Film Factory—moved silently across the hillside, their backs bent under bundles of wood collected for the building of more make-believe thatched huts, each of them larger and more strongly built than their own.

The musical number came to shuffling halt and the dancers went into a huddle with the choreographer, a large Eurasian woman in a grey sweatshirt decorated with a can of Budweiser.

At that moment, Andy McCaffrey, the director of photography from *The Indian Summer* unit, emerged from a side door.

'So how's it going?' asked Charlie, referring to the hair and make-up tests being held in another studio.

'Slowly.' Andy pulled up a chair. 'Ward's being picky about angles and Kate . . . well . . . she's looking as if it's a long time since she got a good night's sleep. How old is she? Thirty-five?'

'Thirty-two.'

The two men began a discussion of angles and filters, colours and make-up bases, in which Kate was analysed as if she were a collection of inanimate elements put together by an inferior craftsman. Although Matt realised that all actors were subjected to this sort of thing he found it unnerving to hear it happening to someone he knew. 'We do our best,' said Andy with a sigh.

On the sound stage, there was a sudden change in the atmosphere—a ripple of excitement heralding the arrival of the star—and Sunny Kumar launched into a dance routine while a peppy line of chorus boys capered around him, swivelling hips and shoulders.

A fan of Indian movie magazines, Matt was firmly hooked on the scandalous adventures of Bombay's alternative pan-

PART ONE

theon with their cute nicknames—Dimple, Goli, Chunkie, Sunny, Jackie—and enjoyed the particular mixture of worship and derision with which their fans regarded them. 'The gods like to fool around,' he had once been told by a temple guide regaling him with one of the jokier Shiva legends and he often thought of that remark when reading about the boozing, the womanising and the quarrelsome arrogance for which the Bollywood icons were much admired. Sunny, however, lacked the Bollywood glamour. Heavy and unco-ordinated, he had the plump, languid look of a neutered tomcat.

Later Matt joined the rest of the party in the small studio where they were to listen to Sunny read for the part of Rajiv.

Sunny arrived only thirty minutes late with his minder—a wiry, excitable man called Mr Roshan who introduced him with much ceremony. Sunny had changed out of the costume he wore for the dance routine and was dressed in black denims. He still had his swagger but his purring self-satisfaction had been replaced by a glum ordinariness of which he seemed poignantly aware. When introduced to Ward he ducked his head and mumbled, as if his lessons in stardom had failed to include tips on how to behave in the glow cast by brighter lights, and Mr Roshan gave him a swift, fierce glance.

Of his three main characters, Matt was fondest of Rajiv. He saw him as an open-hearted, insouciant character who nonetheless was burdened by a melancholy foreknowledge of the limits of his future. He was to fall genuinely in love with Susie against his better judgment and his pleasure in their affair was to be spoilt from the start by his pessimistic view of how it would end.

Sunny was to read with Ward a scene in which Fletcher had just found out about the romance and was enraged, accusing Rajiv, whom he had hired as a guide and translator, of deceit and disloyalty. Rajiv was trying to defend both his honour and Susie's but at the same time felt himself guilty of having betrayed an employer who had made him his friend.

It was a scene in which Fletcher had the lines but Rajiv

had the sympathy of the audience. At least that was the way Matt saw it. But Ward's reading was tricky.

His body relaxed, his jawline went slack and in a matter of moments he took on several extra years. His voice was low and he sounded defeated, the bombast so underdone that it seemed no more than a gesture for the sake of form. It was not a generous reading. 'Beat this,' it said to Sunny Kumar who reacted to it in a high-pitched tone of desperation which effectively robbed Rajiv of all his sad dignity and caused Matt real pain.

After a while he found it so hard to bear that he closed his eyes. Then he no longer heard the lines. There were just the husky, straining cadences of Sunny's voice as he pushed himself to finish.

When at last it was over, there was silence for what seemed like a very long time. Then Hunter stood up and the scene dissolved in a buzz of thank-yous. Mr Roshan backed out of the room, still shaking hands, as Sunny deflated with a soft, eloquent sigh that seemed to echo in the room long after he had left it.

Kate had won the battle to have Susie wear a sari in the later scenes, and in retaliation Hunter had insisted she try on a wig. There was no question of her having to wear this particular wig, he said. 'But I do want to know how longer hair would look with the costumes.' He gave her a cool stare.

As soon as she put it on, she started to laugh at the sight of herself in the mirror and couldn't stop. Infected by her laughter, others joined in until there were several of them, bent over, holding their sides, while Hunter stood by, looking bored, waiting for the madness to pass.

PART ONE

INT. SYDNEY RESTAURANT. NIGHT.

FLETCHER and SUSIE are sitting across from one another in a restaurant booth. Their glasses are full, the bottle of wine on the table is almost empty. FLETCHER is hunched forward gazing into SUSIE's face. He looks slightly dazed—the combined effect of drunkenness and acute sexual desire.

>FLETCHER: Move in with me. Tomorrow. Tonight. Come home with me now and don't leave.

Not nearly as drunk as he is, SUSIE smiles at him fondly.

>Too soon.

>FLETCHER: (Aggrieved) I'm sure. Why aren't you?

>SUSIE: We need a test run.

FLETCHER straightens up, shocked.

>SUSIE: A holiday together.

>FLETCHER: (Perking up) How about Paris? (Swiftly warming to the idea) I suppose you've been?

She nods.

>FLETCHER: You haven't been to the Paris I can show you.

She shakes her head.

FLETCHER tries again, enthusiasm undiminished.

>The States then. A few days in New York, then we head west. South-west. Santa Fe, Arizona, Monument Valley, the Canyons . . .

>SUSIE: No, not the States.

>FLETCHER: (Enjoying the challenge) Africa. The game parks. Zimbabwe's the place . . .

Again she shakes her head.

FLETCHER: Turkey? Istanbul then maybe a sailing holiday along the Mediterranean coast.

SUSIE: No.

FLETCHER slumps, defeated, in the corner of the booth.

SUSIE: India.

He shakes his head in dismay and disbelief.

SUSIE: How long is it since you've been?

FLETCHER: I've never been. Never had to go, thank God.

SUSIE: Then how do you know you wouldn't like it?

FLETCHER: I've never met a giraffe but I know we couldn't have a conversation. The place is a madhouse.

SUSIE: And Africa isn't?

FLETCHER: That's different. In India, they mean to confuse you. British pomposity, Eastern bloody mysticism. Fatal combination.

SUSIE: It's India or nothing.

FLETCHER: Nothing then. (He broods for a while in silence.) Okay, what's all this about?

SUSIE: I have to go. I'm being sent. On a job for the magazine. An Indian government junket. Please. (She grasps his hand, which is lying limply on the table.) Come with me.

CHAPTER TWO

1

The floor was streaked with the droppings of the pigeons nesting high in the vaulted ceilings, and the coins in the dusty glass cases were so tarnished that in the dimness they appeared as identical black stains occurring at eerily symmetrical intervals. Matt knew they were ancient and therefore precious and he peered in a desultory way at their labels which were so faint and so mould-spotted that he couldn't read them. He wandered on, hoping to come across some of the startling sights promised by his guide-book—perhaps the eight-legged, four-eared, preserved goat which rested here somewhere—but every turn took him back to the central courtyard, a large pool of smoky light amid the surrounding murk.

He had queued to get into the museum, waiting for fifteen minutes with a crowd of teachers herding in groups of well-scrubbed schoolboys in impossibly white shirts and well-pressed shorts, while the beggars of Chowringhee worked the line. As always he had been carrying a little money in his pockets, and had given first to the children because their smiles and jokes made him feel better—he had never kidded himself about *their* feelings—then he surrendered to the murmuring, wraith-like figures who took the rupees from him with magical swiftness and shuffled on, the murmurs drifting back like disembodied incantations. Once inside the museum, the crowd had scattered, swallowed up by the gloomy galleries and echoing corridors and he wondered if they had found what they wanted and if so, how.

After a while he gave up his own search. He had even lost the desire to climb to the top floor of the maze and visit the Mughal miniatures which he knew he could find. Instead he went out through the Corinthian portico and started to make his way to the Oberoi Grand for his appointment with Charlie and Hunter.

During every visit to Calcutta, Matt hoped to leave a better person, but this never happened. The city's terrible extremes—of poverty, overcrowding, pollution and squandered wealth—did not make him aware of the triviality of his own concerns. To his great shame and disappointment they stayed with him wherever he went in the city and whatever horrors he saw. While he felt pity, revulsion and helplessness, no matter how much he learnt about what went on here, the life of the streets remained closed to him, unimaginable.

He turned out of the honking bustle of Chowringhee and approached the Georgian facade of the Grand where a liveried doorman showed him into a world effectively sealed off from the one outside—a world of softly glowing surfaces and muted conversation where the colours were brighter and truer than those Matt had just left behind, because here things were not dulled by a patina of dust and there were no gaunt faces and shuffling feet. He couldn't help himself. He was very relieved to be here.

Calcutta was to be their base for the next few weeks. Much of the film's action was to take place in the city, and sets for interior scenes had been built at a studio in the suburb of Tollygunge. They would also film in streets and buildings, and Charlie's suite at the Grand was the organisational hub of things. Here, he and his secretary, Liz, spent their days on the telephone ensuring that the much-worked-over schedule would be carried through. They spoke to politicians, businessmen, municipal and State authorities, police, Customs officers, landlords and newspaper reporters. They liaised with crew members whose job it was to hire trucks, trailers, cars and buses, cast extras and arrange for streets to be cordoned off as needed. To Matt's continuing amazement, Charlie seemed to thrive on this activity.

As Liz showed Matt in, Charlie greeted him with a wave of the hand and a broad smile, interrupting his telephone conversation only for a moment. The receiver was wedged between neck and shoulder while he used his other hand to draw a cigarette from the packet lying open on the desk. 'All right, we'll keep you informed.' He wound up the conversation and slammed down the receiver, taking a deep breath.

'Our Indian investors. Not too happy about us giving the thumbs down to Sunny Kumar. I had to talk very fast. An unknown Bengali actor is not a sexy alternative to a Bollywood big name as far as they're concerned, but in the end I convinced them our Bengali is brilliant.'

'And is he?'

'He will be.'

Charlie glanced up as Liz came into the room. Lean and tanned, with a cheerful, horsey face, she wore Reeboks and cycling pants and was rarely still. She and Charlie communicated in a laconic shorthand which had a calming effect. 'The film festival crowd,' she said. 'They want Hunter there at seven on Tuesday.'

The festival was mounting a retrospective of Hunter's work. Charlie hoped it might do them some good.

'What else?'

She gave him an ironic look and announced: 'The man from the Ministry is here.'

'The one who's going to be with us on the set?'

'Right.'

Matt already knew about this arrangement. A script for a film to be made in India was first vetted by the authorities then a bureaucrat was assigned to the production to ensure that any subsequent changes were also approved.

'Okay, give us a minute,' said Charlie. Then, in a hoarse whisper to Matt: 'Did you hear that they sprung us over the dummy script?'

'What dummy script?'

'One of the minority pressure groups—you know how many of those there are in this city—started making a noise over something they didn't like so we gave them a dummy with the dodgy scenes edited out. Everybody does it. Anyway, we think someone tipped them off because they went to the Ministry and complained. It'll be okay. Unless, of course, any of the others turn up.'

'What others?'

There were a few versions around, Charlie explained gently. 'You know what it's like. Wherever you go, there's another lot of bureaucrats who get worried about something you've never ever dreamt of.'

It was surreal. Matt also found it thoroughly in keeping with the whole slippery process. 'Nothing's finite in this business, is it?'

'Finite?' Charlie seemed perplexed.

A few moments later, Liz reappeared with a tall Bengali with a thin, hawk-nosed face, rimless glasses and a lot of wavy hair: 'Mr Gupta'.

He was dressed in a navy-blue blazer and a shirt of the same glaring whiteness as the schoolboys' shirts at the museum. He looked very young and moved in a rapid, unco-ordinated way which seemed strangely un-Indian. 'Ajay Gupta,' he murmured. He politely refused Liz's offer of coffee and sat down, passing his hand through his hair.

Charlie smiled, his relief obvious. The much-dreaded bureaucrat had turned out to be a polite and biddable boy. He introduced Matt: 'He wrote the damn thing. Anything you don't like, blame him.'

Ajay Gupta looked startled for a moment then he grinned, all trace of self-consciousness gone. 'Mr Matthews.' He began pumping Matt's hand. 'I am a great fan of yours. I read your book a long time ago and I have returned to it several times since.'

Matt was touched. 'It's a presumptuous book in a way . . .'

Ajay Gupta frowned. 'What do you mean?'

'It's always a presumptuous thing for an author to do—to appropriate someone else's country and start doing what he likes with it. People can get upset.'

'I know. So often India is depicted by Westerners as an exotic human zoo of some sort.' Ajay's tone had grown firmer.

PART ONE

'But your book is not at all like that. Nor is your script. You have taken the time to get to know us. Rajiv, for example. Not such a wise person perhaps, but someone I can understand thoroughly.'

It was a long time since Matt had met a genuine reader. In the past months he had watched his book dismembered, sometimes physically, its back broken, its pages torn out and made to bleed with red ink notations while Hunter picked over the pieces; accepting, rejecting and finally encouraging him to transform them into something else. It was gratifying to have it made whole again.

Charlie outlined the script changes to Ajay. The Ministry had approved them in principle but it wanted to be assured of their smooth passage past all the relevant regional and civic authorities. The briefing took ages, yet at the end Ajay seemed invigorated. They had no time to waste, he said. 'I should get together with your location manager immediately.'

When Matt was next in Charlie's office, he noticed a new chart among the collection on the wall—a neat chequerboard in pink, blue and white with meticulous lettering in black ink.

'Ajay,' said Charlie happily. 'The kid's a fast worker.'

Hunter, too, was impressed. He suggested to Matt that they try out one of the new scenes on Ajay.

Matt was doubtful. He didn't really want a witness to the way he behaved while working with Hunter, who often left him floundering—half-finished sentence hanging in the air— or had him back-pedalling furiously to retrieve a beloved line of dialogue all but lost in the free-associating shuffle of ideas that Hunter loved and Matt hated.

Since their arrival in Calcutta, there had been a power shift—expected but not easy to take. For one thing, Hunter had proudly revealed an ability to touch-type. As he said, very rare in a film director.

He no longer paced while Matt took charge of the keyboard. He was already sitting in front of a new laptop computer when Matt arrived, and although Matt hovered at his shoulder as he dictated, trying to make sure that his words were not altered into something unacceptable before hitting the page, Hunter's furious typing kept him well ahead of the game.

There were one or two gambits that Matt especially dreaded. 'No, it won't play,' Hunter would say, shaking his head over one of Matt's favourite lines, or 'Nothing's at stake here,' when Matt had spent an hour adjusting a scene to a point he regarded as perfection.

But it would have been petulant to object to Ajay's presence.

He sat before them reading the new pages.

Matt did not much like the scene under discussion. They had been arguing about it for hours. The lines written for Fletcher made him too aggressive for Matt's taste. He saw the scene as a bridge building to the more dramatic one which followed, but Hunter had wanted fireworks.

Both of them watched Ajay's face as he read. After he had finished he continued to scan the lines, riffling the pages back and forth.

'Come on, tell us what you think. We're not dangerous,' Hunter smiled. 'Only to ourselves.'

Ajay took a deep breath. 'I must confess that the lines sound a bit false to my ears. The scene just does not seem to be in the spirit of the book.'

Nobody spoke for a moment. Ajay looked nervously from Hunter to Matt.

'Tell me exactly what you mean,' said Hunter. 'Exactly.'

Soon they had a new version, remarkably similar to Matt's original, yet Matt did not delude himself. No matter what was on the page, the actual script was inside Hunter's head—an area which remained permanently off limits, no matter how hard he worked in trying to divine its workings.

PART ONE

2

After pocketing Kate's tip, the boy who brought breakfast seemed about to ask for her autograph. But as he stared into her unmade-up face, she could see the doubts multiplying. Was she or wasn't she? Deciding she wasn't, he gave her a weak smile and backed hurriedly out of the door.

She regained her will to live with strong coffee then took a taxi to the studios in Tollygunge, and for a while things were not so bad. A cheery few hours with the wardrobe people helped, then, after lunch with Charlie, she sat down to watch herself in the first rushes-screening and everything fell apart.

It was the hair. How could she have done it? She saw exactly what the bus-boy had seen. She looked old. For the first time.

Andy could have helped her but Andy, she suspected, was not really interested. He had his gaze fixed on a bigger picture than her profile. He was out to photograph India. India in capital letters spelling epic. In Andy's mind, she was no more than a pool of light on the edge of the frame.

Hunter could have helped, but he would have seen the same thing that she had—something far worse than the pallor and the wrinkles. Hunter would have seen the fear.

Ward had received no more favours than she. His wrinkles, too, were a prominent part of what they had just been looking at. But he was not afraid. His bravado—she couldn't quite bring herself to call it courage—shone with every movement he made. Damn Ward. It wasn't nice, but damn him, just the same.

She couldn't think where to go, so the taxi-driver made up her mind for her.

'Shopping. I know a very good place.'

He was an honest taxi-driver and he didn't take her to a stall in the bazaar run by his wife's uncle. He took her to a very respectable government emporium. She was so grateful that she gave him a tip large enough to bring a dazed, joyful expression to his face.

The emporium was cool, dim and orderly with racks of sari lengths and regiments of brass elephants under glass. She bought silk for her mother—a complicated business which involved a trip up three flights of stairs to visit a fierce cashier in a cage.

Only when she reached the street again did she realise that she was two hours late for a meeting with Hunter.

The hotel had to be somewhere nearby but already the light was going and there were no taxis. 'The city of dreadful night.' Kipling? She should know. A real actor would know. It was too late for her and the stage. For the stage, she would have to cultivate more than her memory. A talent for the short take. That's what she had. Perhaps it wasn't even talent. Just willpower. And need. The word gave her a jolt and made her look around—at the faces staring stoically from packed, ancient buses, at the figures weaving through the crowd, at the immensity of the effort being expended on just getting from one place to another. Need? Who was she kidding?

Why weren't they lashing out at one another? Calcutta, they said, was the most law-abiding city in India. 'You will be quite safe in Calcutta, Katharine,' her fellow plane traveller with the wraparound glasses had told her. 'A low crime rate and, unlike Delhi and Bombay, no Eve-teasing.' When she'd laughed at 'Eve-teasing', he'd shaken his head, disapproving. 'Let me tell you, it is no joke.' Of course it wasn't. No joke at all. Only made to sound like one. 'A term invented by a man, no doubt,' she'd said prissily, trying to make up lost ground, and he'd looked hurt.

No, she was not worried about what might happen to her on the streets of Calcutta, only about what she might see.

They were there in the shadows—huddled shapes on the pavement with arms outstretched. Now that the sun was going down, the smog had taken on a hellish glow highlighted by the sparks of the street-vendors' fires. So when the shifting shadows brought a face out of the darkness, she turned her head away.

An uncomplaining rickshaw man edged around her, delicately avoiding a pothole that looked as if it could go all the way to the centre of the earth.

She was lost. Whom could she ask for directions? She pressed on through the crowd until suddenly, as if heaven-sent, there appeared a portly, grey-haired man with a briefcase and spotless white kurta and trousers, looking like a walking monument to order.

He took great pains with the instructions, and even above the hooting and the clamouring she thought she understood, but as he disappeared into the crowd the details magically evaporated with him.

Turning right at the first cross-street, she made out a boulevarde up ahead so choked with traffic that she fancied it must be Chowringhee, yet when she finally reached it nothing about it looked familiar. She came to a halt, standing marooned in the crowd.

Quite near was a boy sitting on a blanket. She had caught only a glimpse and was now willing herself not to look again. If I can get off this corner without having to look at that boy, then everything will be all right, she told herself. It seemed reasonable. But she looked. He had a nice face—even handsome—with large brown eyes, white teeth and a well-formed mouth. But the brown body, impossibly smooth and thin, was without arms or legs and waved back and forth with the motion of the crowd like the stem of a plant in the wind. The shapely mouth was smiling at her, inviting her to smile back. Later, she told herself that she'd made up the smile. It was mindless and unfocused, she maintained. Just a reflex. Carefully avoiding the smile, she thrust some rupees into the bowl on the blanket and darted off into the crowd like a thief.

By now the shutters had gone up on the shops and it was too dark to read the map. She had lost all sense of direction and was looking around for help when a taxi pulled up at the kerb and Hunter got out.

She told him that she had forgotten their meeting.

'Bullshit.' He balled up the paper napkin he had been shredding and dropped it on the table.

'Okay, I took fright at the rushes.' She spoke very fast. 'I bet you did, too. You were right about the hair by the way.'

He gave her a long, steady stare. There was a flicker of something that might have been curiosity. 'No, the hair is okay. Everything else is wrong, but not the hair.' He regained his poise, the anger abandoned. She was sorry about that. You knew where you stood with anger.

'Why do you let Ward walk all over you?'

'His ego,' she said after a moment or two. 'Huge, isn't it?'

Hunter was incredulous. 'Of course it's huge. It's all he's got.'

'He reminds me of my father, since we're talking egos.'

Hunter gave the table a hearty slap which made the cutlery rattle. 'At last—a bit of good news. Unless, of course, you're indifferent to your father.'

No, she was not indifferent to her father.

'What then? Hate, love, lust, rage, resentment, dislike?'

She chose resentment. Hunter looked only slightly disappointed. 'It's something, anyway.' His gaze trailed off into the distance behind her left shoulder. 'I think you know you weren't my first choice for this part.'

She braced herself. 'I do now.'

'But your test was good.' A smile appeared and, against all the odds, warmed the atmosphere. 'You didn't let Ward walk all over you then.'

'I didn't have time to think then.'

He stole a glance at his watch. The last warning or the last rites?

The smile clicked off. 'It's not going to get any easier. Tougher, if anything. Ward thinks it's his picture. It isn't. I will not allow it to be. Whatever happens.'

He let it rest there. A good exit line, she thought. Whichever way you looked at it.

3

Charlie could not go to Hunter's retrospective and asked Matt to take Ajay as a reward for his help. He was turning out to be more liaison man than watchdog and Charlie was full of gratitude.

A large, noisy crowd was already milling about in front of the cinema when they arrived. Matt had to shout to make himself heard. 'I didn't know Hunter's films were so popular here.'

'It's because the word has got around.'

Before Ajay could explain, the doors opened and they were swept up and carried through. Inside, people packed the aisles and stood in rows around the walls, but despite the crush and confusion it was an essentially good-humoured crowd and the shoves and nudges were accompanied by murmured apologies, as if those doing the pushing were amazed at themselves for being capable of such a thing. With some difficulty, Matt and Ajay managed to squeeze in at the back, and Matt found himself absorbing, as if by osmosis, the sense of anticipation in the air.

Ajay explained ruefully that everybody had come for the sex. 'They've heard that it has some quite explicit scenes. The only time you can beat the censor here is during a film festival. The British once made children of us. Now we let our own bureaucrats do it.'

As the film reached the long-awaited scene, there were coughs and throat-clearings. Those lucky enough to have seats lounged back in the tilting chairs, their faces rapt, and as the lovers reached their climax, Matt fancied that the chairs danced and jiggled.

Afterwards there was a press conference for Hunter, dominated by a Sikh who planted himself in the middle of the front row, his turbanned head and massive shoulders making him seem like a large and talkative rock. In a voice which bounced off the walls and boomed throughout the room, he cross-examined Hunter at length on his artistic integrity, with special reference to sexual licence. Had he given serious thought to the effect that scene could have on the day-to-day lives of his actors? Surely such scenes had bearing ever afterwards on the quality of their social discourse?

The Sikh's bombast made Ajay even more despondent. 'The

ignorance, the prudishness . . . There was a riot the other week . . . All it takes is a film with the word 'love' in the title . . . The police were called and of course they brought their lathis. They charged into the crowd so that people were beaten like dogs.'

Later, out in the warm, soupy air, he seemed to cheer up. 'I'm sorry. I am being very dull. And ungrateful. Perhaps I could give you some tea. I live quite near.'

They walked a short distance along the potholed pavement of Lower Circular Road before moving into a twisting maze of lanes and back streets. At last Ajay turned into an alley indistinguishable to Matt from all the others and they crossed a tenement courtyard with doors opening onto dimly lit rooms emitting the mingled smells of paraffin, spices and fried fish.

Ajay's apartment was a box perhaps fifteen feet square, low-ceilinged, with a curtained area at one end. Parting the curtain, he gave Matt a brief glimpse. 'A kitchenette. I share the bathroom off the courtyard with some of the other tenants.'

The rest of the space was taken up by two hard-backed kitchen chairs, a bed covered with cotton homespun, a desk with an Anglepoise light—the handsomest piece of furniture in the room—and bookshelves made up of planks supported by breezeblocks. Ancient hardbacks and tattered paperbacks overflowed the shelving and formed towering stacks lining the walls beside it.

Plato's *Republic* sat on top of a pirated edition of Hemingway's short stories. There were French texts, Shakespeare, Milton, Robert Frost, *Maigret*, Elmore Leonard, Keynes' *Essays in Persuasion* and Freud's *Totem and Taboo*.

While Ajay made tea, he told Matt about his search for the apartment. Before finding it, he had lived in the suburbs, getting up at dawn to catch the bus to work.

He brought in the tea. 'Are you working on another novel?'

Matt shook his head. His future as a writer was not one of his favourite topics, but Ajay pressed him.

'You must at least have another planned?' He made it sound as if the answer truly mattered.

PART ONE

Matt addressed the truth reluctantly. The new novel he was trying to write stubbornly refused to take root in his imagination, and he was now having to face the possibility that *The Indian Summer* may have been a one-shot.

His disappointment was one of his reasons for being here. The job had held out the teasing possibility of change. Any amount of frustration was worth enduring for that. To change the subject, he asked Ajay about his job.

'I'm virtually a clerk, a shuffler of papers. The chance to be on a film set all day is a godsend to me. Just as I thought I would die of boredom I am being liberated for a whole two months.'

Matt got up and wandered across to the bookshelves, spying several scholarly paperbacks on cinema among the piled-up titles. Ajay confessed that all his spare cash went on books and the cinema. 'Not the commercial Hindi moves. I hate all that. Some friends and I started a cinema club.'

'And the job you're doing on our film? Will it be good for your career?'

'Actually, I was not the first choice for the job. The person originally selected was transferred to Delhi just before you all arrived here. My boss, Chowdhury, doesn't particularly like me—possibly because I don't like him. He is an awful toady.' A smile of satisfaction lit up his bony face. 'But I was his only option.'

'Is your family pleased?'

He was silent for a moment, fingering the face of a yellow-eyed tiger painted on the tea-tray: 'I don't see much of my family anymore. My father and I have fallen out.'

'Sorry. None of my business.'

'I don't mind talking about it. All through my childhood we were very close. He is a schoolteacher and my education was very important to him. He sent me away to a school run by the Jesuits. He didn't altogether like the result, however, and when I came home we had many arguments. Unfortunately, the last one was final.'

'Surely not. Fathers expect their sons to rebel. It's part of the relationship.'

'No. Our break is permanent. I am sure of that.'
'How long has it been?'
'A year now. My sin was a very serious one. I refused to have an arranged marriage.'

Matt knew the story. He had heard it two or three times before from young men met in the course of his travels in India, but he could see the effort it had taken Ajay to get this far.

He prompted gently. 'You mean they had a girl picked out for you?'

'Yes. I was taken to see her. The usual thing. All her relatives were there. Her father did all the talking. Mine answered for me. She and I hardly spoke. In fact, I could barely see her face. I don't think she looked at me once. Yet I found myself despising her simply for being part of the ghastly business. When we got home I told my father that that was it. I could not go through with it.'

'If he's an educated man he must have been able to understand how you felt.'

'Perhaps, but for him that was not the point. In his view it was my duty—something for which I should have prepared myself long ago. You see, my sister was married the year before and my parents had to provide her with a dowry. You know the custom. They had to go into debt to do it and the dowry from my marriage was expected to pay the bills.'

He smiled, looking wry and older. 'I send a little money whenever I can but I send it to my mother. If I sent it to him, it would just come straight back.'

It was after midnight when Matt left, and Ajay walked him back through the little streets, waiting for him while he hailed a taxi.

'Don't stop writing,' he said, as he leaned in the car window to say goodnight, then unexpectedly laid on a Peter Sellers parody: 'I am eagerly awaiting your next.'

PART ONE

4

Kate lay awake all night, brooding on Hunter's words, until she could stand it no longer and leapt from the bed to pull back the curtains and open the window to the smoggy air. She guessed it was somewhere near dawn and lay down again, staring at the grey woolly sky in a trance until tinges of pink began to appear.

Then something strange happened. Without thinking, she got up again, switched on the light and went to the mirror. As she stared into it, it suddenly seemed very clear to her that the work could and would be done. Susie was there in the image gazing back at her, her presence so strong that she filled the room with the urgency of her desire to be born.

She spoke the lines. Words that told her that they could show Ward, she and Susie. He would not be allowed to come between them. For that was what was happening. On the set, everything about him said, look at me. And look she did. She was fascinated by the ease, the technique and the monstrous ego. And while she looked, Susie melted away.

Ward wanted her to fail. After all, she was not his idea of a co-star. He wanted somebody bigger and shinier. Yet sometimes, in spite of himself, he began to encourage her. The work took over, the dislike receded and something involuntary came into play. To do his best, he needed her there with him, and every time she failed to make the leap, she saw his contempt grow. That had been the worst of it.

Hunter was on the telephone when she arrived at his poky office at the studio. She sat down outside to wait. He seemed to be pleading with somebody. She was struck by the novelty of it.

'But he's unhappy,' he said. The words were uttered in a choked, unfamiliar voice not at all like the usual fluid baritone, which was so rounded that she had thought he must have picked up some acting lessons somewhere, until she heard about the school debating team.

'I know we've been through it all a million times. Yes, I know you're the one who's on the spot. But that's not fair. Listen . . .'

She got up to go. Her timing was lousy.

'Just think about it. Okay?'

She heard him bang down the receiver. A moment later he appeared. 'Oh, it's you.'

'I'll come back later.'

'Why?'

'You look upset.'

He smiled, embarrassed but not too unfriendly. 'Jess, my wife. We have two kids, both in boarding school. One's okay, the other one isn't . . . Come in.'

'I wanted to talk to you about last night. I know I sounded low.'

'Yes.' His tone said, tell me something new.

'Well, I'm not ready to give up. I really want this part.'

'Glad to hear it.'

He had made a dive for one of the papers on his desk and was holding it up. It quivered with leftover anger from the telephone conversation.

'Look, I will come back later.'

He put down the paper and stared. 'It's now or never. Since you've taken the trouble to come here to convince me you're serious about the part, I want to hear you do it. Go on, convince me.'

She stood up. 'I don't think you're in a mood to be convinced.'

'It's the last chance you're going to get.' As they stared at one another, the telephone rang.

The voice on the other end was so loud that she could hear it from where she stood. It was high-pitched and female. 'Tina,' said Hunter.

Kate turned towards the door. Hunter motioned for her to sit down again.

'This won't take long, will it, Tina? I have someone with me.' He hunched over the receiver, staring at the floor. 'Is she? that's awkward. Can't you stall her? . . . Well, try.'

PART ONE

He looked up at Kate and put his hand over the receiver. 'Okay, you win,' he said to her. 'Give me ten minutes.'

As she left the outer office, she could still hear his voice, much softer than before but still audible over the flimsy plywood. 'I promise you,' it said. 'You won't have to wait much longer.'

She had tried not to think of the other actress waiting in the wings because she knew where the thoughts would lead. Now she couldn't help but think. She thought of Sylvia.

At the time, they had been leading the perfect life, she and Dermott. They'd had a house right on the beach at Malibu. It reminded her of home—except that the beach traffic was far more exotic. Joggers, body-builders, performers of *tai chi* and players of volleyball—a day-long parade of narcissism on the hoof.

The beach had been paradise. It had also produced Sylvia. She had been brought to breakfast by one of their neighbours, and stayed long enough to change everything. Sylvia was blonde and gleaming and conspicuously glad to be alive. She looked unnervingly like Kate herself—except that she was much, much younger.

It was such a cliché. Somehow you expected reality to be ... well, more true to life. Afterwards, one of her friends had asked why it had taken her so long to guess what was going on. The answer was that she had guessed but she hadn't believed it.

Dermott had made a great show of being distraught. Perhaps he was. She knew he still cared for her. He'd shown signs of wanting them both, hinting that he might recover from Sylvia, as if from a traffic accident.

Kate knew that he wouldn't. Sylvia was in for the long haul. At first their friends had made outrageous jokes about her lack of acting talent. Then they had stopped because it was no longer true.

Kate had left the beach and retreated to the hills, which were appropriate but depressing. Her new house was dark with a view of trees from every window. On windy nights they creaked and scraped against the roof, as if begging to be let in.

Ten minutes later, back in Hunter's office, she wasted no time in preliminaries. She had to know, she told him. This woman they had, waiting to take Susie away from her . . . it was Sylvia Elliott, wasn't it?

Poker-faced, he let her sweat for a moment. 'No, it isn't. We didn't think of her.' Then in a tone as dry as ashes: 'Pity. She'd have been perfect.'

5

Matt saw that the chart on Charlie's wall was crisscrossed with notations. Ajay and the location manager had worked at great speed. Permission had been granted for filming on the Howrah Bridge, aboard a ferry on the Hooghly, at a villa in Alipore and at the city's two great colonial show-pieces—the Victoria Memorial and the Tollygunge Club.

While Charlie could not praise Ajay enough, there was one piece missing from the jigsaw.

One set of script changes had been dictated by Hunter's discovery of a Victorian palace hidden away in one of the city's side streets. Built by a princeling of the Raj with large pockets and a passion for antiques, it was run by the government as a museum. Because very little was spent on its upkeep, it existed in a condition of mouldy splendour which so enchanted Hunter that he had decided he must set a sequence there.

Although permission to film in the palace and its grounds had been easily obtained, they also needed the co-operation of the landlord of a neighbouring network of tenements—a powerful businessman with a dubious reputation.

'So who are we dealing with here?' asked Hunter.

Ajay had heard many rumours. 'Ranjan Joshi is a very notorious character.'

PART ONE

'Mafia?' asked Charlie, a constant reader of the crime stories in the Indian papers.

'All I know is that he has his fingers in many pies, which does not make him unusual here.'

A light rain was falling as their driver manoeuvred the Ambassador through the rutted streets, swearing quietly to himself as jaywalkers hurtled to and fro. Matt could never get used to the ferocious drama of Indian roads. It mesmerised him. He gazed out of the window in terror at the macho Sikh taxi-drivers making their kamikaze-like lane changes, one hand pressed hard on the horn, and prayed for the darting scooter-riders with their finely balanced pillion passengers, many of them women in saris riding sidesaddle; the street kids dashing out at the red lights with grimy scraps of rag to rub at car windscreens in exchange for a few notes tossed at them by the drivers; and the beggars, whose macabre exhibitions of entrepreneurial flair eclipsed everything. At the first set of lights, a young man with a clean white shirt and no legs gunned his wooden trolley across three traffic lanes to reach them.

'I am a handicapped man,' he said, as he brought his face up to the window. 'I am having money problems.'

Ajay was talking about Joshi. 'It is well known that he has links with politicians and that he takes kickbacks for services rendered. The old story.' He said that the residents of the tenements depended on Joshi for everything. Some would not hear a word against him. 'He may exploit them but in Calcutta the devil you know is often to be preferred.' Joshi lived in a street arched over with mud-caked trees where the houses were hidden behind high walls of white stucco. Even though the stucco was stained with tide marks of rising damp and the street was no more than a half-mile from Joshi's tenement property, it was a neighbourhood where the rich lived.

The house was a large brick and cement square of two storeys with a stubbly grey lawn and a front door decorated with a brass knocker and panels of amber glass. A boy stood waving a dribbling hose over a flower bed, but the quietly suburban atmosphere was destroyed by the presence of a group of thuggish young men in flared pants and tightly fitted body shirts who sat on the steps smoking.

Charlie's knock was answered by a servant in a creased white coat who murmured something then left them, vanishing soundlessly up the stairs.

The hall had a bumpy parquet floor, a feature wall in polished slate and a picture of the dancing Shiva. Through a half-open door to the right, they could hear loud music underscored by the lazy hum of voices. Matt caught a glimpse of a silky rainbow, which resolved itself into a group of women in saris reclining on cushions before a low table bearing a collection of crumpled chocolate wrappers and teacups stained with lipstick. In the corner was a television set showing a Hindi musical.

They were led upstairs, where a door opened to a sudden gust of laughter. A large, jowly man emerged smiling from the crowded, smoky interior. 'We shall find somewhere more private,' he said. 'Please follow me.'

He ushered them into a small room furnished with leather sofas and carpeted with shag-pile in a garish orange. The sofas exhaled softly when sat upon, making Joshi smile, and they arranged themselves awkwardly, knees bent, while he chose a chair just high enough for them to have to raise their heads to speak to him.

Matt was disappointed. Joshi was boringly prosaic. He was dressed in a khaki bush-jacket which strained to cover his paunch, and his round, fleshy face, with its fat lips and balding forehead, gave him the appearance of a bad-tempered baby.

Hunter explained that they planned just two days of filming in the palace. 'The people who live in the area will be inconvenienced as little as possible.'

Joshi brooded on this. His people had no experience of such a thing. The prospect was making them uneasy.

Hunter reassured him.

'Assurances . . .' He flapped a plump hand. 'I am not just the landlord for these people. They trust me to act in their interest.'

PART ONE

They had come to the crux of the matter. Hunter edged around it cautiously, arriving finally at the words, 'generous fee'. Charlie laid an envelope on the table. Joshi stared at it for a moment, then, with bee-like swiftness, the plump hand descended. He slit the envelope, gazing at the cheque as if the numbers written there were indecipherable symbols from some lost civilisation.

'As I said, a generous sum,' said Hunter.

Joshi allowed the cheque to flutter towards the table.

'Generous? In whose terms? This film you are making? What is it about?'

Hunter politely reminded him that he had been sent an outline.

'I have no time to read stories. Stories are for children.'

Undeterred, Hunter embarked on a synopsis of the script. Matt settled down to enjoy what promised to be a polished performance. Hunter's technique had been honed by many such recitals given over lunch to non-reading film industry executives, but before he had gone far, Joshi interrupted.

'Westerners do not understand India.' His hands were again folded across his belly. 'You see only what you expect to see. My people know that. They think you are depicting them and their neighbourhood in a bad light.'

When Hunter tried to continue, he raised his hand. 'It does not matter what I think of it. We're talking of the people under my protection. They are hearing things they do not like.'

Hunter persevered. Having heard the story, Joshi would be able to calm their fears.

'How do I know you are telling me the truth?'

Hunter brought the Ministry into play. With the Ministry vetting the script, any slur on the city and its people would be out of the question.

'The government . . .' Again the plump hand took flight. 'I am not talking about the government. The government is one thing, the people are another. To me it is the people who matter.'

Charlie had edged so far forward on the ridiculously low sofa that his chest was pressed against his thighs. 'Of course, and we want to make it worth their while.'

'The people are not to be bought off so easily.'

Charlie produced a queasy smile. 'Tell me, Mr Joshi, what do you think would be an acceptable sum?'

Later, when Joshi was showing them out, Matt was interested to see that all traces of babyish ill-temper had vanished, replaced by a bubbly jollity. He was delighted to have done business with them. He slapped backs, pumped hands, radiated approval.

'Pleased to meet you, Mr Gupta,' he said when it came to Ajay's turn for a farewell handshake. 'And what is your role in this affair?'

Ajay's explanation was received as a great joke. 'The man from the Ministry. Then any complaints I am having will be directed straight to you. Be warned.'

His Santa Claus laugh followed them down the stairs.

PART ONE

INT. VICTORIA MEMORIAL. DAY.

RAJIV, FLETCHER and SUSIE are in the Queen's Hall, the echoing expanse under the dome, being lectured by TAPAN, an excitable young guide. We come in on his summing up . . .

>TAPAN: Did you know that the Queen herself took lessons in Hindustani? It's all in here. The whole story.

He motions them on. SUSIE falls into step beside him. RAJIV and FLETCHER follow.

>RAJIV: (In a low voice) Tapan has dreams of impressing some rich tourist and being offered a job in Europe or America. He's learning French and Italian in preparation.

>FLETCHER: (Faintly mocking) And you, Rajiv? What's your dream?

>RAJIV: Not that one. I'm here to stay.

They have arrived in the portrait gallery. FLETCHER loiters by the Duke of Wellington, looking contemptuous.

>FLETCHER: The cant, Rajiv. The red tape. The self-importance. How can you stand it?

>RAJIV: (Lightly) Born to it.

>FLETCHER: No. You're a modern man. (With urgency verging on panic) Rajiv, there's no logic here.

>RAJIV: (Amused) No, you're wrong. There are rules. The main one to remember is that we all want to make our mark—even on the passing stranger. Indians don't like to disappoint. Saying no is a no-no (Laughing) Remember that, Mr Fletcher, and you save time and aggravation.

CHAPTER THREE

1

The whole world seemed to Kate to be shrouded and smoky—the muffled sky; the ferry with its decks of battleship-grey; and the distant figures on the ghats, dunking themselves in the murky waters of the Hooghly in their never-ending efforts to wash away the dirt of the world.

Against the grey, the few flashes of colour—the orange sails of passing dhows, the saris of the women on the shore—seemed luminescent. Gaudiest of all was the bright blue shirt worn by Girish Bannerjee, who was squatting on the deck, imprisoning them with his brown eyes and white smile.

'I became arrogant, you see,' he told them. 'I went back to my old ways.'

He was to be Rajiv. Tall and feline, he would be elegant one day but was now kittenish and slightly out of control with a touch of the alley cat about him. He was telling them his story, which was worth hearing, although obviously an old routine. He showed no sign of being bored with it. It wasn't clear if he expected to be believed. He spun it out like a long-running joke.

It began with his childhood in the city's slums and the days spent begging and picking pockets to help feed himself and his family, then it took a leap into wonderland with his 'discovery' by a visiting film company looking for children who could be taught to act.

Ward entered into the spirit of it, zestfully playing the sceptic. 'Come on, kid, you don't expect us to believe that.'

Girish shifted on his haunches and laughed up at them, swearing every word was true. 'I think it was my wheatish complexion that got me the job.'

Ward was baffled.

'I am not very dark. Not as dark as him, for instance.' He pointed at one of the grips. 'It is a very big thing here. Anyway, I watched very closely and I learned very fast—so fast that they gave me a big part. At the age of twelve, I was a film star. It could not continue, of course, but I would not accept that.' He paused dramatically. 'So three years later at the age of fifteen, I decided I no longer wanted to work at the sort of jobs they are giving me. I have been a big-time actor. I am not going to work as a runner, fetching the coffee, so I quit. I also stopped attending the classes the film company is arranging for me.'

He paused again—reflectively this time. The past had taken over.

'So what happened?' Ward really wanted to know.

'Oh . . . finally I came to my senses.' He was charmingly vague. 'I grew up. That is what happened.' His smile lit up his face. 'I returned to school and here I am.'

He glanced around at the small army of technicians, some picking their way around the tangle of electrical cords snaking across the deck; at the lamps poised to send beams of light slicing through the greyness; at the extras huddled against the breeze coming off the water, warming themselves with coffee in styrofoam cups.

'It is not easy to make a film in Calcutta. Thomas is very brave.' Girish was the only one to call Hunter by his first name.

Ward grunted. 'It's the producer who's brave. Let's hope he's put money in the right pockets.'

Girish turned to Kate. 'You must think we are very corrupt people.'

Ward answered for her. 'How could she? She lives in LA.'

'People survive the best way they can,' she said.

Girish nodded approvingly, eyes lustrous. 'Tell me what it is like in LA.'

'It's all business, Girish.'

Now that he had finished his story she was longing for quiet. Somewhere to go and think. Not too much. Just enough to get her through.

She wasn't sure how much longer she had. She had tried to convince Hunter of the Susie she knew was just beneath the skin and she had talked about Ward's effect on her, all the time expecting him to say that if she couldn't handle Ward, then she couldn't handle the part. But he'd heard her out in silence and at the end, sounding bored with the whole business, had said: 'All right. We'll see how it goes.'

So here they were—seeing how it went.

Everybody must know, she thought as she sat in make-up, which was a curtained cubicle on the lower deck. Hunter would have talked to Andy McCaffrey. And Andy would have talked to anybody who'd listen. George would have heard. He did hair and was staring at her now, eyes glinting behind Gauloise smoke, as Melanie prepared to make her up.

Melanie and George were light and shade. She was a creamy-skinned blonde; he was dark, thin and permanently poised to meet the worst.

'Charlie's been in,' he said, staring at her steadily.

She nodded. Charlie would have been trying to help. He would have said, 'For Christ's sake, spend a bit of time on her.' He would have told them to do their utmost, making the situation sound truly desperate.

'Ward's nervous,' said Melanie helpfully. 'He's been giving me hell.'

'It's his capillaries,' said George. 'And the new boy, of course. He doesn't know what to make of him.'

'None of us do.'

'Very beautiful.'

Melanie agreed. 'And knows it.'

George thought that was only reasonable. 'If I were you, though, I'd be keeping my wits about me.'

PART ONE

They both smiled at her in the mirror—Melanie's smile, benign and sunny; George's slightly twisted from a lifetime's scepticism. The smiles cheered her. It was quite possible, she decided, that George and Melanie were on her side.

Suddenly the curtain parted and Hunter appeared. 'Just come for a look.' He turned to her image in the mirror and gave it a long, non-committal stare. The room held its breath.

'Don't be long,' he said and was gone.

George winked at her. 'God has spoken and God alone knows what it meant.'

Sitting among the extras on the upper deck, Matt viewed the action with a sense of remoteness and disorientation. It was months since he and Hunter had finished writing the scene about to be shot, and he no longer had any idea how it fitted into the scheme of things.

He knew what it should achieve. It should dramatise Fletcher's troubled, ambivalent fascination with India and show up the strains that were starting to develop in his relationship with Susie. He read it again. The words rolled around in his head without making any connections. He had even forgotten which were his and which were Hunter's. He thought there should be a laugh in there somewhere but couldn't find the place.

At the point at which the scene occurred, Fletcher had become obsessive about what he read in the papers, vituperative about India's politicians and bureaucrats and itched to be at work, putting it all down on paper. Instead he was having to trail around with Susie and Rajiv, pretending to enjoy himself. The scene in progress took place during a so-called pleasure trip on the Hooghly to watch the sunset.

Matt wished he had something to do. Everybody else did. They may not have been doing it—the extras, for example, were leaning miserably against the ship's rail or stamping up and down, trying to stay warm—but they knew they were needed. Even Ajay, whose official job it was to sit and watch, was busy with something else. He had gone off with Hunter to talk to the actor who was to play the ferry tour-guide. Matt, on the other hand, felt that the caravan had moved on without him.

There was a call for quiet. A small space in the centre of the deck became the focus of everybody's attention. Within this island, enclosed by cameras, lights and peering faces, were Kate, Ward and Girish Bannerjee. They were seated together on one of the ferry's benches while Hunter leaned over them, speaking in a tone so soft that Matt could catch no more than the odd word. 'The emphasis . . .' said Hunter, '. . . dialogue . . . overlap . . .'

The technicians hovered about the cables, lights and lenses, observing the islanded figures dispassionately as features in a landscape. Matt wished he were a technician. In particular, he would have liked to be Andy McCaffrey, who glided through the scene making mysterious adjustments which would go on right up until the call for action. Matt envied Andy his tools—his light meter, gels and filters, his range of film stocks. Andy painted with light which seemed to Matt a much more reliable instrument than the words he himself used. Andy saw the results of what he did. He could get instant playback on the video screen which sat to one side, recording every move the actors made. In contrast, even though Matt was holding his own work in his hands, its essence seemed lost to him.

Hunter's first assistant, Nick Thornton, shepherded a group of extras into the rows behind Kate, Ward and Girish. Matt moved around to the area near the camera. Although he could see and hear clearly, the three actors, wrapped in their bubble of light, seemed to him to have slid off into some other dimension, parallel but unreachable.

The rehearsal began and although every line of dialogue was perfectly audible, Matt found it hard to listen. Instead he watched, mesmerised by the body language of the trio on the bench. He saw how Girish leant forward eagerly, talking into the faces of the others; how Ward staked out his space in the frame by resting his arm along the back of the bench; how Kate leaned into the hollow of his arm so that she had to turn her head to speak to him, arching her neck in a coquettish, sensual movement which effectively stole the scene.

PART ONE

Hunter smiled, saying nothing until abruptly the bubble burst. Kate broke off in mid-sentence. 'That's a terrible line. I can't say that.'

Everybody turned toward Matt—even the technicians, no longer priestly in their devotion to the job but grinning like schoolboys at the prospect of someone else's humiliation at the hands of the teacher.

'One of Hunter's,' he said smoothly.

Everybody laughed—even Kate. Especially Kate. Matt was caught up and lapped in laughter.

The next run-through left Hunter looking doubtful. He dropped to one knee in front of Ward. 'You're not giving me enough. Fletcher's on edge here. He's twitchy. I want more movement.'

Ward now had both arms stretched along the back of the seat. To Matt he looked like a cartoonist's impression of the state of relaxation.

'Okay, chief.' He gazed down on Hunter. 'Edgy it is.'

This time the dynamics of the scene altered radically. Ward changed places with Kate so that he sat between her and Girish and proceeded to use his dialogue like scatter-shot to disrupt the flow of their conversation. An extra note of dissonance was added by the restless jiggling of his leg against the seat. When it was over he cocked his head at Hunter with a look that said, 'What about *that*.'

Perversely, Hunter stood rubbing his face, refusing to respond.

'There's something I'd like to try,' said Kate.

This time, when Ward's leg started jiggling, she laid her hand on his thigh and smiled into his eyes. Only a few seconds were involved but they effectively restored the eroticism of the first run-through and permitted her to recapture centre stage.

Now Hunter didn't hold back. 'Terrific. Let's do it.'

Ward had faltered and lost his rhythm. Such a little thing, she thought. She had surprised him, that was all. Made him think. And for Ward's kind of actor, thinking was disastrous.

Afterwards, Girish sat with her, wanting to talk.

'I liked it when you did this.' He touched her knee and held his head in the flirtatious way she had in the scene. She started to laugh: he was such a perfect mimic.

'When I was a child,' he said, 'we liked to sneak into the cinema to sit in the front row. The musicals were our favourite. Dancing around under the screen until they caught us and threw us out.' He gave her a hearty jab in the ribs. 'I don't think Jake was very pleased with you.' He grinned with delight. 'Excuse me, that was not a wise thing to say. You must let me know when I am behaving badly. By nature I am not a very tactful person, so I shall be relying on you.'

Later in the day, Ward's anger at her boiled over and they started to fight about everything. It seemed to her that he didn't care too much about winning, only about the damage he could inflict. If there was a winner, it was Girish, who stole each take, entrancing Hunter with his ability to produce infinite variations on a single move.

As soon as it was over, she saw what she should have done. Instead of wrangling with Ward, she should have been working with Girish. They should have been a team, she and Girish. He was a gift and she should have appreciated him.

Ajay had told Hunter and Matt about a speech he'd once heard one of the city tour-guides deliver aboard the ferry. He'd remembered all of it, almost word for word. Hunter had liked it so much he had discarded the one Matt had written and used it instead. Now, instead of the actor hired for the scene, he wanted Ajay to play the guide.

At first Ajay refused, yet Hunter continued to press him. He must repeat the speech exactly as he had reported it.

They had planned to shoot at sunset, no more than an hour away. Andy McCaffrey and his team were already working furiously to arrange the lighting.

'It's a long speech,' said Ajay. 'It will take several takes. More, if you use me.'

Hunter didn't think so.

PART ONE

After rehearsing with Hunter in a quiet corner, Ajay stepped before the camera with surprising confidence. At least surprising to Matt, who had nothing of the actor in him and expected serious people of Ajay's sort to be the same. He was amazed when Ajay got to the end of the first run-through without missing a beat.

'There are one hundred and fifty factories which discharge effluent into the Hooghly yet every Hindi in this city begins his day by drinking Ganga water. You ask us why we do this and the answer is that it is our religion. You cannot take it away from us, for without it we would be crazy. It is our inspiration and our refreshment. I, too, must have my Ganga water. But I am an educated man . . .' He scanned his audience. 'And first I boil the water and drop in a purifying tablet.' Another pause and a radiant smile. 'As we all know, the gods help those who help themselves.'

The crew applauded and Kate went over and hugged him. Charlie sighed with relief, but before Andy and his camera operator were quite ready, a high-pitched babble in Hindi was heard coming from the gangway.

Joshi loomed in hulking silhouette, accompanied by a man of competing bulk and shining baldness with a moustache curving over round, firm cheeks. Escorting them were two of Joshi's strongmen who hung back, surveying the scene darkly.

The glossy man was introduced as Mr Singh. In contrast to Joshi, who had resumed his expression of pouting discontent, Mr Singh was full of unctuous smiles and twinklings.

'We heard you were here and we were nearby so we thought we would take the opportunity. Mr Joshi is naturally very interested to see the way you cinema types work. I hope we are arriving in time to witness some action.'

'One more scene before we wrap.' Charlie produced a courtly smile. 'That is, before we pack up for the day.'

Ajay glanced up nervously then began his speech again. It was a more subdued reading this time. When it was finished, he and Hunter went into a huddle. Joshi and Singh muttered ominously in Hindi.

There were three more takes before Hunter was satisfied. By then the sun had become a blood orange, its rim balanced against the flaring horizon. Hunter had just shouted 'Cut!' for the last time when it dipped and vanished from the sky.

Joshi's voice came rumbling out of the gloom. 'Is that a copy of the script of this film?'

He plucked the pages from Matt's hands. 'The speech we have been hearing—show me where it is written.'

Matt said it was too dark to read.

Joshi pointed towards the only unextinguished lamp.

'We may not be using this scene,' said Charlie.

'Not using?' Singh gave the phrase a high, rising inflection.

'Just an idea we were trying.'

'How can that be?' Joshi's pout curled into a snarl. 'You have distinctly told me that your script has been vetted by the Ministry and is not to be changed. It is an objectionable speech. The kind which reinforces Western prejudices about our city.'

'Oh?' Charlie refused to understand.

'The factories that are mentioned. "Discharging their effluent" . . .'

Singh chipped in sorrowfully. 'Untrue and unfair. A concoction.'

'Worse,' said Joshi.

'Yes, a condescending speech concocted in ignorance.' No longer sorrowful, Singh turned up the heat, glittering with Joshi's reflected anger.

Hunter joined them, a figure of exaggerated calm, his hands in his pockets.

Joshi greeted him with a predatory growl. At the same moment, he remembered where he had seen Ajay. 'A civil servant, not an actor. So why is he in your film?'

'He's not,' said Charlie. 'He's advising us. Trying it out. The speech, I mean.'

'So he is the one who made up this lie,' said Singh. 'A civil servant and he is peddling these distortions about his own city.'

'Are you saying that there is no chemical effluent in this river?' Hunter's tone was recklessly tinged with amusement.

'An inaccurate and contemptible speech,' said Joshi.

'We're not using it.' Charlie glared at Hunter.

'I will be wanting your word of honour on that.'
'Of course.'
Joshi heaved himself to his feet and turned toward the gangway. Taken by surprise, Singh stumbled after him.
'Goodbye then,' said Joshi ferociously. 'I am going to be counting on it.'

2

Matt joined the cast and crew to watch a new batch of rushes. Charlie had had to fight Customs for them and his ulcer had been reactivated. He sat rubbing his diaphragm. Hunter offered little sympathy, saying that his gut was finally saying no to all the chilli he fed it.

When Ajay appeared on the screen, there was much stamping and whistling, causing him to look embarrassed but pleased. Watching the four takes, Matt admired his naturalness in front of the camera.

'Number three's the one,' murmured Hunter.
Charlie made a face. 'Do we really need it?'
'Joshi'll never know.'
Matt said he would when the film came out
'Joshi's just trying it on,' said Hunter.

It was so easy when it worked, Kate thought, gazing at her own magnified image. So sinfully easy. A complete negation of everything your mother ever told you about working hard and being good. Goodness had nothing to do with what she was looking at. To hell with logic and hard work, too. As she had sat on the bench, confidently upstaging Ward, all she had felt was a delight in the assertion of her own ego. Alive and well, after all. What looked like sensuality was an expression of neither lust nor affection. Indeed it had nothing to do with anybody but herself. Self-love.

It was Dermott who had taught her the knack. Could it be that that was all he had taught her? Not love. Not the real thing. Just this, its mirror image. Best not to think about that. Best not to think about anything. Floating free was the trick. If only she could master it.

In the next take, she had lost it altogether. All the radiance had gone. Even her proportions seemed wrong, the set of neck and chin made ugly by the tension in her shoulders. She looked heavy and dull while Girish drew all the light, shimmering with it.

She glanced at him, but he didn't notice. He was enthralled. Lucky, lucky, Girish. He had his feet drawn up on the chair and sat cross-legged, gazing at the projected images as if seeing himself for the first time.

She thought again of Dermott, who hadn't properly looked at her until he had seen her face on the screen. They had met in her agent's office soon after she had arrived in London. In Sydney she had done some student productions and a television soap. Her agent had to talk very hard to get him to test her. But the test had done it. The test had altered everything.

Up on the screen Ward was now in close-up. He looked slightly ill, the wrinkles and hollows pitilessly exposed, the blue eyes shining with watery brilliance. They had been taking more care with her. In these new takes, she looked years younger. She should have known exactly how they had done it. She should have known enough to demand it in the first place. With Dermott, she had never bothered to learn about lights or lenses. She never needed to.

She looked young, Fletcher looked old. The contrast was startling, yet somehow it worked. This tired, edgy, all-knowing Ward was Fletcher to the life.

She glanced across at the real Ward. He was sitting with his arms folded across his chest, his jaw clamped so hard that she could see the muscle twitching under the skin.

'Jake is a lot older than I thought.' Girish smiled. 'Maybe a lot older than Jake thought.'

It was 3 a.m. and Matt very much wanted to go to bed but was too tired to walk along the corridor to his room. There was also the possibility of missing something.

PART ONE

Hunter was sprawled in a chair, head back, eyes closed, a drink at his side. Charlie stood with an empty glass pressed against the wall and his ear pressed against the glass.

'He's calling LA again.'

'He's always calling LA. And when's not calling LA, he's faxing LA. This is not news, Charlie.'

'Tonight there's a lot more traffic than usual.'

Matt's laughter verged on the uncontrollable, the sound of his voice telling him how drunk he was. 'You mean you stand here every night with a glass against the wall monitoring Jake Ward's calls?'

'Only when I can't sleep, which is . . . Well, I don't do it for long.'

Hunter opened his eyes. 'Jake's speaking to Tina. He's in love.'

Charlie removed the glass from the wall and slopped some whisky into it. 'He's scared, that's what he is.'

'I would be, too, if I were in love with Tina.'

'Of himself. He's scared of himself.' Charlie's voice skidded on the 's' sounds.

'You're right.' Matt wanted to reward Charlie for being as drunk as he was. 'Fletcher's making him feel old.'

'Yeah. He's afraid Tina won't love him anymore.'

'For God's sake, she sleeps with him. She knows exactly how old he is.'

Hunter's perfectly enunciated sibilants made Matt want to argue with him. 'It doesn't matter what *she* thinks,' he said. 'It's the way he feels about himself. He's abandoning his vanity . . . A lifetime of devotion and he's letting it all go.' His hand fluttered shakily in the air, pantomiming a limp goodbye to Ward's vanity.

'He's not,' said Hunter crisply. 'He's redirecting it. For the first time in his life he's realised he can act. If he wants to. And I am going to make pretty damn sure that he does want to.'

The force of these words silenced them. Charlie stared into his glass. Beyond the wall all was quiet.

'I think I'll . . .' Charlie was interrupted by the clunk of a door closing softly. His head jerked up at the sound of someone moving about in the corridor. 'What the hell is he up to now?' There was a knock on the door.

'Jesus.'

Ward was wearing a crumpled shirt with a button missing. The grey stubble on his cheeks gave him a fuzzy, out-of-focus look, yet there was nothing tentative about his entrance. Energy levels rose all round. Hunter sat up, Matt was miraculously sober again.

'Sorry to bust in on you but there's no time like the present.'

They absorbed these ominous words in silence.

'I've just been on to Tina in LA.'

'Nothing new in that, Jake,' said Hunter.

Ward's smile, unexpectedly boyish, brought him back into focus. 'Well, I miss her. Anyway, to cut to the chase, she's coming over.'

'No.' Charlie shook his head. 'No.' For a moment he seemed unable to move beyond the word, then, regaining the power of speech: 'We had an arrangement. She was to look after everybody at that end while I took care of things here.'

'I know.' Ward's boyishness persisted. He perched jauntily on the arm of a chair. 'That's why I came straight in to tell you. She's just coming out here for a few days. There is one thing, though. Now that she and the guys from Acorn have seen the rushes, they think we're in real trouble with Kate.'

3

Kate watched Girish splash about in the hotel pool. He swam, duck-like, with his head up, turned over on his back and blew a jet of water into the air. When he was bored with floating, he paddled back to the edge of the pool and smiled up at her. 'I have an idea. For this afternoon.'

Before she could say no, he went on. 'This outing I am planning will provide valuable research for you. I know Hunter will agree.'

Hunter was strolling across the lawn towards them, wear-

PART ONE

ing a polo shirt and shorts and carrying a copy of the script under his arm. He looked suspiciously relaxed and friendly.

Girish was proposing a trip to a Hindi film. He had one picked out. 'A real blockbuster in the old style.'

She was tempted. An afternoon spent with Girish would almost certainly do more to help her than more hours of brooding alone. May be she could talk him out of the musical and get him to take her sightseeing.

'There won't be any subtitles.'

Girish's wet face shone with enthusiasm. He had already seen the film and would tell her the story in advance.

Hunter spread a towel on the sun-lounge next to her. 'How would you feel if I came too?'

As they waited in line on the steps of the theatre, Girish began his synopsis. Soon a crowd gathered and he was surrounded by an enraptured audience. In response, his voice rose and his gestures grew. Before long he was acting out the main parts, with different voices for each. At the end there were appreciative murmurs and some discreet clapping.

Kate slipped her arm through his. He had cheered her up. He began shepherding them into the theatre. 'Quickly, we must find good seats.'

First came the commercials—with families rejoicing in their rediscovery of the time-tested qualities of clove oil in their toothpaste; adolescents whose blemishes were banished by Skinnocence with Lacto-Calamine; and young executives toting their lightweight nylon Skybags en route to business meetings in Bombay and Delhi—then the movie, in which everything was as promised: a confection of music, swordplay and doll-faced pantomime in glittering fancy dress. Kate kept glancing away from it to spy on Girish, who was so caught up with it all that he never noticed her. He hummed and swayed to the songs and his lips moved silently in synchronisation with those on the screen.

They watched for about an hour then out of the darkness came Hunter's voice, pitched low enough for Girish not to hear. 'I don't think he'll mind if we leave now.'

She thought of refusing but there was no point. All this time, she had been sitting waiting for it. Better to get it over with. Still lost in the film, Girish nodded at them happily as they went.

Out on the street, Hunter asked her if she'd like a beer.

'Shouldn't you be somewhere?'

'Not for a while. Come on. There's a place near here.'

She found his choice of watering hole as mysterious as everything else about him. The Fairlawn Hotel had a broad paved entrance bordered with dusty potted palms, a pillared porch and a garden courtyard hung with vines threaded with fairy lights. Looking onto the courtyard was a small dining-room lined with postcards and photographs of English royal families past and present. The patrons were backpackers and English tourists with braying Home Counties voices, who looked unnaturally pale in the reflected light of the Fairlawn's sea-green walls. Except for the terracotta floor and the banana-chairs of multicoloured wicker, everything was sea-green—even the hatstand and the safari suit worn by the Indian waiter.

Inspired by the decor, Kate asked for fresh lime and soda but the waiter, who was short and muscular with a military moustache, answered with a fierce shake of the head.

'All right then, a Kingfisher and a Thums Up,' said Hunter. The waiter turned smartly on his heel and melted into the green.

'How did you find this place?'

'Don't you like it?' He grinned. 'Charlie will never find me here.'

It annoyed her to hear him make fun of Charlie. She frowned, which only made him laugh.

'I'm not being disloyal. Charlie's a worrier and he likes to have someone to worry with. Preferably me. How long have you known him?'

'A long time. But only in certain contexts. He comes to Los Angeles and we have lunch. Sometimes dinner, but mostly lunch. Before India I'd never seen him outside a restaurant. These days, he's possibly my best friend.'

'Mine, too.' Hunter smiled remotely, staring off into the surrounding greenery.

The waiter arrived with the drinks, putting them down hard and making the table wobble.

Hunter told her about Maggie, Charlie's wife. 'A firm hand. Occasionally a touch of the whip.' He poured his beer, watching it fizz.

'Charlie tells me you get nervous when you don't work. Hence the bad pictures.'

She told him she didn't get nervous. She got terrified.

'Why?'

He was still studying the froth in his glass, controlling the pace of the conversation.

'Simple, really. After Dermott left me, I had a breakdown—assisted by an obliging doctor and an excess of prescription drugs. Not working gives me the feeling that it could all happen again. Okay?'

He regarded her curiously. 'Not really. This was over a year ago, wasn't it?'

When she didn't answer, he persisted. 'You should be able to work by now. You should be able to put it into your work.'

'You'll do well in Los Angeles,' she said bitterly. 'You already speak the language.'

She was pleased to see him blush, but the embarrassment didn't last. He leaned forward. The table lurched. 'You're an artist, aren't you? For God's sake. You sit here, a bundle of exposed nerve endings and quivering bloody sensitivity. But when I put you in front of a camera, it all vanishes. *You* vanish. You're just not there. It's like trying to catch smoke in a bottle. The other morning on the boat. In the first scene. Quite suddenly it all came together. Thank God, I thought. She just needed time. Then nothing. All day. Not another damn thing from you.'

The anger evaporated. He looked disconcertingly human. 'I've waited a long time for this picture—knocked other things back because they weren't right. I've also given Jess a very hard time in the process. Our marriage isn't up to much anymore, and if I'm honest, which occasionally I can be, I'd have to admit that it's my fault. Envy gets under your skin after a while. Into your life, into your work.' On the table, he traced a line through the wet rings left by their glasses. A fragile bridge of understanding.

'So how long have I got?'

He had the answer ready before she finished speaking.

'Twenty-four hours. If tomorrow is no good, then we have to do something.'

She wanted to take a taxi back but he insisted they walk across the *Maidan* to the Victoria Memorial, where he got her to sit down on the steps in the sun. As if lulled by the symmetry of white marble and British landscaping, scattered groups of men and women sat cross-legged on the tiled, checkerboard expanse in front of the monument and gazed out over the gravelled walkways and the dusty green rectangles with their marigold borders and puffball trees.

She sat down reluctantly. She felt unbearably restless, itchy with it. Twenty-four hours. The words rustled in her head.

Hunter leaned back and spoke into the air. 'What was he like, this Dermott character? To leave you with such a powerful hangover?'

She was about to say that it was none of his business, then it seemed easier just to tell him so that they could get up and go. 'It wasn't just him. The work was part of it. A big part.' She hadn't been looking at Hunter. As she turned to him it occurred to her that she had never told anyone else the next bit. 'While we were together I felt understood. He could see things about me that I couldn't. I miss his imagination.' She held up her hands, making a square of them, the camera's eye. 'I suppose all the time we were together, he must have been looking at me like this.'

Hunter sat up. 'And now you need to show him an angle he never discovered.'

'He doesn't care anymore.'

'If you're good enough, he'll care.'

She tried to make it sound like a new thought. 'Maybe.'

PART ONE

4

Girish had been asking about Hollywood. He wanted it painted in word pictures; he had told his story and now he wanted theirs—anecdotes, memoirs, a West Coast Arabian Nights. Kate couldn't help; she lacked the background. She had not met John Wayne and had never been to the Oscars. Ward had done both and much, much more but was in no mood to talk about it.

They were sitting on the terrace of the Peacock Palace, looking out onto a garden with banyan trees and an old stone fountain. Mynah birds perched there and tiny vivid flowers sprouted through the cracks in the stone. Stepping at a stately pace across the yellowing grass were peacocks with pelicans waddling along behind.

Beyond the wrought-iron fence surrounding the garden was one of the most populous streets in Calcutta, a bustling strip hardly wide enough for a car, edged by vendors' stalls and overhung by tenements, their windows and balconies filled with people staring at the grips who were hauling their cargo of cameras and lights along the rutted bitumen.

Extras mingled with people who had come from the streets and buildings to join the crowd. The assistant directors and the liaison people were waving their arms and shouting at the ring of rapt faces forming around them, while the palace guard, a mountainous figure in khaki shorts and long socks, jovially flourished his stave at the bodies pressed against the wrought iron.

Girish gazed up happily at the audience in the gallery from his position centre stage. 'Everybody is wanting to be in on the action.'

'Always the way,' said Ward gruffly. He was already made up for the scene with tissues stuck in his collar, and the pancake made him glow in the morning sunlight. Even so, he looked withdrawn and remote from the scene. He pushed his chair back into the shadows and concentrated on the script.

Kate was called to the make-up trailer, parked at the quiet end of the garden.

'Jake's losing his grip,' George said, taking out the gel and shaping her hair into Susie's spiky, stand-to-attention style. 'He's been complaining that Andy isn't lighting him properly.'

'Lots of fireworks?'

'Not fireworks exactly, was it, Mel?'

'No.' Gazing into the mirror as if viewing the scene replaying there, Melanie began to describe it in her little-girl voice. 'Jake was sort of . . . embarrassed.'

'To be making such a thing out of it.' George had cut in, too excited to wait for her to finish.

Melanie was still thinking about it. 'He was trying to make a joke out of it . . . He sort of said that if he looked as old as he did in the rushes, nobody would believe that he and Susie could be a couple.' She pondered this. 'I s'pose they wouldn't.'

'Oh, I don't know,' said George. 'I always think that rugged, beaten-up look has got quite a lot going for it. Presumably that's what she thinks.'

'Susie? I'm sure she does,' said Kate.

'Not Susie. Tina Epstein. Anyway, we'll soon see.'

'What do you mean?'

'She's coming. Ward was full of it.'

'Girish doesn't help, of course.' Melanie had been pursuing her own line of thought. 'The fact that he's so beautiful.'

'And so pushy,' said George. 'I imagine he's keeping you both as busy as bees.'

Kate turned away from George, who saw everything, to Melanie's softer gaze. 'When does she arrive?'

'Any day now.'

George stood back and surveyed his handiwork. 'Those spikes do wonders. You look perky and full of fight. Go out there and give 'em hell.'

They were filming inside the palace, a Victorian wonderland of kitsch and fine art jumbled together in the gloom. Titians, Turners and Rembrandts mingled with an Olympus of athletic gods and voluptuous goddesses in bronze and marble; filigree cobwebs stretched across the cornices and the mantles, and over it all hung the stink of mould.

PART ONE

In the scene they were about to shoot, Rajiv was showing Fletcher and Susie over the palace as they expressed astonishment at the surreal medley of riches and junk. Fletcher had to be persuaded that the Old Masters were real, which made Rajiv quietly indignant. Susie, who had read about the palace, backed him up, helping to cement their developing friendship.

After the first rehearsal, Ward suddenly told Hunter that he wanted to try something different. As he elaborated, his gruffness disappeared and he seemed to light up from within. 'Okay. Now Fletcher's a cantankerous, impatient bastard who likes to make his own discoveries. So he races ahead of the others and when they get up here, he's nowhere. As they start looking around, the camera does a slow pan and there he is, in a corner, posing eye to eye with this character.' He walked across to a bust of Mars in a war helmet and stood so that the light slanted artistically across his left cheek. Girish watched intently.

They played it out and Hunter liked it. As they started down to the bottom of the stairs for another rehearsal, Ward shot off ahead and Girish turned to Kate: 'I, too, want to try something.' It was nothing radical—just a change in the tempo of his delivery so that Rajiv's dignified responses were magically transformed into playful banter. But Kate was thrown by it. 'It doesn't work,' she said.

Hunter mouthed the lines to himself. Ward leaned against Mars, looking thunderous. Hunter repeated her line, giving it a new lilt. Suspiciously, she tried it for herself. To her surprise, she found it suggested a rhythm for the rest of the take. She went ahead and did it. Ward's frown deepened and he shook his head.

'I like it,' she said.

The crew moved around quietly, tinkering with lights and cables; George flicked a brush through Kate's spikes; Melanie hovered.

Still glaring at her, Ward asked: 'And what does our leader think?'

Hunter smiled, 'I like it too.'

'Then you're making a goddamned mistake.' Ward

emphasised the words with a brief, rictus-like smile. It was a frightening sight. Girish observed it nervously.

'Come on, Jake,' Hunter said. 'You set the tone yourself with that bit of business.' He clapped his hands quickly to signal a take.

Girish's gaze flipped back and forth between the two men and settled finally on Kate. She took him by the hand and led him back down the marble steps.

'One to us.'

Girish giggled. 'Jake is a good actor, but not a very reasonable person.'

'Of course he's not. None of us are. We can't afford to be.'

'Oh, I think Thomas is different. He seems to me to be very reasonable.'

Afterwards, in the make-up trailer, George was still excited. 'Oh, I love it, I love it. The shoot's only a few days old and we're already into the subtext.'

The camera had been set up on dolly tracks laid in the street beyond the palace gates. Although the second assistant was working at crowd control with a loud-hailer, the crowd kept spilling out behind him and swelling, tide-like, towards the fence.

One of the grips had rigged up a beach umbrella to shade Kate and Ward as they waited at one end of the street, but the heat was getting to Ward. His make-up was starting to cake.

Girish was busy conferring with Hunter. Someone had hung a saffron-coloured *kurta* and white *dhoti* on the palace gates to dry and Girish had led Hunter across to them. From the miming and arm-waving that was going on, Kate was beginning to see what he was up to and sat waiting for the explosion.

Hunter approached them. 'Girish has an idea. As the three of you reach the gate, he'll snatch up the washing and make a joke about it in Hindi to the guard. He's good talent, the guard, and I think we should use him.'

'And what the hell are we supposed to be doing while this bit of local colour is being dished up?' said Ward, glaring at Kate because she was nearest. She looked into his sweating face with the eyes screwed up against the sun and, almost without thinking, said: 'I know what I want to do.' She fingered the camera hanging from a strap around her neck. 'I'd like to be taking a picture of Girish and the guard.'

'Show me,' said Hunter.

She improvised, making a little silent comedy out of the business of posing them. Somebody laughed. Then somebody else. When she had finished, she turned round to find Hunter watching her curiously.

'We'll go with that.'

'Great,' said Ward in disgust. 'Just great.'

Smiling faintly, Hunter headed towards the palace.

'Smartarse bastard,' muttered Ward under his breath.

Nick Thornton prepared to walk them through the first rehearsal. The crowd was hushed and all available grips formed a cordon in an effort to keep the spectators out of shot. Kate and Ward started forward with Girish slightly ahead of them and on cue he turned his head slightly to deliver his first line.

But before he could speak, Kate felt a rush of air near her cheek and suddenly Girish fell backwards, holding his leg. A great cry went up from the crowd and people scattered, desperate to reach safety, out of range of the stones that were raining down on them from the tenement rooftops.

One stone had caught Andy McCaffrey, knocking him sideways. He scrambled to his feet, shouting to the grips to unfasten the camera from the dolly, when suddenly, in the midst of the crowd, there was a whirlpool of violent movement. A flash of red appeared on someone's cheek. There were men lashing about with lumps of wood. People cannoned into one another and were knocked to the ground. Only the crush of bodies kept Kate standing.

The grips reached the camera in time but one went down under a blow from one of the sticks. Nick Thornton had the loud-hailer and was shouting to the crew to gather everything and get it into the palace. Kate had lost sight of Ward, but Girish had struggled to his feet and had hold of her hand.

'Come on, Katharine. Inside. We must get inside.'

Still limping, he began forcing a path through the crowd. Nick Thornton saw them and shouted for help and some of the grips moved towards them. As they surged through the palace gates, she took one quick, compulsive look at the scene behind her. All she could see were the clubs rising and falling into the press of bodies.

'You told me you took care of everything.' Ward was shouting at Charlie, who was nervously moving from one foot to the other. 'Know the right people, grease the right goddamned palms . . .' The speech subsided in a mutter of contempt.

They had done all they could, Charlie repeated patiently. 'Nothing is foolproof in this city. Christ, demonstrations here are as natural as bloody breathing.'

Ward's tantrum had a large audience. The cast and key members of the crew had crammed into Charlie's suite. Implicit in their silence was the suggestion that Ward might be speaking for them all. He had taken a glancing blow on the shoulder from a stone and there were numerous minor injuries suffered by others in the cast and crew but miraculously no one had been seriously hurt. The demonstration had ended as suddenly as it had begun. The thugs had disappeared into the crowd, and although the police had been quick to arrive and had swarmed through the tenements interviewing witnesses, they had little to go on.

Ward's tirade continued. He stared fiercely at Kate, who was confirming his opinion of her by refusing to back him up. Going for broke, she gave Charlie a look of wholehearted sympathy.

When Hunter took the floor there was a quickening of interest. The crew seemed to find him consistently fascinating.

Charlie was right, he said. They had done all they could. 'But we can't guarantee your safety. It's impossible, so all those who want to go home . . .' He scanned the faces in the room. 'Let me know now. You'll be paid off and put on the first available flight.' He looked around the room again. Ward opened his mouth to speak, then closed it again and gazed at the floor.

'Nobody?' Hunter kept on staring. No one moved. 'I don't want anyone here who is not completely committed to the production.'

There was silence.

Afterwards, Kate helped Girish hop back to his room.

'For me it is most interesting,' he said, 'that Jake has so much to say about the violence when he was present for such a short time. I only hope that when I reach his age, I am moving as fast.'

Hunter, Kate discovered, had a sense of occasion. To tell her what he had decided, he took her back to the Fairlawn. He waited for the surly waiter to dump two Thums Up in front of them on the rickety table, then he told her.

'Well, aren't you pleased?'

Relief had made her numb. 'How did you make up your mind?'

'The way you worked with Girish in handling Ward. It's only the beginning, by the way. Ward's going to get much worse. He hates both of you, but you the most.' He gave her a satisfied smile.

She was curious. 'Is it always like this on your sets?'

'Only when the dynamics dictate.' He leaned back in his chair and made a square with his hands, gazing through them at her. 'Through the camera's eye. Was it always like that?'

'Pretty much.'

'Even in bed?'

She was astonished. He dropped his hands and grinned. 'Sorry, I'm not usually so crass. Must be over-excited. You intrigue me. The way your face shows everything. No secrets.' He went on staring, taking her in feature by feature. 'No secrets at all,' he said dreamily. 'None. That's why I got so mad when you closed up on me in front of the camera. We're going to make a very good film together. You'll see.'

5

Harold Matthews, whom Kate now called Matt, was telling her about the end of his marriage. She had had to tease it out of him, but now that he had started, he seemed pleased to be telling somebody. She suspected that people seldom asked him anything personal; that he'd made a habit out of being the one who asked the questions.

'It's something that journalists do,' he said, when she voiced the thought. 'Anyway, what are you doing asking me? Actors only talk about themselves.'

'You've caught me on a good day.'

He had been waiting for a taxi in the lobby of the hotel when she came out of the restaurant after breakfast. She didn't want to go back to her room. She wanted to celebrate. She hadn't told anyone but Charlie about her conversation with Hunter. There was no one else to tell. And Charlie had just kissed her and heaved a great sigh of relief. To Charlie she had just become one less thing to worry about. So the elation had been left to bubble along on its own.

Matt had been on his way to one of the locations, an Art Deco house in a suburb called Alipore. It had curved ocean liner walls and iron-railed balconies painted the aquamarine of swimming pools. He had been astonished when she had asked to go with him.

The house was empty except for the servant who let them in then disappeared. They wandered around, fingering the sharp-angled furniture and gazing at the eggshell-blue walls and scalloped cornices. The only sound was the faint twitter of birds, the first she had heard in Calcutta.

'Was there a real Susie?'

He suddenly became interested in a piece of zigzag plasterwork.

'You don't have to tell me.'

He turned away from the plasterwork and scratched his cheek. She liked his reticence. The people she knew needed no prompting to talk about their love lives.

'Yes, there was a Susie. I had an affair with her. It broke

up my marriage.' He took a deep breath. Kate guessed that she was about to get the abridged version, perfected for general use.

'It was an attraction of opposites. Barbara—my wife—couldn't understand what we saw in one another. I'm not sure I can either.'

'Divine intervention, was it?'

He looked startled. She had put him off. Never mind. She was only bothering because she liked him. Sitting in on his conversations with Ajay, she had been put back in touch with the outside world. She also recognised him. Recognised his diffidence and the frustration that lay behind it. Watching him work with Hunter, she saw mirrored in his strained smiles and determined affability her own fears. Like her, he seemed becalmed, waiting to be blown in a new direction, which seemed odd because he looked so reassuringly solid in his creased linen jacket and baggy cotton trousers. The blunt features, the heavy walk and the self-deprecation could have made him seem dull. Soft and comfortable. But there was a glint in the brown eyes that said, so far and no further.

She wondered if his wife had felt cheated—if she had married him for his companionable air then been shocked to see how quickly the drawbridge could come up. Yes, she liked him.

'Come on,' she said. 'Don't stop now. It's good for you.'

She gave him a smile as sunny as a schoolgirl's. He smiled back doubtfully. Her face fascinated him. In repose, it assumed a strangely melancholy air. Cool grey eyes and a nose a little too fine and straight for perfection both hinted at an arrogance at odds with the sensuality of bee-stung lips. The effect, he thought, was to make you wonder how anyone so beautiful had the right to look so gravely on the world.

He had not counted on giving anything away. He had been getting by so far on his amiable-artist-buffeted-by-life routine, honed through countless sessions with Hunter and Charlie, and he still didn't fancy spreading his life out in front of her simply because she had a spare half-hour.

The smile was encouraging. It looked real enough. But how could you tell? She was an actress.

'Divine intervention?' He attempted a good-humoured laugh. 'I suppose Barbara could call it that. She's remarried. Very happily.'

The need to escape Barbara's happiness had been one of the reasons for taking on the screenwriting job. She had been determined that he share in it, adopting him as her new best friend. She had been much more enthusiastic about this than she had ever been about their marriage. He received regular letters. She would probably start introducing him to other women soon.

He guiltily admitted not putting enough time into being a husband. 'I was away for a lot of the time and she wouldn't come with me. Liked her job too much. She works for a cosmetic company—earns more money than I do.'

They moved upstairs, wandering through the bedrooms. The main one was attached to a bathroom with a shower screen sandblasted with fairytale images of mermaids and angelfish.

She asked what had happened to Susie.

'Oh, the affair ended at the same time as the marriage. By mutual consent. By then we were getting on one another's nerves.'

She thought he sounded more bewildered than sorry; as if he would like to know the reason so he could file it away for future reference.

'And what about Barbara?'

'Not by mutual consent.' He laughed weakly, the laugh dissolving into a sigh.

She had been tracing the sandblasted outlines of a mermaid's tail and turned back to him curiously.

'It was very painful for a while. We both did a lot of shouting. And crying. A lot of that. I think we exhausted one another.' He paused, not much wanting to go on. She could tell that he was wondering how he'd got this far. He shrugged. 'Now I hardly even think about her.' He stopped pretending and looked very sad. 'Everything passes in the end. It's supposed to be a comforting thought, that. Time heals. It makes you wonder, though, doesn't it? Why bother at all?'

CHAPTER 4

1

Matt and Hunter brought up the rear as Ward and Charlie piloted Tina Epstein out of the airport terminal and into the bonfire stench of the Calcutta night.

Even though the unit liaison man was there to deal with the touts eager for the privilege of carrying her mound of matched luggage, the confusion was spectacular. Watched by a voluble crowd, the party milled around the open boot of the Ambassador for some time, discussing ways and means of wedging everything into it.

When at last it was done and everybody was tightly jammed into the car, Matt heard Tina's laugh for the first time—a throaty crackle which bounced off the windows and startled the driver into grating the gears.

'Why didn't you warn me?' she asked.

The question dipped in the middle before swooping up at the end and prompted Ward to produce his own *basso profundo* roar of amusement, a sound nobody had heard in some time. While far from musical, the conjunction of the two laughs gave Matt the first hint of what Ward and Tina had going for them. The laughs declared them a pair—good-time people warmly admiring of one another's ability to move and shake the surrounding atmosphere.

'I did, honey. I did.'

Unable to see them from his seat next to the driver, Matt

could tell by instinct that Ward had embraced her, unconcerned about squashing those on either side of them hard against the doors. With Tina beside him, he was virtually reinflating—regaining the old macho exuberance knocked out of him by life with Hunter.

At dinner in the hotel, Tina hung on Ward's arm, letting go only to allow him to lift his glass or knife. She nagged him about the three whiskies he drank, tut-tutted over the cigar he smoked and worried about the effect of the Calcutta smog on his lungs. When not entirely preoccupied with Ward, she surveyed the rest of the table with daring green eyes and tossed questions into the midst of the conversation. She ignored the answers.

She was lithe and pale and her carrot-coloured hair was done in a basin cut with a long fringe to the eyebrows. She had a wide mouth with large, square white teeth and she wore scarlet lipstick and clanking earrings shaped like Chinese pagodas.

Her effect on Charlie was electric. He functioned at double speed, a blur of action and anecdote. He recounted his adventures with Indian Customs, relived his battles with city officials and treated them to a potted guide to the tortuous political networks he'd had to explore in order to make things happen. He gabbled as if on borrowed time, and so it turned out, for as soon as they had finished dinner, Ward gave Tina a besotted smile and suggested they have an early night. She patted his hand. 'You go ahead, hon. I won't be long.'

The atmosphere changed before he reached the door. Tina's gaze ceased to dart and flicker and became concentrated into an inquiring beam focused on Charlie and Hunter.

'First the good news. Everybody likes the Bannerjee kid. Which is lucky for all of us. Now comes the bad. Number one. Acorn is freaking over the schedule. One week and already you're behind.'

Charlie hunched his shoulders and reminded her of the riot.

'Yeah, the riot. The riot would go down very well with

Acorn. If I'd made a big thing of the riot, you wouldn't just be entertaining *me*. As it was, it's a wonder they didn't send some suit out on the same flight.'

Charlie repeated the story of Joshi. Tina only half-listened. Puffing furiously on a cigarette, she shot questioning glances towards Hunter, who remained wilfully silent. Finally, as Charlie was about to run down, she cut him off. 'So . . .' she said ominously. 'The schedule. What are you going to do about it Hunter?'

The dazzle of Hunter's smile suggested that the question was the most entertaining thing he had heard in many days. 'My best, Tina. I will do my best. As always.'

'Hun-ter.' Charlie turned the two syllables into a groan. With lightning swiftness, Hunter rounded on him.

'Is that not good enough for you, Charlie? Tell me now if it isn't. I'd like to know.'

At the whiff of discord, Tina perked up instantly. She turned away from Hunter and Charlie and, for the first time, Matt felt her focus on him—felt rather than saw, for the experience was so like sitting under a hot light that he flushed and put a finger against his neck, as if to put air between it and a tight collar.

She laid a hand on his arm. 'One thing we do have,' she flashed another snaky glance at Hunter, 'is a great script from a great book. I think we should keep that in mind. Just how great the book is.'

'You mean you've read it?' said Matt weakly.

Her laugh startled a resting waiter out of his doze. 'Jesus, Hunter has been grinding you down. Listen, Hunter . . .' The snakiness had gone, replaced by an even more frightening joviality. 'Give this guy a break. He's talent. A genuine talent.' She paused. 'Which brings me back to the real problem here. Kate isn't. Talent, I mean. And we've got to replace her.'

There was silence. Matt was startled by his own sense of outrage. How dare she? He suddenly realised that in the short time he had spent with her, Kate had worked her way so thoroughly into his imagination that her Susie now existed in tandem with his. 'No, you're wrong.'

Tina gave him an amused, indulgent look which said, this is a decision for us big kids. We'll get back to you later.

Charlie pitched in, red-faced: 'You haven't seen her new stuff. It's good. Really good. Hunter'll tell you . . .'

Hunter was delicately breaking a toothpick into small pieces. He did not look up.

Matt willed him to speak and when he didn't, burst out, 'Charlie's right. The work she's done in the past two days . . .'

Tina put her hand on his arm again then swept on, Chinese earrings jangling. 'Look, I know it's not nice. But this business is not about nice. She's got to go. We've just got to decide who's going to tell her.'

'No,' said Charlie.

Tina ignored him. 'Now the next item on the agenda. Jake. He's doing great work, but Hunter, you and Andy have got to make him look better.'

Now, at last, Hunter spoke. Now, over something that doesn't matter, thought Matt bitterly, he finally speaks.

'Come on, Tina,' Hunter said. 'We've got him looking like Fletcher. For the first time in his long and very lucky career, the man is acting.'

'Fix it.' Her head suddenly shot up. 'Uh oh.' Ward was standing in the doorway, beckoning her. 'I'm out of here. But the Kate thing. I'm telling you. It has to be done.'

As they watched her cross the room, Charlie turned to Hunter. 'You bastard.'

As if he hadn't heard, Hunter finished the rest of his drink and stood up. 'Good night,' he said cordially to Matt then, without looking at Charlie, he walked off.

PART ONE

EXT. CALCUTTA STREET. DAY.

FLETCHER and SUSIE are under siege from two bright-eyed beggar children as RAJIV tries to hail a taxi. He stands with arm raised, a slim, immaculate figure in blue blazer and grey trousers.

Taxis whiz by, all occupied. He shrugs ruefully at SUSIE as FLETCHER empties his pockets of small change.

> SUSIE: What about those little three-wheelers?
>
> RAJIV: Auto-rickshaws? (Glancing at FLETCHER) A rough ride.
>
> SUSIE: Doesn't matter.
>
> RAJIV: (To FLETCHER) Are you sure?
>
> SUSIE: (Before he can answer) It'll be fun.

An auto-rickshaw comes to a stop in front of them. They pile in, SUSIE in the middle. While they are still settling themselves, the auto-rickshaw swings back into the traffic stream, jolting them backwards.

FLETCHER is hypnotised by the closeness of the traffic in the next lane. A car's mudguard almost grazes his elbow.

SUSIE looks up, laughing, into his face.

When he ignores her, transfixed by the driver's lightning lane changes, she turns to RAJIV. He immediately leans forward, trying to look around her and check on FLETCHER.

> SUSIE: (Amused, flirtatious) He's fine, really. He's a reporter. Used to wars.

The auto-rickshaw sways and rattles; the air is thick with petrol fumes; a lorry looms above; a Vespa zigzags in front of them, making the DRIVER curse.

FLETCHER has gone stiff, eyes glazed.

INT. AIRLINES OFFICE.

RAJIV, SUSIE and FLETCHER are seated before a booking desk. On the other side, a CLERK stares into a blank computer screen.

>FLETCHER: What's he think it is? A crystal ball?

The CLERK glares at him.

>RAJIV: (Pained) It's about to come on line.

FLETCHER slumps in his chair, arms folded and lets his head flop onto his chest, simulating narcolepsy.

>SUSIE: Give him a chance, Will.

She smiles reassuringly at RAJIV.
   The screen suddenly lights up. RAJIV returns SUSIE's smile and they come together to confer with the CLERK as FLETCHER fades into the background.

PART ONE

2

Kate browsed dully among the terracotta figurines and straw table-mats of the Bengal Home Industries store. A few feet away, Tina was in a huddle with Girish over a brass lamp she might or might not buy. It had been a long morning. They had done the West Bengal Government Sales Emporium, Cottage Industries and the New Market, where Girish had manfully fought off the touts desperate to escort them into the dusty warren of little shops, and Tina had bought sari lengths and kurtas, jewellery and shawls.

There had been one bad moment. As they walked along Lower Circular Road, an unsmiling young man placed himself in front of Tina—in Rodeo Drive outfit of short skirt and bodysuit—blocked her path and gravely poked a finger into her right breast as if testing a mattress in a furniture store. The incident was over in a second. The man headed off, vanishing into the diesel fume haze. To her credit, Tina produced what Kate already thought of as The Laugh, but Girish was appalled and would have set off after the man if he had not still been limping from the blow to his ankle.

Now Tina was going to pack away her LA wardrobe and go Indian—saris in the evening, white cotton pyjama suits by day. Kate was reminded of Susie. There was a lot about Tina that reminded her of Susie. She agreed with Ward. The two were alike—so much so that she was unnerved.

Their morning together had been Charlie's idea. A bonding experience. 'Take her shopping,' he had said, eyes shining with desperation.

At their first meeting, Tina had greeted her with a thin smile, a surprisingly limp handshake and a rapid once-over, during which Kate had seen herself thoroughly written off. Tina had seen wariness and read it as weakness. Kate recognised an old enemy—the introvert-hating extrovert. She had known Tinas all her life. They were proud of never changing their minds. 'I know about people. I can tell the first time I set eyes on them. It's a gift I have.' That's what the Tinas said.

They went back out to the street, leaving behind the brass lamp, and as Girish went off to find a taxi they were surrounded by beggars.

Following Matt's example, Kate now carried rupee notes in her pockets, doling them out as long as they lasted. She had no idea if this was right or wrong and had decided already that towards the end of her stay in India she would do as sensible people advised and donate to some accredited charity. Meanwhile, she had to cope with the faces in the street, so she laughed with the children, responded to the buccaneering swagger of the older and bolder ones and had got used to thrusting rupees into the bowls of the cripples on the pavement without breaking her stride. Beside her, Tina gazed off into the distance, avoiding eye contact.

'I mean, are you telling me that those kids are going to get to keep those rupees?' she asked later in the taxi. 'Girish tells me that these people break the legs of babies to make them better beggars.'

She rolled her eyes and Girish shrugged helplessly but even the thought of the mutilated babies couldn't depress him for long. In Tina's company he was incandescent. No matter that she had never met John Wayne. She had brought Los Angeles with her. He breathed it in with her perfume, which was by Armani. Tina's conversation was dotted with the names of restaurants, designer labels and Hollywood executives, minor and major. Kate had heard of some, not of others. All blended together in a monologue which rolled on without punctuation. Girish splashed about in it joyfully, moving with its currents and eddies and occasionally beating back the tide with a question or two.

'Tell me again. He is one of the agents at CAA or do I have it wrong and he is an ICM man?'

The monologue flowed all the way back to the hotel. In the coffee shop, Tina got interested in Girish's story.

'You really worked in a brothel?'

'No, no, not *in* the brothel. I worked as a tea-boy in the neighbourhood of the brothel and it was on my daily round.' He had been eleven at the time.

'Wow!'

PART ONE

In the midst of their conversation Ward arrived, looking ruddy-faced and well-scrubbed from a morning in the hotel health club. He gave Girish a sour look. 'So Girish has got started on the sins of his childhood, has he?'

Girish nodded cheerfully and went on with his story. Ward settled down to wait. Ignoring Kate, he lit a cigarette and looked off across the room. Glad of a chance to escape, she was rising to her feet when he suddenly spoke, cutting off Girish in mid-flow. He told Tina there had been further negotiations with Joshi. 'He's turning the meeting into a goddamn party. He wants all of us along.'

'So the money's not enough,' said Tina. 'He wants a little stardust, too, does he?'

Girish shook his head. The incandescence had gone. He looked more annoyed. 'This trouble is all because of Ajay Gupta.'

There had been ill feeling between Ajay and Girish for some time. Kate had watched Girish glowering at the sight of Hunter and Charlie seeking Ajay's advice on the set and had witnessed his indignation over the casting of Ajay in the role of the tour-guide. 'What does he know?' he had complained. 'He's just a pen-pusher, a watchdog of the bureaucrats.'

Kate said that it wasn't Ajay's fault. 'Joshi would have found something to complain about. He's just hopping on the bandwagon.'

Girish looked even more annoyed, saying that only someone who lived in Calcutta could understand a person like Joshi. 'Some of the people in the tenements and the *bustee* he controls on the other side of the bridge see him as the only person who will help them in times of trouble. Nobody else is interested.'

'Meanwhile, he's screwing them for everything they've got for the privilege of squatting in a tarpaper shack on some shitheap,' said Ward. 'Oh, yeah, he's a great guy, Girish, a great guy.'

'You can never understand.' Girish's bright eyes flashed and Tina patted his cheek, causing Ward's smile to vanish.

'What the hell?' she said. 'He wants a dog-and-pony show, we give him a dog-and-pony show.'

3

Kate recognised the fat man sprawled in the biggest armchair as Joshi. Singh, whom she also remembered from the ferry, sat beside him, and perched on stiff-backed chairs were several other men looking like actors waiting for the curtain to rise. It was a gloomy room except for the rosy glow cast by dusty sunbeams shining through two long, pink-curtained windows, but in one corner was a parrot-bright splash of colour. There, the women of the house lounged on low sofas, watching the door.

As they entered, Singh leapt up to greet them. He was dressed in white, moustache sleek, cheeks smooth. He pumped hands enthusiastically. 'We are very happy to see you here.'

Joshi was slower to rise. His paunch was constrained by a tight-fitting jacket and he grunted and puffed as he got to his feet. Kate took his outstretched hand, which was remarkably small and soft, then, with a quick indifferent nod, he moved on. It seemed to be Singh's job to entertain the ladies—at least the visiting ladies. The ladies of the house remained in animated isolation in their corner.

Singh drew Kate and Tina aside, ordered them fresh lime juice and proceeded to tell them about Calcutta. 'As you must know, it is entirely the wrong place for a town. You have read the history?'

The novelty of this thought provoked one of Tina's laughs and Singh blinked brown button eyes before plunging on. 'A place of swamps, fever, miasma. The fault of the British who chose the site. But we have overcome. That is our special talent. To persevere and overcome. Calcutta is my adopted city. I am a Marwari.'

Singh swept on quickly, perhaps fearing another laugh. 'We are from Rajasthan and have become the businessmen of Calcutta. Mr Joshi is not a Marwari—he is from Bombay—but he, too, is a very good businessman. So we have come together.'

He paused for breath. Kate asked if Joshi's wife was among the women on the sofa.

'Yes, yes. You shall meet them. All in good time. First we shall eat.'

A buffet had been laid. They were led across and handed plates. Tina took some naan and looked doubtfully at the rest.

'Please,' said Singh. 'It is all very delicious. Nothing here to upset delicate Western stomachs.'

Tina explained that she had an allergy to chilli and he listened attentively, never having heard of such a thing. 'You will be safe here. Not a shred of chilli will pass your lips. I guarantee it.'

Throughout lunch he treated them to stirring tales of the ancient Rajput rulers, but once the eating and drinking was done, the small talk came to an abrupt end and there was some adroit social manoeuvring. Tina was swept off with Hunter, Charlie and Matt to another room to do business. After some whispered discussion, Ward was invited to go with them, leaving Kate behind with Girish. Singh took them to join the ladies.

'Aha,' said Mrs Joshi, leaning forward on broad thighs, swathed in apricot silk. 'So we were wrong. We have been playing a game among ourselves.'

Kate instantly guessed its nature but Girish responded eagerly. 'What sort of game?'

'We were trying to decide which of the two ladies—this one or the other—was the actress.'

'Oh, I see.' Girish laughed heartily. 'And what do you say to that, Kate?'

A plump, pretty girl, with an emerald-green sari and a ring of kohl around her eyes, cut in, answering for her. 'It is because you wear so little make-up. It is very unusual.'

Kate explained that she wore so much when working that it was a relief to go without when she was not.

'You are very pale,' said Mrs Joshi, not at all solicitously.

Kate changed the subject. 'You are all related?'

'My daughters-in-law.' Mrs Joshi was not to be diverted. 'You are singing in the film you are making?'

'Goodness, no. I can't sing.'

There were murmurs of surprise.

'I imagine that you have seen our Bombay film stars?'

'Yes, I have.'

Another of the daughters, indifferent till now, leaned forward. 'Who is your favourite?'

'They are all very glamorous.'

'That is true,' said Mrs Joshi. 'Their fans expect it of them.'

'Glamorous but not always professional, I believe.'

'Professional? In what sense?'

'In the sense of arriving for work on time.'

Mrs Joshi waved a dismissive hand. There was a clinking of bracelets. 'Stars will be stars. It is expected. They are not wage slaves. What do you think, Mr Bannerjee?'

Girish gazed at the girl in the green sari. His eyes shone with the urge to tease. 'I think they are a crowd of spoilt, pampered creatures indulged far beyond their worth. They are not gods, after all. Yet they are treated as such.'

Mrs Joshi tut-tuttered but the pretty daughter-in-law was intrigued. 'How do we know this is not just sour grapes on your part?'

'Sour grapes? Let me tell you something about the way the motion picture industry is working . . .'

In the other room Joshi presided, vitality restored now that the pleasantries were done. Here, too, the curtains were drawn and it was so dim that they might have been taking part in a seance with Joshi as the medium. He sat centre stage in a pool of light shed by a standard lamp with a fringed shade, flanked by the sinister figures of his beetle-browed sons. Singh had been relegated to a minor position.

Tina had placed herself between Hunter and Charlie, and Matt watched, fascinated, looking for clues to the balance of power. Was Hunter strong enough to stand up to Tina and how much did he want to? Why hadn't he spoken up earlier when Tina insisted Kate must go?

When Matt had asked Charlie these questions, he had grumbled about Hunter's petulance. 'He's annoyed with me. He thinks I'm hassling him. I'm not hassling him.' His face had taken on a tired, jowly look. 'No more than usual. I've always had to ride him a bit. It's a part of our routine.'

Joshi told the room at large that he had no idea who had organised the demonstration. He spread his hands. 'Of course, there are many rumours. Naturally enough. Because you have stirred things up. People did not trust you when you arrived and now they trust you even less.'

'And why would that be?' Tina lit a cigarette. For a moment, everybody was transfixed by the snap of the Dunhill lighter and the plume of tobacco smoke.

'They are more than ever convinced that your film will be depicting them and their city in a bad light.' Joshi reminded them of the scene on the Hooghly ferry.

'Nothing to worry about.' Charlie shook his head emphatically. 'A bit of improvisation. You objected and we took it out.'

Joshi's frown created shadows, throwing his baby face into glowering relief. 'How can I be sure of that?'

'You have my word. And Mr Hunter's.'

Joshi thought this a less than reliable guarantee. Singh suggested they substitute a speech that more accurately reflected the spirit of the people.

'What sort of speech?' asked Charlie cautiously.

Before Singh could answer, Hunter spoke from the shadows, where he sat back in his chair, looking too relaxed. Charlie regarded him nervously. 'There will be no new speech.' Hunter leaned forward into the light. His mouth was tilted up at the corners. He looked dangerously close to laughter. 'The one we have is already a great tribute to the spirit of the people.'

Charlie seemed to bounce in his chair. Twisting round to face Joshi, he almost slipped on to the floor. 'I assure you, Mr Joshi. The speech will not be used.'

'There is only one form of reassurance we can accept. You must bring me the negative of the objectionable scene and we will destroy it here together.'

At the word 'negative' all traces of Hunter's smile vanished. 'Out of the question.'

Joshi glared at him. Charlie looked anguished. Hunter

directed his next remark to the coffee table, as if to the only rational being in the room. 'It would set a dangerous precedent. We'd be open to demands from all sorts of pressure groups.'

Joshi folded his hands over his paunch. An air of stillness descended. 'Then we cannot do business.'

For a moment no one moved, then Tina made a lunge at an ashtray on the table and slowly stubbed out her cigarette, working at it until nothing remained but a mash of crumpled paper and spilt tobacco. Even Joshi was mesmerised. She straightened up, gave Hunter a long, cool stare and spoke to the room at large. 'You can have the negative, Mr Joshi. Guarantee us effective protection and you can have it this afternoon.'

4

On the morning of their return to the Peacock Palace, Kate sailed through her scenes with the conviction that she could do no wrong. Nothing fazed her—neither Ward's sulks nor Girish's games. Hunter watched and smiled. The smiles buoyed her up and carried her even further and there were no uncertainties, no breaks in the rhythm. She sailed on, feeling nothing but delight.

When it was finished, she didn't want to come back to earth. Ducking away, she climbed the smooth stairs of the palace to the sculpture gallery, where she drifted, peering into the marble faces which were not bland and perfect as she had thought at first, but all different—sly, sad, pompous and ingratiating, with grooves and wrinkles, smiles and frowns, so that they gave off a ghostly sense of intimacy.

Downstairs, mingling with the others, were Mr Singh and two bodyguards, whose Harley Davidsons had caused a flurry among the pelicans. Tina had taken Singh in hand and given him a tour, explaining everything. She had bantered with him and encouraged him to play the film fan. He had responded by taking her arm and patting her hand.

PART ONE

Kate had passed them on her way to wardrobe. Tina had given her a quick glare, then five minutes later had brought Singh to make-up and invited him to sit and watch Melanie at work. It had been such a blatant and ingenious act of hostility that Kate had felt invigorated by it. This was something to fight, something to get truly angry about. The thought provoked a perverse rush of optimism and she smiled into the mirror. An odd, secretive smile which had drawn a satisfying look of puzzlement from Tina.

She moved across to the window and was gazing down on to the street when she heard footsteps. A moment later, a tall figure came towards her out of the gloom. Hunter.

'I've been looking for you. We've organised a car.'

'The heat was too much for me. That and Mr Singh.'

Below in the street, Singh was bidding Tina a fulsome goodbye. Kate beckoned to Hunter to come and look.

'I suppose you heard about Joshi and the negative,' he said.

'Yes.' Charlie had told her, complaining about Hunter, accusing him of flippancy.

'Joshi was bluffing,' he said. 'He'd have been happy with just the money. He didn't really care about that speech of Ajay's. Tina let him get the better of her.' He sighed. 'And I let her get the better of me. Now we've lost the negative.'

Beneath the window, Tina was haranguing Charlie, who looked hot and miserable.

Hunter went on, sounding rueful. 'I wasn't concentrating. I was annoyed with Charlie. He always expects the worst, so sometimes I make it happen. Just so he won't be disappointed.'

Tina was now in the midst of a group which included Andy McCaffrey and the first assistant, Nick Thornton. All were regarding her with strained expressions as she waved her arms furiously. Shouted syllables wafted up, full of heat and bluster.

'Tina hates me,' said Kate.

'Don't worry about Tina. I'll take care of her.'

He drew her away from the window, back to the marble figures. They paused by a winsome sculpture of a Victorian angel. On the wall was a Titian, alongside it a musty battle scene full of raised sabres and white-eyed horses with flaring nostrils. As she gazed at the paintings decaying together in the gloom, it seemed to her that age and neglect had levelled them, cancelling out goodness and badness, so that all that mattered was the fact of their continued existence.

'What a waste.'

Hunter ran his finger lightly over the blackened canvas of the Titian. 'No, not a waste. Good work is never a waste.'

He turned from the painting and put his hand on her cheek. She reached up to touch the hand, which felt cool and a little clammy. His hair was dark with sweat, lying flat from the hat he had worn all day, and as he went to embrace her he faltered for a moment, staring into her face to see if it was all right. It was not all right. Not wise, not advisable, but certainly inevitable. If it did not happen, nothing else would. She had no doubt of this. No doubts at all, but if she had, his moment of hesitation would have dealt with them. So they kissed beneath a statue of a strangely maternal-looking Diana with Wolfhound, and she wished very hard that in the twilight room all the gods might be smiling.

CHAPTER 5

1

'Cut,' called Hunter. He stood, with his hands on his hips, looking down on Ward.

It was Ward's close-up. The sixth take. 'You're the director. Tell me what you want,' he growled, squinting into the sun.

'Anything would be nice.'

There was a long silence. Ward made a sour face and spat into the grass.

They were in the gardens of the Tollygunge Club, an oasis of true green on the city's southern edge. The Tolly, with its wedding-cake curlicues and blue shutters, rose above emerald lawns. Here, the leaves of the trees did not droop under a grey burden of oil and dust, but grew magically lush and glossy.

In the scene they were shooting, Fletcher and Susie were guests at an official garden party. Ward and Kate sat on gilt chairs upholstered in red velvet, next to a portly old Indian actor cast as an influential Bengali politician. Extras dressed as guests stood smoking and chatting with others got up as servants in ceremonial turbans and red and gold livery. Buffet tables were draped with linen cloths and laid with white china, silverware and centrepieces of orange and gold.

During his conversation with the politician, Fletcher had been critical of the continued existence of relics of the Raj like the Tollygunge Club, offending the Bengali with his bad manners and amusing Susie against her better judgment. Kate liked the scene, which was written with sharp lines and abrupt shifts in mood. It was to end with Fletcher and Susie exchanging a glance of complicity. Everything was to go into this glance—delight, outrageousness, sexual attraction, the pleasure of two people convinced they are a match. Two against the world.

Kate had breezed through her part, but Ward stalled. Every time he looked into her face, his eyes went blank and hard and his smile faltered and froze.

Hunter knelt by his chair. 'You're just not getting it.' His voice was loud enough for everyone to hear. Practised in the art of pretending not to listen, the technicians busied themselves with reflectors and sound levels.

'Okay,' said Hunter, 'we'll take a break.'

Kate went to sit under the trees. Girish's voice wafted across from where he was sitting with Tina, reading aloud from an interview in an Indian movie magazine. '"You've allowed yourself to become fat. Your short height further accentuates your circumference . . . Your acting is becoming a joke . . . You have become a confirmed boozard and cannot resist the temptation of the bottle. How do you manage to get offers?"' Girish was an authority on the excesses of the Bombay film stars and read with great feeling, deftly switching voices as he went—a bored, velvety tenor for the delinquent star, a bossy baritone for his interrogator.

Tina followed intently, wanting more. 'Jesus, how did Jackie handle that one?'

'Oh, he admits he is having a booze problem. Listen, he says, "I can't handle my drinking, it is true. I drink till I go ding."' Girish gazed at Tina fondly and she rewarded him with The Laugh. As Ward seldom left the hotel except to work, Girish had appointed himself Tina's guide to Calcutta. That morning they had been shopping and sightseeing together.

Girish had told Kate all about it. 'Tina says she can sit in a hotel room any time she likes back home in LA. If Jake wants her here, she says, he's got to be prepared to let her have a little fun.' He smiled slyly. 'Only reasonable, don't you think?'

PART ONE

Ward was coming back from the make-up trailer. Tina looked up in time to catch his scowl. 'How's it going, hon?' she cried brightly. When he ignored her, she leapt up and followed him.

They did another take, no better than the last. Tina stood at Hunter's elbow, slapping nervously at non-existent mosquitoes. 'Listen . . .' she whispered.

'What?' replied Hunter very loudly, making everybody look. To Kate's surprise, Tina blushed.

She grasped Hunter's elbow and tried to lead him across the lawn out of earshot, but at that moment Ward suddenly straightened up and gave a great bellow. 'For Christ's sake, Tina, shut up. Just bloody shut up.' He paused, shook himself and turned to Hunter: 'Let's get on with it, shall we?'

The next morning, Matt was eating breakfast in the coffee shop when Charlie arrived. His face was pale and puffy and his hand was shaking as he held out his cup for coffee. 'Tina was on to me first thing this morning. She's definite about it. Kate's off the picture. She says Hunter's got to tell her.'

Matt was overwhelmed by the news. A form of alchemy had occurred and Kate's Susie had impressed herself upon his version, changing it in some mysterious and fundamental way.

'What does Hunter say?'

'He doesn't know yet. She's been trying to tell him but he won't pick up his phone. And I haven't had a chance to look for him. Anyway, he's not telling me anything these days.'

Charlie fell silent, dwelling on his troubles, which stretched all the way to Jaisalmer in the east and Madurai in the south. In Charlie's office were bulging folders of airline tickets, permits, request forms, endorsements and authorisations which he distractedly shuffled and rearranged in the early hours of the morning when he couldn't sleep. While Hunter filmed, Charlie and his production manager trooped in and out of bureaucrats' offices or sat beside telex machines firing off messages to police departments, electricity boards and the secretaries of Maharajahs all over India.

'And there's the schedule,' he said. 'Hunter's taking his bloody time over everything—shooting way over ratio—and they want to know why. If we replace Kate, the whole thing will just . . .' He shrugged hopelessly. 'And there's another thing. Kate. I mean, it would finish her if she lost the part.'

Matt made up his mind. 'I'll go and look for him.'

He didn't have to look far. Crossing the lawn, he found Hunter by the pool, marking one of the new scenes they had written with red ink slashes.

He nodded calmly at Matt's news. 'I was expecting it.'

'Well, what are you going to do?'

'What do you think of the work she's doing?'

'What do I think? I think it's extraordinary.' His voice rose out of his control. A dead giveaway, but he didn't care.

Hunter looked at him curiously and said nothing.

'So what are you going to do?' Matt repeated.

Still Hunter didn't answer. His gaze had shifted to something behind Matt's shoulder. He turned to look. Kate was coming across the grass towards them, looking absurdly happy.

'I'm going to talk to her. That's what I'm going to do.' He turned back to Matt and said very deliberately, 'I'll see you later.'

Hunter touched her shoulder. They had not been alone together since the kiss in the Peacock Palace.

'How about a swim?'

She went to her room to change. When she returned, he was floating on his back in the centre of the pool, arms and legs extended, an upturned starfish.

She dived in, coming up next to one of the outstretched arms. He turned over and wrapped himself around her. They moved together through the water, his hands resting lightly on her waist. Then they dived and swam underwater, sliding dolphin-like against one another, their breath rising in bubbles to the surface. When they came up, he took her hand.

PART ONE

Because his room was next to Charlie's, they went to hers, where they showered together, splashing about like children, and made love in a patch of sunlight warming the bed.

Afterwards, Hunter lay on his back, gazing at the ceiling. 'I've wanted that for a long time. The suspense was getting to me. Will she? Won't she?' He ran the tip of his finger along her thigh lightly, hardly touching. 'Bad for my work.' Stroking her cheek. The finger halted its delicate progress. 'Did you know we have the same birthday?'

'What?'

'It's true. October 10. Charlie told me when we first met.'

She felt at ease lying with him in the patch of sunlight. 'I'm coming back to life.'

'You mean this is the first time since what's-his-name?'

'Yes.'

'I don't know whether to be pleased or jealous. I can't imagine anyone taking that long to get over me.'

'I told you, it wasn't just him. It was the life. The whole thing.'

'So tell me more about it.' He propped himself on his elbow ready to listen. 'Did he visit you in, ah, whatever it was you were in?'

'The bin, you mean. He tried, but I said no. I would never have got better if I'd had to see him.'

'Where did you go when you got out?'

'Back to Sydney.' She grinned. 'Home to mother.'

'Heart to hearts, hot drinks, back to the womb, was it?'

'No, not exactly.'

She tried to tell him about it. She and her mother had rattled around the Darling Point apartment together, calling one another 'darling', while her mother invented excuses not to talk. Her mother was a great fan of incidentals. She filled her days with them and they seemed to do their job well enough, successfully edging out alarms and disappointments. If her father was devoted to 'style', her mother's household god was 'taste'. She derived comfort from getting things right. In this way, she had just about succeeded in eliminating the unexpected from her life.

'You could never be like that, if that's what you're worried about. You didn't let her get away with it either, did you? I bet you made her listen to you. I bet you really let her have it, all of it.'

She admitted it. She had driven her mother out of the flat with her misery. Now she and Hunter rolled around together in the patch of sunlight, laughing, as if it had all happened in somebody else's life.

When they were quiet again, Hunter said: 'I've got something to tell you.'

'What?' she asked, already apprehensive.

'Tina's ordered me to sack you.'

He lay on his back, staring up at the ceiling, while she stayed very still, panic clutching at heart and gut. 'And?'

He turned towards her. 'You mean what am I going to do?'

'Yes.'

'What do you think I'm going to do?'

'I don't know.'

'God, you're as bad as Charlie . . . I'm going to tell her, that's what I'm going to do. I'm going to tell her. If you go, I go.'

For the next hour, she waited by the phone and finally it rang, but the voice she heard was not Hunter's.

'Listen,' said Tina, 'I need to talk to you but I can't leave the room. I'm waiting on a call from LA. How about you come round here?'

'All right.'

She knew there was no call. Tina just wanted them to meet on her ground. There was no point in arguing or delaying. Her nerves wouldn't stand it.

Minutes later, prepared for the worst, she entered Tina's room.

'Sit down.'

Tina sank down next to her on the sofa, plumping cushions, lighting a cigarette, stringing things out.

The coffee table was streaked with ash from an overflowing ashtray. There was a fax machine by the telephone and a copy of *Variety* dumped on the floor, its pages forming a small paper tent. Falling from one of the chairs was a cascade of coloured silks from one of Tina's shopping trips. Kate dwelt on all these things. Her mind wanted to come back later when everything was over.

Tina picked up one of the silks and draped it over the sofa arm. 'Hunter's quite an operator.' She let the silk slide back on to the floor. 'But I guess you know that. You must be quite an operator yourself, if it comes to that. "If she goes, I go." That's quite a line. I can't say any man's ever done that for me.' She produced a cat-like smile which made Kate think of Mr Singh grinning at her in the make-up mirror.

'What do you want to say, Tina?'

'Oh, nothing that you don't know already. Oh, there is one thing. Hunter gave me a little lecture on looking at rushes. Very few people know how to judge rushes, he said, when I told him what I thought of yours.' She lowered her voice and started popping her consonants in a parody of Hunter. It sounded like a Bette Davis imitation. '"Have you looked at them, really looked at them?" he said. "With due respect, it's an art and if you can't see how much better her work is now, then you haven't got it."' Her voice returned to normal. 'So yes, you're staying. But I just want to tell you one more thing . . .' She threw back her head and blew a curling smoke cloud. 'This is Jake's picture. He's the only one I care about. He's the only one the audience is going to care about.'

She lay her arm along the back of the sofa, the cigarette clamped upright between her fingers like a firecracker about to fizz. The smoke drifted into Kate's eyes. She stood up. Enough was enough. 'You're wrong about that,' she said.

Faced with having to look up at her, Tina sprang to her feet, but Kate was already on her way out. She paused at the door and felt herself start to smile—a curve of happiness going all the way to her eyes. Tina observed the smile in puzzlement, silent at last.

2

Kate woke early to a city of ghosts. The buildings she could see from her window were visible only as faint outlines in the smog. Overhead, a flock of crows beat its wings against the flannel sky. She marvelled at them. Where did they find the breath to fly?

Downstairs in the foyer she came across Matt, wearing a fiercely ironed white shirt and cotton trousers and with his hair still damp from the shower. He had a camera slung around his neck. 'They've been trying to ring you from the coffee shop. You're not wanted till nine.'

They were going to film on the Howrah Bridge—the great steel highway over the Hooghly crossed by millions each day en route between central Calcutta and the slums and docks of Howrah on the other bank. The busiest bridge in the world. Charlie had pulled strings all over Calcutta to get permission.

'I'm going to walk across the bridge to the flower market on the other side,' said Matt. 'Want to come?'

The bridge was already full of traffic. There were bullock carts, a jam of the city's ancient, rattling buses and a gathering stream of pedestrians, most of them *kulis* padding barefoot and straight-backed while carrying on their heads massive loads of marigold garlands bundled in cloth or piled into straw baskets.

On the ghats below, the morning ritual was well underway. Soapy bodies slithered about in the filmy waters and women knelt pounding and kneading wet cotton on the stepped stones above.

Dust was everywhere. Kate could feel grit on her face, under her fingernails and in her hair. The skin of her sandalled feet was grey with it.

Halfway across the bridge, they met the crew, already setting up. Only a few passers-by stopped to stare. The people on the Howrah Bridge were there only because they urgently needed to be somewhere else.

PART ONE

Kate had brought her own camera. She leaned on the bridge rail, staring through the viewfinder at the river craft, the *kulis* with the marigold bundles, the women on the latticed balconies of the nearby apartments. Behind the lens she felt invisible.

On the Howrah side of the bridge was a flight of stone steps where she stood with Matt, looking down on the market stalls. Posies of blood red and cornflower blue, white wreaths and stars trimmed with tinsel stood out among the gold and orange marigolds which carpeted the ground in great coiled ropes.

At the bottom of the steps, Kate grew bolder, moving in close with her camera and ignoring the glares of the flower sellers. This was a serious place—business was being done. She knew that she was intruding but went on clicking.

'You're shameless.' Matt grinned at her and she put the camera away, suddenly self-conscious.

'By the way,' he said. 'I was ready to go on strike over you. Not that Hunter would have noticed. But I'm very glad you're staying.'

'Thank you.' She touched his arm shyly. She had left Tina's room on a high, feeling that the battle was finally won. Then the doubts had returned—the sense of the daily battles to come, with the camera and with Ward. But happiness must help. She thought of Hunter and smiled, seeing the smile reflected in Matt's glance of surprise and pleasure.

Hunter had joined the knot of film people in the centre of the bridge. Ward and Tina were with him. Kate turned to Matt. 'Playtime's over.' She moved off, threading her way through the crowd on the way to the make-up trailer.

Tina watched her go then came across to Matt, wrinkling her nose at the pall of traffic fumes. She tried to brush the grit from her hands, fluttering them in the air like a small child with jammy fingers.

Matt felt the wayward beam of her attention settle on him and move systematically upwards from his dusty shoes.

'Little Miss Prim filling you in on recent developments, was she?'

Matt assumed the blank expression he used with policemen

and immigration officers. 'I've always thought she was fine as Susie.'

She regarded him with disbelief. 'So you're happy, are you?'

'Are we talking about life in general? In the cosmic sense?'

She gave him a burst of The Laugh and linked her arm in his, bouncing along at his side so that they proceeded at a jaunty, arrhythmic pace which set his teeth on edge.

'Are you always this cagey?'

'More or less. We Australians are a tight-arsed bunch.'

On one side of the bridge the crew had become an island unto itself. The continuity girl had set up her card table and portable typewriter; the third assistant darted about with her walkie-talkie; Ajay and Nick Thornton were huddled with a city official.

As they watched, a snake-charmer materialised out of the passing throng and squatted in front of the card table. 'Mem, mem,' he called, enticing a sluggish-looking reptile into uncoiling from its basket.

'Yuk.' Tina gripped Matt's arm more tightly as the snake was lifted into the air and encouraged to wrap itself languorously around the snake-charmer's forearm.

Hunter stood gazing at it in an abstracted way, causing the snake-charmer much excitement. 'Would the Maharajah like to hold the snake?'

The crew gathered around as Hunter took the gently writhing creature, permitting it to loop itself around his arm. Slowly it worked its way towards his shoulder. Snake and Hunter were soon eye to eye.

Everybody stood motionless, watching. Matt could feel Tina's fingernails biting into his arm. Then at a signal from its master, the snake neatly unwound itself and was returned to its basket. Telling the snake-charmer to wait, Hunter conferred with Andy McCaffrey.

'What the hell is he doing?' Tina still had hold of Matt's arm.

'As you know, Hunter likes to improvise.' He grasped her hand, offering false comfort, seized with the desire to tease and upset. 'Let's go and see.'

PART ONE

Tina dragged mulishly on his arm. 'No, I'm staying right here.' But as Hunter moved across to Ward, she changed her mind—just in time to hear Hunter outlining his plans.

'We've got Fletcher and Susie walking across the bridge when our friend comes out of the crowd with his basket—just as he did here this morning . . .' Hunter went on explaining. Fletcher was to stop in a moment of weakness and start fumbling for a rupee. With that, the snake was to be produced from the basket and the snake-charmer would try to drape it around Fletcher's shoulders.

'No. No way,' said Tina. 'This is a goddamned python we're talking about.'

'Cobra.' Matt was really enjoying himself.

'Whatever. They're all fucking horror shows to me. And Jake. Jake hates snakes, don't you hon?'

Ward, who had been regarding the snake with silent loathing, suddenly became non-committal.

'All the better because Fletcher does, too,' said Hunter. 'The old macho pride won't allow him to run so he has to stand there bravely while the thing . . .'

'I told you. No way.' Tina laid a protective hand on Ward's shoulder. He patted the hand awkwardly and removed it. He turned to Hunter. 'Now nobody appreciates a good bit of business more than I do. You know that and I know that, but all we're going to have here is Fletcher mugging for the camera. That's not him and it's certainly not me.'

'Who said anything about mugging? The man's a stoic. Scared out of his wits but determined not to show it. It's a nice bit of character revelation. Worth at least six pages of dialogue.' Hunter's face was a blithe, ingenuous mask. He bestowed a brilliant smile on the surrounding crew members.

Ward reflected on the cobra, which had grown livelier in the sun and was winding itself around its master's shoulders while the snake-charmer rolled his eyes in enthusiasm.

Tina was getting desperate. 'Listen, I think it's time for me to pull a little rank here . . .'

Roughly drawing her to him, Ward kissed her firmly. Before her lips could open again, he nodded to Hunter who gripped him by the shoulder in a comradely way before moving off to arrange the scene.

'You damn well let him get away with it.' Tina's pale hands curled into small fists.

'What the hell.' Ward seemed intoxicated by his decision. He swaggered off, leaving Tina sighing after him.

Hunter made the most of the snake. They did eight takes, after which Ward was sweating and shaking, the cobra had fallen asleep from over-work and the snake-charmer was a rich man.

Charlie was straining to read the menu by the light of the candle on the table. 'The food is very good here. The real thing. None of that bland garbage they're always trying to pass off on the tourists.'

Tina said she would eat anything as long as there was no chilli in it.

'You don't eat chilli?'

She told him about her allergy and Charlie sighed, more depressed by this news than anything else so far. He plunged back into the menu. Menus were therapy for him, and by the time he emerged with the necessary decisions made, he looked almost happy.

'Look, Tina, Hunter's doing good work. Who else could keep his nerve in this city?'

'Just tell him to lay off Jake. I mean Jake is not as tough as he likes to make out. The strong, silent type, sure, but inside it's a different story.' Her voice dropped. 'Believe me, I know.'

She turned to Matt. 'How do you think he's doing?'

After hanging onto his arm throughout the snake's performance, she had been reluctant to let him go. Across the table, Girish was regarding him suspiciously.

'I think he's doing well.' Ward had already confounded his initial doubts. Beneath the vanity and the self-absorption was a bullish determination to do the job properly. While Hunter aroused Ward's anger, he also aroused his hopes, and Matt saw something poignant in that.

Tina took out another cigarette, searching in her bag for

her lighter. Girish was too quick for her and struck a match from the book on the table. He asked her if she was coming with them to Rajasthan.

'No, she's not,' said Charlie briskly. 'She's got too much to do back in LA.'

Tina squinted through the smoke. 'Maybe. Maybe not.'

The food began to arrive, filling all available table space and causing the hasty rearrangement of plates and glasses. In the confusion, Charlie was unable to identify the dishes flavoured with chilli and the waiter was called back. After he had moved off again, Tina was still uncertain. 'I just have to get near the stuff and I stop breathing.'

This time Charlie tasted everything. 'This one and that one. I promise you.'

Still she hesitated.

'Please, allow me,' said Girish, and as the tasting ritual was completed and the plates sorted: 'So there is a chance you will be accompanying us?'

Gazing steadily at Charlie, Tina said there just might be.

Charlie bit his lip, seemed about to speak, changed his mind and began to eat. Tina continued to stare at him. 'Got any problem with that plan, Charlie?'

Matt tried for a postponement. 'Tell us about the train, Charlie.'

'Yes, yes. The train is very interesting. I, too, am looking forward to the train,' said Girish.

The train on which they were to travel through Rajasthan was made up of carriages once reserved exclusively for the Rajput princes. The carriages were now used to transport tourists across the State, giving them what was meant to be an experience of Raj luxury.

'Yes, well, don't get too excited. There's not a lot of room in the carriages, you'll have to share compartments and there's a ton of dust. My main worry is how to stop the crew banging on a mutiny when they find out where they're sleeping. Not to mention temperamental actors.'

'You're not putting me off,' said Tina.

3

Kate and Hunter fell into a routine—a strange word to describe the secret, dream-like nature of their meetings, yet these occurred regularly, arranged by signs, nods, notes passed on the set and phone calls made late at night. Nobody knew. They were both sure of that, although she worried about Tina who might not know but would certainly have guessed.

Hunter was gamer than Kate. He liked to spend the whole night with her and slipped back to his own room just before breakfast. Sometimes, too, they slept in his room, where the phone often rang.

If it was Charlie, Hunter would lie in bed, inventing excuses to discourage him from coming round, while Kate shut herself in the bathroom. The conversations still drifted through to her. 'Christ, Charlie, I haven't been able to sleep all night,' she heard Hunter say one morning. 'Reviewed my whole damn life and I have to tell you the news wasn't good. I just got to sleep before you rang. Give me half an hour and I'll be okay.' When she came out of the bathroom, he gave her a wicked grin.

The insomnia was genuine enough. When the love-making was done, they lay exchanging memories and scraps of life history, fixing these so precisely in time that it became a game. The same birthday, the same places, the same times. They had shared the same teenage acquaintances, the same Sydney, yet had never met. Or had they? They wondered about this—if somewhere they had passed one another without seeing.

He was exactly two years older and had grown up on Sydney's North Shore, a doctor's son. His mother had done good work for Catholic charities and insisted he have piano and guitar lessons. He was a good Catholic until the age of sixteen. 'The Jesuits were such good teachers. That was the thing.' He frowned, still taking it personally. 'All that disciplined thought. In the end it did away with belief.'

Now he just liked the music. She woke to Bach and Handel and the sight of Hunter in reading glasses, sitting by the window, poring over script or storyboard, with an old cardigan draped over the chair and a row of ironed shirts hanging in the wardrobe. Bizarre as it seemed, he was cosy to be with.

All that spoiled things was the photograph of his two boys—ten and twelve years old with straight, floppy hair like his and gravely staring blue eyes.

Sometimes Hunter talked to her about them. 'Will's okay. I never have to worry about him. He's one of those kids, you know, who'll get on anywhere. It's the younger one, Pete.' He stared sadly at the photograph. 'He's a dreamy character. Too much imagination.'

'You can never have too much of that.' She hoped she sounded sympathetic, but could not dwell on the worried-looking face of Pete, who would grow even more miserable if he were ever to know what she and his father were up to together. For most of the time, she was able to think of herself and the boys as existing in different worlds. They were part of Hunter's past and future while her thoughts of him moved no further than the here and now.

She refused to analyse whatever it was that they had together. Did she feel for him when he was unhappy? She had no idea. Hunter's periods of unhappiness were so brief and his air of being in charge so convincing that concern for him seemed irrelevant. Yet there was no question that she wanted to be with him. She woke every morning to a day brightened by the prospect.

With Charlie, she was glib and offhand—especially when he mentioned Hunter's wife, Jess. Charlie liked Jess. 'I hope you get the chance to meet her,' he said. 'They're a good team, she and Hunter. Been together for years. Through all the pictures he's done.'

She felt bad about deceiving Charlie because he was having such a hard time. Tina nagged him tirelessly and sent daily faxes to Acorn, keeping their contents secret from everybody. On the set, she hovered at Hunter's shoulder, countering everything he said to Ward, and when he took no notice, she went back to Charlie to complain. It was a busy routine. Even so, she had time to go shopping with Girish and spent hours in the make-up trailer gossiping about the sex lives of the crew.

She had infuriated Charlie by having the wardrobe department make up the silks from her shopping trips into saris and Punjabi pyjamas, which she wore at night when she drank with Matt and Ward in the bar or danced with Girish in the discotheque. She looked glossy and pleased with herself and ready for action.

Ward, on the other hand, grew more agitated and irascible, as if he were the donor in a mysterious exchange of energy. Everything about Calcutta oppressed him. He muttered at the beggars, coughed in the smog and wilted in the heat. He drank beer, dosed himself with Lomotil in reply to his grumbling digestive system and refused to eat for fear of further contamination. Whenever he seemed abstracted, Hunter would think of yet another way of goading him into responsiveness. He seemed permanently in touch with Ward's state of mind, as if the actor were an old and stubborn instrument continually in need of tuning.

Kate thought of this as the antithesis of the way she herself was treated by Hunter, who now seemed intent on shielding her from all criticism—keeping her out of harm's way. A little too obvious, this. Even when they made love, she felt soothed and monitored as if passion, too, could be regulated for safety's sake.

4

Their last day in Calcutta was spent filming more scenes at the Tollygunge Club and afterwards there was to be a party.

By the time the last set-up was completed, it was dusk and the hazy sky was bronzed. Long shadows crept across the grass and the leaves of the shade trees had a gilding of orange light.

As the equipment was packed away, a team of waiters appeared, carrying planks, trestles and folded white cloths. Tables were set up and laid with food and drink. It was the usual food—the puri, the dhosas and the bland meat dishes served at lunch and dinner during each day's filming, but Charlie had bought whisky and gin, and a troupe of Indian musicians established themselves in the centre of the lawn and started up a wailing rhythm with their tablas and sitars.

Outside the gate, the music inspired a small group of protesters—a half-hearted bunch with hand-lettered placards saying 'Hollywood Go Home' and 'Do Not Take the Name of Our City in Vain'. Their chanting rose in ragged counterpoint to the music then died away again.

Sitting with a drink in his hand, Matt quietly observed the change in atmosphere. Instead of lights and cords, cameras and clipboards, there were glasses and cigarettes. The pace had slowed, the body language altered. Actors and crew were no longer two armies going about their separate businesses. Distinctions blurred, arms curled around shoulders and waists. Elegant, sari-clad women turned confidentially towards young men in torn jeans and T-shirts. The noise level rose.

Along with a large crowd of Indian extras, there were some Europeans, most of them recruited from the embassies, and a hard-drinking English character actor called Teddy Dawson had been flown in for a few days' work playing an expatriate businessman befriended by Fletcher. Teddy had already appropriated a bottle of Scotch and had settled down to enjoy it in the company of Ward and the old Indian actor cast as the Governor of West Bengal.

Warmed by the whisky and the talk, Ward had cheered up noticeably. He had used one of the club's bathrooms to shower, and in his well-pressed bush shirt and white cotton trousers had assumed some of his pre-Calcutta shine. As Matt watched, Tina walked across to him and settled herself on his knee, and as they sat centre stage in the glowing, theatrical light cast by the setting sun, Ward looked triumphant—the old, craggy allure fully restored.

Matt felt pleasantly exhausted. He wanted only to sit in the friendly twilight and think about nothing much. He was also hoping to consume enough gin and tonic so that at some point in the evening, before he got too drunk, he would find a way of breaking through the invisible barrier that stalled his conversations with Kate.

He thought about her all the time now. An amazing development, given his sexual torpor since the breakdown of his marriage. That hadn't been perfect but it had suited him. 'Of course it did,' Barbara had said bitterly during their final row. 'It was marriage on your terms.'

It had not been entirely true. Before her career had become so important to her, she had enjoyed travelling with him. And later, at home in Sydney, she had also had one or two affairs which he had never admitted to knowing about—even at the end. As he looked back on it now, their union seemed so fragile that he wondered how it had lasted so long. He saw that he had deliberately ignored the signs of her loneliness and that he had missed the point at which it had turned to boredom. After that, there was nothing to be done.

Now he couldn't consider love—or sex—without thinking of failure, an association of ideas which had effectively killed desire—or so he had thought.

Sitting in a chair next to his, Kate was arguing amiably with Ajay.

'But you should read Matt's novel. You really should,' he told her.

'I will. After the picture is finished.'

'No, you should read it now.' In his desire to persuade, he picked up his chair and moved it closer to hers. 'It will help you. You see, so many Westerners write about India as if it were a circus and we were all clowns. A nation of children and madmen.'

'And you would do the same if you wrote about America. It's natural, Ajay. Not nice, but natural. We're all clowns.' She gestured at the scene before them. 'God knows, this is no occupation for grown-ups.'

Ajay didn't agree. He saw the film as serious business. 'Matt's India is not a circus. And Rajiv is not a clown. At least he wasn't.' He flopped back in his chair. 'Before Girish.'

'Have you ever done any acting, Ajay?' she asked him.

'He's done a lot,' said Matt, who had learnt that Ajay was a member of a Calcutta drama group and that he cherished a hopeless dream of one day giving up his dreary job in the Civil Service for a life in the theatre.

'Amateur only.'

'Doesn't matter,' said Kate. 'It explains why you were so good in that scene on the ferry.'

'Oh, please. I'd rather forget about that. It caused so many nasty complications.'

'That wasn't your fault. Joshi was just looking for an excuse to make trouble. Anything would have done. But you're wrong about Girish. He's an instinctive actor.' She smiled. 'He's been very good for me.'

Ajay shrugged. 'I'm sorry. You can't convince me. I think he betrays Rajiv with every word. He's a little boy. The Rajiv of the book is a man.' He looked up, hearing his name called. Charlie was waving to him. 'I'll see you later. But I'm not going to rest, Kate, until you have read the book.'

Kate watched him walk away. 'He's working so hard. I hope we're not taking advantage of him. We move in, sort of take him over for three months then leave again.'

Matt said he knew the feeling.

She laughed. 'No, you don't. You're making more money out of this than Ajay is likely to see if he lives to be two hundred.'

'Could we have a truce? Nothing too ambitious. The rest of the evening, say?'

It had got dark. Flares had been placed at intervals around the garden, the Indian musicians had put away their instruments, and a rock group—slim young men in jeans and sneakers with drums and guitars—were getting ready to replace them. Meanwhile, someone had brought out an outsize ghetto-blaster and set it up on the buffet table. The atmosphere was instantly transformed. The peaceful, languid mood vanished, and booming through the jasmine-scented air came the sound of the Rolling Stones and 'Jumping Jack Flash'.

The extras, who had been milling elegantly, moved to the centre of the lawn and started jerking about to the music; the women restricted by the folds of their saris to a stately version of the twist. Liz, Charlie's secretary, had dragged Andy

McCaffrey out to join them, Charlie was with Melanie, and even Ajay had joined in and was dancing with the continuity girl.

Kate startled Matt by taking his hand and gesturing in the direction of the dancers.

Matt never danced. He looked across at the crowd—a jostling press of bodies rising and falling raggedly to the beat—and imagined how silly he would look if he gave in. His chances with Kate were slim enough, but as long as the two of them stayed put, there was the possibility that they might move beyond banter and actually start talking to one another. If they danced, it would all be over before it started. He would look stupid and others would come between them. He would lose her to the mood of slightly stoned abandonment that was intensifying with the scent of marijuana smoke now mingling with the jasmine.

'I want to tell you something.'

'What about?'

What about? He didn't yet feel up to the truth. 'About Susie. The original one.'

A flicker of interest. She inched back into her chair.

'It's uncanny. How close you've got to her. I mean, it's different. As I said earlier . . .' He was improvising fast. 'How did you do that? You get off the plane straight from some other picture . . .'

She smiled, relaxed. 'It wasn't easy. Tina will tell you it took me too long to get her. I did cheat a bit, though . . . gave myself time.'

He was intrigued when she told him about Juhu Beach. He was still dwelling on the thought of her there when she astonished him by saying how much Tina reminded her of Susie. 'What about it? Shall I give her The Laugh? Just a couple of bursts.'

He was appalled, but as he watched Tina gazing dreamily at the dancers, he had to admit it. In the softening light there was something of the real Susie about her. Maybe his younger self might have found her attractive. If so, he had become another person. All he could see now in the silhouetted figure on Ward's knee was trouble.

He had unwisely allowed the conversation to lapse.

'Come on, dance with me.'

Reluctantly, he let Kate pull him to his feet and slowly followed her across the lawn. They inserted themselves into the crush and he fell into a sedate jog, making perfunctory shoulder movements which kept him vaguely in touch with the music.

Everyone was dancing except for the group centred on Tina and Ward. She was still sitting on Ward's lap but was otherwise detached from him. Her upper body swayed, her hands clapped to the beat and she perched—a bird contemplating flight—while Ward turned the other way to talk to Teddy.

Girish was sitting a few feet from her, looking like a kitten too frightened to pounce. Suddenly, she made up her mind and with magpie swiftness rose from Ward's knee, took Girish's hand and bolted in the direction of the dancers.

The Stones wound up 'Jumping Jack Flash' and swung into 'Satisfaction'. Next came a slow track, and some couples fell into a embrace while others melted away into the shadows. Matt settled for old-fashioned formality, drawing Kate to him, one hand across the small of her back, the other clasping her hand, holding her so that their bodies just touched and his chin grazed the top of her head. He planned to ease her gradually closer with awkward adolescent stealth.

Tina and Girish were not touching. He moved on the spot, staring soulfully at her while she weaved around, hair tousled, eyes glazed, with one leg of her silk pyjamas caught up around her ankle and her bare feet black and grass-stained. She had kicked off her shoes because the heels were sinking into the turf, so that for a second or so she had whirled like a dervish pinned to the spot.

When the slow track came to an end, the Indian rock group was ready and the beat resumed at twice the volume. Matt cursed under his breath, then, against all the odds, Kate was suddenly smiling up at him: 'I've had enough. Let's sit down.'

'Let's walk. So we can talk away from the noise.'

For a moment she hesitated, then they strolled across the soft grass and into the shadows.

'I used to have a routine,' he said. 'Four drinks to lose my inhibitions then make a pass. To be honest, it worked best with women I'd never met before.' He went on, trying to spell out the way it was between them. 'When I'm with you, the things I'm saying are never what I'm thinking. Like being in a time lag. I'm like that with most people these days. Usually I don't care.'

She didn't answer, but she didn't move away either.

'I didn't want us to slide past one another never making contact. I wanted to make the effort.'

She turned to look at him, frowning slightly. Her face was neatly divided in two by the light, half completely lost in shadow. Visible was a pale mask, tilted towards him, gravely appraising. She smiled.

'I'd written you off,' she said. 'You looked as if you'd sort of closed the books on people.'

'Just about.'

She put her arm through his. He felt it snug against his ribs.

'So why had you closed the books?'

'Loss of nerve, I suppose.'

'The marriage. The marriage that ran out of steam.'

'Without me noticing.'

'And you can't forgive yourself?'

'Well, it does make me wonder what I thought I was doing at the time.'

'Why did you get married in the first place?'

'The usual reasons. I thought I was in love and couldn't live without her.'

'Then you found out you could.'

'Sort of. Marriage was very comforting. I enjoyed the fact of it.'

'Perhaps that's the way it is with most people after a while. We don't miss the person. Only the things we did and made together.'

Matt recognised a fellow pessimist.

She admitted it. 'Worse than that. At least you don't mind your ex-wife being happy.'

He supposed he didn't. He just wasn't quite ready yet to watch her at it.

PART ONE

'You're a much more benevolent character than I am then.' She started to talk about the English director who had been her lover. 'It's not at all nice—how I feel. I love it when I hear that something is going wrong for him. A great surge of malice. Very exciting.' She produced a resonant laugh which lost itself in the music. 'I ought to be over it by now, but I'm not. I can't imagine ever wishing him well. Now some people might call that love, but it's not. It's the opposite—proof that I never loved him. And that's sad. That's the saddest thing of all.'

They had arrived back at the circle of light and hovered at its edge, reluctant to re-enter it. Matt made the first move. 'How about a drink?'

As he crossed to the bar, he saw that the protesters had joined the party. Their 'Hollywood Go Home' placards were propped upside-down against a tree trunk and they were lining up for drinks at the bar. One of the waiters shrugged. 'They are not bad men. Just doing their jobs. Now they are off duty and can enjoy themselves.'

Matt laughed at this absurdity, feeling light-headed, buoyed up by an optimism he had not felt in years. He contemplated a new prospect and, curiously, only a minor part of it was coloured by sexual desire. He visualised conversations—rich, relaxed, discursive talks going on forever.

He started to hurry back with the drinks. When he cleared the press of bodies around the bar, Kate was no longer where he had left her.

He spied the tall figure of Hunter. Kate was with him. They stood talking, nudged by the dancers either side of them, and as he watched, they, too, started to dance, swaying in a desultory, preoccupied way as their conversation continued.

His sense of anticipation evaporated and with a sigh so heavy it left him dizzy, he upturned one of the glasses, watching the liquid sink into the grass.

Under cover of the music, she whispered to Hunter: 'Where have you been? I missed you.'

'Seeing to things. Let's go back to the hotel.'

'No, I want to stay here.' It seemed important not to break the spell. The garden was now a magical place with its flickering torch-light and its dark-leaved trees, each of them sheltering embracing couples swaying to the music.

They left the dancers and headed into the shadows, walking in step, hip to hip, thigh to thigh, and while she briefly considered breaking away from him for fear of being seen, it was more convenient to decide that an aspect of the garden's magic was to confer invisibility on those in need.

'The party girl. Not like you.'

'You don't know everything.'

'I will, though.'

'You already know much more than I'm ever likely to know about you.'

They had reached the shadow of the make-up trailer. He turned and kissed her. 'No.' He whispered the word, turning it into a long, aggrieved sigh and stroked her cheek. 'All you have to do is ask.'

'It's better if I don't know too much.'

'But if I want to tell you?'

'Just don't tell me now.'

'No, not now.'

He silently opened the door to the trailer and they slipped inside. The music was still blaring and, enveloped in sound, they kissed again, not even pausing to look around and grow accustomed to the darkness.

They kissed for what seemed like a very long time then beneath the pounding of the music, there was another noise. And light. Lots of light.

She looked towards the open doorway, blinking and indignant, feeling as if woken roughly from a delicious dream. It took a moment for her eyes to focus and another moment to identify the figures standing there.

One of them was Charlie, staring, with his mouth open, at her and Hunter. The other, Jake Ward, was not looking at them at all. He was gazing past them towards the far end of the trailer where Tina was lying naked on the sofa with the smooth, brown body of Girish stretched out on top of her.

PART TWO

CHAPTER ONE

1

They had left behind the fuming air and crumbling streets of Calcutta for a dazzle of blue sky, sunlit water and white marble.

Kate was lazing on the terrace at the most splendid palace hotel in Udaipur—a filigree citadel which rose, mirage-like, out of an island in the midst of a glassy lake. Lake Pichola. The manager had just finished lecturing her enthusiastically on the building's history as the palace fortress of an eighteenth-century Rajput prince beset by many enemies.

She had been sitting in the sun all afternoon, reading and drowsing, with no sound except for the occasional voice, the putt-putt of a motor launch and the muted whirr of Matt's printer in one of the rooms above, turning out yet another page of script.

Hunter and Charlie were with the rest of the crew at the railway station, making preparations for their journey into the desert. Tina and Girish were there with them, but Ward was not. Kate guessed that he was in his room, communing by telephone with his agent in LA. She had spotted him only once since they had flown in. He had been in the lobby, quarrelling with the desk clerk and had just grunted at her bad-temperedly. Several people had tried to talk to him but Tina, the only one who could possibly make an impression, had not.

Since the night of the party, friendships had ruptured and new alliances had been formed. Kate had not spoken to Matt. She had felt a twinge of guilt about abandoning him at the party, then had forgotten about it till the next day. She hadn't taken him seriously when he flirted with her. Now she saw she had been wrong and didn't know what to do about it. He was avoiding her, and although Tina denied having told him or anyone else about the events in the make-up trailer, she knew better.

From the moment the light had been snapped on, Tina had taken charge. As Girish scrabbled for his clothes, she waved her arm, dismissing everybody, and Ward staggered out into the darkness with the others close behind.

'Quick, back to the hotel,' Hunter whispered, taking Kate's hand and starting across the lawn, but the thickset figure of Charlie blocked their path.

'No, Hunter, you're going to stay here and help me deal with this shit.'

'I'm getting Kate out of here first.'

'Damn you, Hunter. Damn you both. You're staying.'

'I'm sorry,' Hunter said to Kate. 'Why don't you wait for me by the gate?'

'No, we'll both stay.'

At that moment, Tina and Girish emerged from the trailer and, before anyone could stop him, Ward swung a punch at Girish, knocking him back against the wall. Thump. At Girish's yelp of pain, the music stopped. Across the lawn, the silhouetted figures of the dancers turned to watch.

'Please.' Girish did not try to hit back but steadied himself, looking unhappily from Ward to Charlie.

'You slut,' said Ward to Tina in an offhand tone edged with a faint note of surprise. In contrast to this mildness, his eyes blazed, bloodshot and furious.

Tina looked at him and sighed. An exhalation of pure boredom. Kate felt enervated just listening to it whistle past her ear. But once it was out, Tina seemed invigorated.

'Come on, Girish, we're out of here.'

Taking his hand, she marched across the lawn, cutting a path through the dancers, and disappeared.

Charlie was outraged. Kate was crazy, he said. Hunter would never leave Jess; he was married for life. They were a perfect match. 'And I should bloody well know. I haven't been through three marriages without learning something on the way. Don't get involved, Kate. Not with Hunter.'

Hunter told her that Charlie should mind his own business. 'He doesn't know anything about us.' His smooth features creased in irritation. 'He doesn't look at people. He's too busy thinking up ways of getting round them. Practical bloody man. That's Charlie. No matter what he tells you about Jess and me, he doesn't know.'

'Doesn't he?'

'No, he doesn't. I told you. It's a very rocky marriage. It has been for years.' He told her that he and Jess were rarely together. 'When the kids were smaller, she wouldn't leave them to come on location with me and now, when she could, she won't.' He hesitated. 'Anyway, she's had one or two affairs of her own and . . .'

'And?'

'Well, I have too.'

She silently assessed this information, not sure if it made things better or worse. As the 'affairs' lined up in her mind—anonymous faces, each bringing its sharp stab of jealousy—he watched her gravely, knowing exactly what she was thinking. Was this a good sign? A sign of his determination not to insult her intelligence? She shouldn't even think about it.

She would have liked to confide in someone, but there was only Tina. Alarmingly, Tina was being almost friendly and enjoying handing out unwelcome advice. She still didn't think Kate should be in the picture. She had told her so again that morning by the pool. 'Take it from me, it's going to be the hardest job you ever took on. And don't expect any help from Jake. He's as mad as hell.'

Kate regarded Tina gloomily. She was wearing a bikini and sat cross-legged on a sun-lounge, like a Shiva statue, all taut lines and sharp angles. Her green eyes narrowed. 'I don't know what you see in Hunter. He's such a cold fish.'

She started to talk about herself. And about Girish, Ward, her father, her ex-husband and her shrink. It had been the shrink's idea that she have an affair with Ward. 'It's because I have a thing about my father. Wanting to kill him, wanting to fuck him. The usual stuff. And since he's unavailable, the shrink thought that Jake would be a good substitute. Made sense. I mean, that's why I fell for Jake in the first place. The older man syndrome. Even the setting was right. We were at a party at somebody's house on the old Barrymore estate. He came up out of the bushes, looking as if he knew where all the bodies were buried, and said, "Hiya, kid." That was enough for me.'

She stretched out on her back, offering up her pale body to the sun, eyes hidden behind round dark glasses with wire frames. Anarchists' glasses.

'You've got a watch. I don't want to burn. Tell me when three minutes are up. That's all it takes with my skin. I read it somewhere.'

On this kind of thing she went by the book. Many books. She had a bag full of them—on macrobiotics, bio-rhythms, rebirthing and herbal cures. A row of pill bottles stood on the table beside her sun-lounge. 'It used to be coke. Now it's vitamins. That's got to be an improvement.'

She returned to the subject of Ward. For the first few days in Calcutta, they'd had a great time. 'But older men . . . I don't know . . . it seems to me that their attitude to life in general is more or less the same as their attitude to sex. Jake's good in bed—don't get me wrong—but a little goes a long way with older men. They like to get back to what they were doing before you came into the room—which is probably talking to their share-trader or their agent, or in Jake's case, some old stuntman who remembers what it was like doing a John Ford picture.'

She raised the dark glasses and sat up to heave the sun-lounge into the shade. After taking time for some deep breathing in the lotus position, she went on. 'He's the same about life. You go out, see a few people, have a few drinks, take in a few sights, then it's back to base for a week. Especially in a country like this. I mean, every time he breathes in, he thinks he's going to drop dead. But he won't help himself. I used to try. Jesus, how I used to try. He's got a trunk load of vitamins my naturopath fixed for him, but he doesn't take them.'

When Kate asked her why she didn't go home and leave him to it, The Laugh rang out so loudly that it seemed to ruffle the water in the pool. 'Yeah, you'd like that, wouldn't you? No way. No, you need me here. You may not know it, but you do. Anyway, I'm having a good time.'

'What if Girish really falls for you?'

'Don't worry about Girish. He can look after himself. He's adaptable. Cute. And adaptable. I'm going to have fun while it lasts. How about you?'

She looked so predatory in her anarchists' glasses that Kate was tempted into lying. 'I think it's probably over already.'

Tina spluttered with amusement. 'Give me a break.' She uncrossed her legs and lay flat again. 'So the obvious answer to my question is that you're not going to have fun with it. Bad mistake. Bad, bad mistake.'

Matt had stopped typing and was rocking back in his chair with his hands behind his head, gazing at the ceiling with its glimmering light show, reflected from the fountain on the terrace below. He was intensely aware of Kate's presence beneath his window. Because of it, he couldn't work. His chair was surrounded by screwed-up balls of paper. Working meant working for Hunter—not a great prospect.

Tina had briefed him fully on all that he had missed at the party, taking a seat next to him on the flight from Calcutta expressly for the purpose. He wasn't sure why—except that she knew how he felt about Kate. For one so insensitive, she was remarkably intuitive. She had a nose for weakness and a genius for exploiting it.

She maintained that she was telling him about Kate and Hunter for his own good, although at first she pretended ignorance of his feelings. She was simply telling a funny story—entertaining him. 'Just my lousy luck,' she said, working up to the punchline with a burst of The Laugh. 'A little bit later in the night and the bodies on the sofa would have been theirs instead of ours.'

As he sat struggling to hide his hurt, she studied him as if he were something trapped in a jar. The worst thing was that he had no right to his bitterness. Kate had not led him on. Led him on? God, what a term. He was relapsing into adolescence.

He couldn't look at Tina, who was still checking his symptoms. 'You really go for her, don't you?' she said finally. 'I thought you did. Jesus . . .' She shook her head. 'I mean, why?' She swung round to face him, pinning him to his seat. 'She's no threat. That's it, isn't it? Little Miss Weak-as-Water. She makes you feel like a big man. You and Hunter.'

No longer interested, she picked up a copy of *Variety* and left him alone for the rest of the flight.

It was no use. He got up from his typing and wandered over to the window, careful not to be seen from below.

Kate's chair was empty and as he stared at the space where she had been, he felt such a heaviness in mind and body that he didn't want to go on. So that's how it feels, he thought. It's not even sadness, just boredom. A profound disinclination to continue.

It lasted only a moment, then he felt frightened. The room was cold, he was shivering. He turned off the air-conditioning and picked up the papers. I must get out of here, he thought. I must keep moving.

There was a knock at the door and he went to open it gratefully, expecting the usual flock of housemen and chambermaids, poised to dazzle him with the daily ritual of towel-changing and bed-making. Instead, there was Kate in a faded blue cotton shirt and cream pants, her damp hair combed back, her eyes and mouth without make-up. She smiled at him.

On hired bicycles, they wound their way carefully through the narrow streets—past peeling shopfronts and slow-moving pedestrians who turned to stare at the sportive sight. Kate rode ahead, straight-backed, her brown feet in *chappals*, her trousers rolled up past her ankles. Matt laboured along, wiping the sweat out of his eyes, the front wheel of his bike wobbling as children laughed and women giggled behind their hands.

At Udaipur's City Palace hotel they stopped for tea, riding through a wrought-iron gate in a high white wall to sit on a terrace beside a pool coloured by floating petals of bougainvillea.

Here she apologised for deserting him at the party—a hesitant little speech in which she was careful not to presume too much. 'I'm sorry. I didn't think you'd mind . . .' Then, drily: 'I imagine Tina told you the whole story.'

'Yes, you can rely on Tina.'

All his bitterness went into the words and he was pleased to see her flush. After a moment, she rose and walked to the edge of the pool. 'Come over here. It's cooler.'

She sat dangling her legs in the water. She looked so young and, beneath the awkwardness and embarrassment, so happy, that he was stunned, as if dealt a blow by a carelessly thrown object.

'Look, it's okay. The other night I was wishing for something. It's not going to happen but that's not your fault.'

'So we can be friends?'

The words reminded him of Barbara. When she had used them, he had thought of them as cancelling out everything they had ever had together. Now they put paid to hope for the future.

'Yes, of course.'

Kate turned away from him, her happiness dulled to the point where he could just bear it, and stirred the surface of the water with her toes—a delicate signal that his message had been received and understood. They were silent, watching the bougainvillea bob and drift, propelled by draughts of warm air.

EXT. SOMEWHERE IN RAJASTHAN. DAY.

The Maharajah's train has come to a stop so that its passengers can stretch their legs and take a closer look at the landscape.

FLETCHER sits on a large stone, looking at ease with the world; SUSIE walks about gingerly, while RAJIV stands by, ready to help if she slips on the stony ground.

> RAJIV: Are you glad you decided to stay, Will?

> FLETCHER: Yes, I am. Now that we're out here I'm very glad.

> SUSIE: (Addressing RAJIV but looking ironically at FLETCHER) Fletcher loves deserts. All those tough, prickly little plants living on nothing.

> FLETCHER: (With a blithe smile) That's right. An example to us all.

PART TWO

2

Kate and Tina sat knee to knee in the saloon compartment of their shared carriage, wedged in fast by Tina's matched luggage. Kamal, their cabin captain, found their situation interesting but not hopeless. 'Don't worry. My assistant and I are taking care of it. You will see. Ours will be the happiest saloon on the train.'

Kate guessed Kamal to be about six foot four. His chest and shoulders were so broad that the armholes of his uniform were giving at the seams, and glimpses of shoulder pad were revealed with every gesture. He wore a Rajput moustache and a dusty gold turban and the hem of his coat trailed around his trousers.

Kamal and his assistant, Tampi would be sleeping in the kitchenette behind a screen of long underwear hanging from a makeshift clothesline. Some of Tina's luggage had already gone in with them and the rest was being magically manhandled into odd spaces and empty corners while Tina and Kamal argued over ways and means.

Kamal referred to Kate and Tina in the third person as the Maharanis and, despite his smiles, was firm with them. By the time the train left the station, he had them sitting down to tea while he stood in the doorway of the kitchenette with his arms folded, making sure that they drank it.

Kate had not expected to share a compartment with Tina and had followed Kamal into his lair behind the underwear screen to tell him so.

'No, it is all down here on the list I am given. We will all be very happy together.'

Tina was being suspiciously docile. As they drank their tea, she asked Kamal ladylike questions about his life with the train and his cousin in New York who ran a restaurant in the West Village. Even the bathroom, with its rudimentary shower, failed to upset her. After they had inspected it, she followed Kate into her compartment to sit on the bed and watch her unpack. As Kate lay the clothes on the bed, her long fingers picked them over, seeking the labels in the linings. The cloud of cigarette smoke around her head gave her a murky aura and Kate thought of bad fairies gathering up nail parings and hair combings for the casting of lethal spells. At last she protested feebly: 'Do you have to smoke in here? We can hardly breathe as it is.'

Tina peeled off the jacket she had been trying on, tossed it on the bed and leant against the mirror, hand on hip.

'You're weird, you know that. You should try meditation. Twenty minutes a day, morning and night. A lot of actors do it.'

'I know. I've met them.' She put away the last of her clothes. 'What's on your mind, Tina?'

'I've patched it up with Jake.'

'Why aren't you with him, then?'

'He wants to make me suffer a little before we get back in bed together.' She smiled complacently. 'He's so busy being a hypochondriac, he's happier sleeping alone for the time being. Meanwhile . . .'

She slipped out into the corridor and could be heard asking Kamal for an ashtray. A moment later she reappeared.

'Meanwhile I want to spend some more time with Girish. And since you and Hunter feel the same way about one another, I thought we could make a deal.'

Kate felt a sharp pang of envy. It must be nice to be Tina. For all the talk about her shrink, she gave no sign of having an inner life. If it felt good, she did it. If one door closed, another was bound to open. If not, she would force it. Kate doubted that she knew anything about regret.

Tina's excitement at the prospect of a little intrigue and subterfuge was almost seductive. But the image of the bad fairy persisted. Going along with Tina meant being in Tina's power. She shook her head.

'Well, that's too bad,' said Tina, the gleefulness replaced by mockery, 'because Hunter already said yes. After we finish shooting tonight, he's coming in here with you and I'm sneaking into the compartment he's sharing with Girish. It's all arranged.'

PART TWO

Kate and Hunter stepped from the train into a lunar landscape, eerily silver under the stars, and sat down on a convenient boulder. Hunter was dressed as usual in cotton trousers and a denim shirt in washed-out blue, the sleeves rolled up to the elbows. The plainness of these clothes suited him so well that she wondered how much vanity had gone into their choosing.

He dismissed her misgivings. 'I'll handle Tina. Don't worry about her. We're getting on better now—since we had our run-in over you. It cleared the air. She'll probably start telling you how good you are soon.'

'Never.'

He put his arm around her. 'Then never mind. You know you're doing good work. We both know it.'

She nodded. It was true. She had her nerve back. She could forget about the flaws and fissures exposed by her illness and feel herself soaring beyond the point where calculation ended and intuition began.

'You're going to be a star.'

'Then I wish . . .' She threw her head back and gazed at the train—a series of lonely capsules of light and sound.

He pressed his lips against her cheek. 'What do you wish?'

She was still thinking of Tina's recklessness. Just a little of it would do. 'Oh, I wish I had red lips and breasts like monuments.'

'Is that what you want to be? Larger than life?'

'Larger than my life.'

'Then you will be.'

His smile glittered in the darkness and she felt a rush of optimism. He took her hand and led her across the stony path towards the capsules of light.

Kamal brought morning tea in bed, smiling down on them from his great height. Kate minded less than she had expected. She and Hunter were already used to being looked at. On waking, they had raised the blind to find that the train had stopped at a station and people were peering at them through the glass.

Some were gipsy-like women, dressed in orange and gold, with beaten silver nose-rings and bangles studded with amber and turquoise; others were schoolboys, spruce in white shirts and grey shorts.

'We are studying commerce, sir,' one shouted as Hunter pushed up the window. 'We collect foreign coins.' Kate found some Australian twenty-cent pieces in her purse and Hunter smoothed out three American dollars and passed them to the waiting hands just as the train pulled out.

After their tea, they shut themselves in again and made love, laughing as the rocking train suddenly accelerated. Kamal was wearing a broader smile than usual when they finally came to breakfast and Kate smiled back, overwhelmed by the pleasure of having Hunter to herself.

By mid-morning it had grown so hot that they threw open all the doors and windows. Kate was dressed in a sarong and Hunter was in shorts and they sat in the doorway swinging their legs over the side and watching the desert go by.

As the train crossed a narrow bridge, they spied peacocks picking their way daintily across a stony ravine far below, their tails blue-black against the dun-coloured expanse, then, as the engine slowed for a twisting hill climb, they looked back to see the other carriages curving snake-like behind them.

They were only partway through their winding, upward course when the train stopped. They were to film on the hillside and right on cue, encouraged by chapatis tossed from the train by the kitchen boys, a pack of chimpanzees appeared out of nowhere and obligingly posed on the rocks.

Kate and Hunter moved inside the carriage as people began to leave the train and clamber down the slope. Some wore shorts or sarongs, one was in a bathrobe and there was a variety of straw hats. She thought they looked like holiday-makers on the moon—a hot moon, bathed in shimmering waves of air.

It was time for Hunter to leave. She sat on the bed watching him stow his things into his cracked leather briefcase. When he was finished he crouched on the floor in front of her, leaning his elbows on her knees. She took his face in her hands and kissed him hard on the lips.

'It'll be all right,' he said. 'You'll see. You'll live happily ever after.'

Somebody had found a cloth of embroidered cotton in red, green and gold with inlaid mirrors which flashed in the sun and set it up on four poles to provide shade. Ward put his canvas chair beneath it and Tina joined him in her white cotton Punjabi pyjamas and new Rajasthan jewellery.

'The royal couple,' muttered one of the grips.

Now that they were reconciled—at least in public—Ward's health had improved dramatically, and while Tina did not fuss over him as she had in the days before Girish, she paid attention. In response to his stories The Laugh was working overtime, while Girish sat glumly on the sidelines.

He had become a creature of the night when what he really wanted was to shine by day before an appreciative audience. Only when it was his turn to do a scene did he come to life, then Hunter spoiled things with complaints about his timing. His hurt expression made Ward smile.

Afterwards, Kate tried to cheer him up. 'It'll be a good scene. You'll see. That's why Hunter took so much trouble with it.'

He plucked irritably at his shirt, trying to put some air between it and his perspiring back. 'Everybody is against me now because of Tina. If she really had some feelings for me we would not be skulking around in this manner.'

'And things would be unbearable on set. It's better this way.'

'You mean it is better that I am made a scapegoat so that Jake can save face.'

'She's very overpowering.' Her gaze drifted across to Tina, enthroned under the embroidered canopy. 'And often very thoughtless. Girish, if this thing with her is making you miserable, then perhaps you should end it.'

'Oh, no. Not while there is a chance.'

'A chance of what?'

Girish was silent. They both knew what he was thinking. He was dreaming of a future in which he lived with Tina in a mansion in Beverly Hills.

3

That night Hunter did not sleep in her compartment since he had to stay up late in the dining-car with Andy McCaffrey and Frank Lipscombe, the special effects co-ordinator, planning the next day's shooting in Jaisalmer.

Tina was in the compartment instead, wanting to talk. She stretched out on the sofa in the saloon and, despite her slimness, seemed to fill the room. Kate settled back in a nest of cushions with a copy of the script and tried to concentrate on her lines. Behind the scene of underwear in the kitchenette, Tampi was making tea while Kamal moved along the corridor with a cloth, disturbing that day's dust.

'I'll tell you something . . .' The smoke from Tina's cigarette drifted upwards, spiralling into the currents of air around the ceiling fan. 'I'm starting to think again about Hunter. Nothing radical but I've got to hand it to him. He's getting good work out of Jake. And Girish.' She paused to emphasise Kate's omission from the list. 'I mean, I thought he was one of your regulation boy wonders—full of bright ideas when everything's swinging along but when the going gets rough, they fall apart. But he hasn't fallen apart.' She paused. 'Oh, sure, there is the teeny problem of the schedule. We're way behind. But that's India for you.'

She threw up her hands, performing a horizontal shimmy of distaste. Kamal looked on interestedly. He had finished dusting and had taken up his usual post in the doorway. Tampi came through with the tea.

'No offence,' said Tina to both of them as she swung her feet to the floor. 'Anyway, we've got some brilliant stuff.'

After tea, she became restless again and started asking about Australia and Kate's childhood, brightening considerably when Kate talked about her father.

'Do you still see him?'

'Mmm. He likes having an actor in the family.'

'The bastard,' Tina said comfortably. 'What about your mother?'

Kate did her best to describe her mother but she wasn't nearly such good talent. Her Anglo-Saxon forbearance was too much for Tina. 'One thing you can say for the Jews. At least we know how to make the most of trouble.'

4

They climbed an ascending maze of stone pathways to the city palace, then beyond to Jaisalmer's complex of Jain temples where they found a priest tending one of the shrines, his mouth veiled against the possibility that he might unwittingly take life by ingesting a dust mite. Afterwards, they meandered back down the hill to explore the alleyways of the town.

The path was narrow. Matt dropped back and Kate took Ajay's arm. The three of them had spent the whole morning together. Friendship seemed easier when Ajay was with them. They talked to one another through him.

Matt relied a great deal on Ajay, showing him every page of script as it came off the printer. To everyone else these pages were merely blueprints—rough guides to the job in hand. It was only Ajay who still saw them as part of a continuing narrative. To Matt he was a touchstone.

Ajay was laughing at something that Kate had said. They had long discussions about acting and he had finally persuaded her to read the book. 'You see, I was right, wasn't I?' he said, eyes sparkling, when she told them both how good it was.

At the bottom of the hill they stopped and Ajay looked at his watch. He had changed his Calcutta uniform of dark trousers and white business shirt for jeans and a T-shirt with *The Indian Summer* inscribed across the chest, and now looked like a member of the crew. He was relaxed and lighthearted and in the train had sat by the window, delighting in the dun-coloured miles unrolling before them. 'You know, this is the first real chance I have ever had to see my country. I cannot even tell you when I was last out of the city.'

He saw that he was late for an appointment. 'I have to meet Kalelkar, the representative from the local authority here. At the location.'

'We might as well come too,' said Matt a little too quickly, not ready to be left alone with Kate. 'Kate hasn't seen the *havelis* yet.'

They were just as he remembered them, amber-coloured in the morning sun. Shadows slanted across the arched doorways and the carved sandstone filigree stood out in delicate relief against the play of light and shade. Above were ornate pillared balconies and gracefully formed window bays, jutting from the walls like a succession of ships' figureheads.

Matt told Kate about the rich Jaisalmer gem trader who had had them built for his five sons in the town's heyday as a desert trading post. In the script, one of the grandest of the *haveli* had to catch fire and later in the day, they would be filming its facade. As he and Kate climbed the rickety wooden stairs, they came across Ajay and Kalelkar, a youngish, soft-looking man in white kurta pyjamas, whose plump features were clouded with concern as he watched two special effects men plant smoke pellets behind the lattice-work windows.

'Jaisalmer is such a tinder-box town,' he said. 'The thought of a fire of any sort. If it were to spread . . .'

Ajay tried to soothe him. 'The main set we are building is well away from everything. And the safety experts have all worked in Hollywood, some on very big and expensive productions requiring elaborate stunts. The head of the safety department will be here soon. You will meet him . . .'

The burly, reassuring figure of Frank Lipscombe was already coming up the stairs. Matt and Kate made their escape, going on up to the flat roof where they stood gazing out over the honey-coloured landscape.

To one side of them lay the lanes and alleyways of the

PART TWO

town. Some of the flat roofs served as extra bedrooms with *charpoys* and neatly rolled mattresses waiting for the night. The other side offered a view of the sandstone fort and its battlements—a ridge of glaring yellow sandcastles, baking in the haze.

A moment later Ajay joined them. 'Ah, the perils of being a liaison man. Thank God for Frank is all I can say. Now, let's see . . .' He drew a tattered guide-book from his pocket and began reading to Kate. 'This house is not so old. Not nearly as old as those in other parts of the city. Perhaps 1860. I think the sandstone carvers were Muslims. What a great place it must have been in its day.'

Kate was still thinking of Kalelkar and the scene downstairs. 'I hope they all realise what a bargain they've got in you Ajay.'

He beamed at her. 'I don't really care. I'm here.' He gestured so vigorously with the guide-book that a loose page slipped out and fluttered over the rooftops.

Matt took Kate back into town to shop, but without Ajay there were long silences. In his presence, smiles, jokes and moments of mild flirtation had all been possible. Now they walked along like sedate acquaintances.

He had once fancied that it was not the actual Kate who obsessed him, but her great luminous image which had so often wrapped itself around him in the darkness of the theatre. Now he know better. It was her flesh-and-blood ordinariness that he loved. He had discovered that he did not always find her beautiful, and that at these times his feelings ran deepest. Once she had invited him into the make-up trailer so he could read her a page of script. Watching her strip her face bare of make-up and examine it under the lights as if it were a weapon or an instrument, for practical use only, he had felt closer to her than ever.

They had one moment of spontaneity. Turning into one of the maze-like streets, they came upon a wandering cow having trouble edging past a sharply angled bend, and as they shooed and coaxed it around the corner, they started to laugh, reeling drunkenly against the mudbrick walls.

Matt tried to hang on to the lightness but when he got his

breath back, his self-consciousness came with it. It weighed him down and they made their way to the street of the *Patwon ki Haveli* in polite silence.

They found the area around the street of the *havelis* filled with people. A noisy mass pressed against a cordon closing off one end of the street, and in the cleared space stood Girish and Ward, made-up for the take.

Fletcher and Rajiv were to be alone in one of the uninhabited and more dilapidated *havelis* and, against Rajiv's advice, Fletcher would insist on climbing its unstable staircase to see the view. On the way down they were to smell smoke and discover that a fire had started on the second floor. The fire was to start licking at one side of the staircase and, in the downward scramble, Fletcher was to be overcome by smoke, trip and knock himself out. Rajiv was to save him.

As Kate and Matt watched, a billowing white cloud issued from one of the upper windows of the *haveli*. There were cries of alarm from the crowd which pressed forward, straining the cordon.

'Somebody get those people out of here!' Tina was wearing a coolie hat of plaited straw tied under the chin. As she whirled about, waving her arms, Kate was put in mind of a sharp object, dangerously out of control.

'What is happening?' Mr Kalelkar was standing nearby, his face glistening in the heat.

'It's all right,' said Ajay, 'they are just testing one of the smoke pellets.'

'It's damn well not all right,' snapped Tina. 'Who are you, by the way?' She rounded on Kalelkar, who stepped back in fright. When Ajay introduced them, Kalelkar's identity made her more furious then ever. 'Then why aren't you keeping these goddamned people under control?' Ajay tried to draw her aside, but she shook him off. 'Where the hell is Hunter?' She sped away.

'Who is that person?' Kalelkar was still quivering.

Everybody spoke at once. 'She didn't mean to upset . . .'

said Ajay. 'She didn't understand . . .' said Kate. 'Tempers run very high on film sets,' said Matt.

Their voices trailed into silence as the *haveli* starting spewing smoke from every window. The extras stood transfixed with pretended panic and a moment later, Girish appeared on cue in the doorway, staggering under the weight of the drooping Ward.

At the sight of them, a spontaneous shout went up from the crowd and it pressed forward, snapping the cordon like string. Hundreds of people rushed before the cameras, surrounding the two actors, and the air was filled with expressions of hysterical concern.

'Cut!' yelled Nick Thornton. 'For God's sake, cut!'

The smoke began to clear. Looking abashed and confused, people allowed themselves to be led back behind the cordon.

Kalelkar took out a spotless white handkerchief and wiped his brow. Ajay touched him reassuringly on the shoulder and was about to speak, but it was too late. Kalelkar's sorrowful eyes were already flashing in alarm at the sight of Tina bearing down on them.

'I thought you had these people under control!'

Ajay bravely placed himself between them. 'You have to understand . . .'

Tina pounced on the phrase, cutting him off. 'I don't have to understand anything. We are trying to get a goddamned picture made here—a picture that's going to do a lot for this . . .' She paused for a spine-tingling moment then flashed a savage smile. '. . . country. This lovely country.' With a final withering glance at Kalelkar, she turned and strode off, leaving him gazing after her.

'What a truly terrible woman.'

'It's that damned Ajay's fault.' Tina gathered up some rice with her fork, scrutinising it closely before putting it into her mouth.

'Rubbish, Kalelkar has nothing to do with crowd control. He's a city official. He didn't know what you were talking about.'

'What would you know? You're an actress.'

'Tell her, Hunter. Please.'

Hunter was watching Tina's fork as it stabbed at the grains of rice on her plate, sifting and sorting. 'What does your therapist say about you, Tina?'

She looked at him darkly then the green eyes softened and she grinned. 'None of your goddamned business.'

5

Charlie was pacing back and forth in the dust. Beneath his natty Panama, his eyes were bloodshot and his features had lost their usual rosiness and taken on a sallow tinge.

'Gut trouble. I've been up all night. You heard what's happened, I suppose.'

'No.'

'The fuel that Frank's people bought in Delhi was below strength and we couldn't get the gel to work properly.'

The set on the town's outskirts, built to duplicate the interior of the *haveli*, was to be set alight with a flammable gel made up of silica mixed with fuel. Drums of petrol bought in Delhi had been trucked across to Jaisalmer.

'Frank's found some fuel in town. We can get by if we do the whole thing in wide shot, but Hunter's holding out. He wants cutaways, close-ups, the whole deal. He thinks we should wait and send somebody into Bikaner for more stuff. I've been trying to talk him out of it.' His mouth turned down. 'Without success.'

Matt walked across to the group around the camera, which had been placed so that it framed the plywood staircase connecting the four floors of the set. The front wall, which Matt had learnt to call by its technical name, 'a floating flat', had been detached from the rest so as to provide space. Girish stood beside it with the two stuntmen, Henry and Anil.

Charlie had followed Matt across. 'We can't waste any more time,' he said to Hunter. 'We're too far behind already.'

Hunter shook his head. He was as calm as ever. 'It's not a

waste of time. It's a big scene. It must be done right. Tina agrees.'

Charlie was aghast. 'You don't, do you?'

Tina's face was half-hidden by a floppy straw hat. 'Hunter's right. It's a big scene.'

Matt watched Girish approach the circle around the camera and wait tentatively on its edge. 'I have a solution,' he said, so quietly that the others failed to hear. He repeated himself more loudly. 'I have a solution.' Now that they were listening, he spoke very fast. 'I have watched Henry and Anil rehearse the fire gag and I am sure I could do it myself. That way there would be no need for the cutaways. After all, we don't have to see Jake's face as we come down the stairs because Fletcher is out to it.'

'Absolutely not,' said Charlie.

Girish gave no sign of having heard. 'Please, Hunter, I am perfectly confident.'

'It's a bad idea, Girish,' said Frank.

Girish flashed his old smile, a reminder of what a blithe spirit he had been before Tina. He had complete confidence in Frank and his team. All would go as clockwork. The staircase would collapse exactly on cue and not a moment before. There were no trick falls involved, and, in any case, Henry would keep him out of trouble. 'I am betting that he could be holding me up instead of the other way round and nobody would be any the wiser.'

Frank shook his head, worried about the vapour that would be building up on the stairs, making it hard to breathe.

Ward had joined the group. 'It's only a movie, Girish.' He sounded oddly sympathetic.

Hunter regarded Girish curiously. 'Why, Girish? Why do you want to do it?'

'I know I can.'

'Gag', stunt'. Matt rolled these euphemisms around on his tongue, considering their inadequacy. He was witnessing a ritual—an exclusive ceremony with its own mysteries, comprehended only by the special effects team and the stuntmen.

Now that the decision was made, they showed no sign of doubt. Their concentration was absolute. By the time the preparations had been made, the only note of protest was registered by Mr Kalelkar who had arrived late and took time to realise the significance of what was taking place.

'My God,' he muttered. 'Is that Girish who is going to run through the fire?'

'Not through,' said Ajay dutifully. 'The fire will only be licking at the back of the stairs. It is perfectly safe.'

As the moment approached, Henry, Frank and Anil gathered around Girish in a circle and, out of view of the crowd, he stripped to his underpants to be anointed with a jelly-like substance that left him sticky and glistening in the sunshine.

'What is happening now?' whispered Kalelkar, even more disturbed by this development.

'It's a protective substance they are putting on,' said Ajay, who had learned his lines well. 'A fire suppressant. If a spark should happen to touch his body, it will not hurt him. You remember, Frank Lipscombe explained it to us when you talked to him in the *haveli*.'

Kalelkar wiped sweat from his upper lip while continuing to stare at Girish, who was putting on his costume over the gel. Frank and the two stuntmen whispered last-minute words of advice.

'There go the fire-extinguishers,' said Matt in his heartiest tone, feeling Ajay needed some support. 'They'll allow the fire to burn for only a very short time.'

At last, Henry and Girish were standing at the top of the staircase, waiting for the effects crew to finish painting the set with the flammable gel. Girish stood very straight, like a man about to dive from a great height. Matt could detect no sign of nervousness. Gleaming under lights set up to eliminate the lengthening shadows, he looked as if he were exactly where he wanted to be.

The set was now coated thoroughly with the gel. Frank bounded down the stairs to stand by the camera, and an effects man, with a gas bottle and a long wand fitted with an attachment which looked like an oversize paint scraper, stepped forward and ignited the mixture. There was an orange flash at the side of the staircase, a puff of thick grey smoke and, after an agonisingly long moment in which the flash had become a slender tongue of flame snaking along the casing of the stairs, Hunter cried: 'Action!'

Afterwards, when it was all over, Matt had trouble recalling the precise sequence of events. People seemed to come from everywhere, obscuring his view, so what he remembered best was the whoosh of hot air and the noise—a popping and splintering which memory had amplified and turned into an explosion.

It was not an explosion—just the sound of wood splitting as the staircase fell in a heap of sparks and charred beams which everybody agreed, later on, looked spectacular on film. The next thing that he remembered was the sight of the ominously still forms of Girish and Henry being dragged clear of the set.

Henry was the first to revive. Groggily hauling himself up, he rasped, 'Girish. Look after Girish.'

Anil had already turned Girish over and was busy pressing his chest and breathing into his mouth. There was no sign of life—just the rising and falling of the stuntman's shoulders as he breathed in and out.

Beside Matt, Kalelkar was wringing his hands and staring in horror at the set, where the men with fire-extinguishers were working furiously to stop the blaze spreading across the second floor. The unit doctor forced his way through the crowd to Girish's side. Matt strained to see over him and the crush of onlookers to where Girish lay. Long moments passed. Then he heard a feeble cough. The doctor moved aside. Blinking back sooty tears, Girish scanned the faces gazing down at him until he found Hunter's.

It took a while, but finally he managed a faint croak. 'How did it look?'

By evening, Girish was well enough to have visitors. As Kate approached his compartment, she could hear Charlie's raised voice and hesitated, tempted to turn back. Before she could move, the door was flung open by Hunter. He gave her a swift, blank smile and ushered her into the saloon where Girish lay propped up against a mound of pillows on one of the sofas.

'Hello, Kate. As you can see I am much better.'

The 'wheatish' complexion of which he was so proud looked yellowish in the pale light, and because his eyebrows had been badly singed, his face seemed sadly asymmetrical.

Sitting in a chair by the bed, Tina leaned forward on her elbows, nursing her inevitable cigarette. Charlie fanned the smoke away impatiently as it curled past his face and up to the ceiling. They both nodded wordlessly at Kate.

'I just wanted to see that you were all right,' she said to Girish. 'I won't stay.'

'No, don't go.' She looked at him doubtfully. 'Please. I want you to stay.'

She perched on the edge of a brocaded armchair. Hunter was staring into the darkness beyond the window while Tina and Charlie persisted in some Cold War of their own.

Suddenly, Tina broke the silence. 'I blame Frank Lipscombe. He said it would be safe and it wasn't. End of story.'

'Not at all. Not a bit of it. Frank didn't want Girish to do the stunt.' Charlie beat a tattoo on the table with his forefinger. 'You heard him, I heard him.' Even though Hunter's name had not been mentioned, it occurred to Kate that he was being put on trial. Ominously, Charlie seemed to have assumed the role of prosecutor.

Tina continued to blame Frank. 'Then why did he go ahead with it? He'd written a safety report on the picture, specifying a stunt guy for the scene. He should have stuck to his guns.'

Hunter glanced wearily from one to the other—although, to Kate, the weariness seemed assumed. 'He did it out of loyalty to me. It was my fault.'

Everybody was silent. Charlie seemed about to speak then changed his mind. Finally, he said gruffly: 'I guess there's nothing more to say.'

'Is that so?' Tina's voice rose. 'The fact that Hunter's willing to carry the can doesn't seem to me . . .'

'Please.' Girish was overcome by a fit of coughing. His eyes streamed with tears. 'I am to blame. I alone. It was my decision and my fault.'

Anguish produced a second flood of tears. He wiped them away with the flat of his hand, leaving his face streaky and smudged. His misery was too much for Kate.

'Let's go. Leave him in peace.'

'No, please. I must apologise to you all. And to Frank, too.'

Charlie rose from his seat in sudden embarrassment. 'All in good time, Girish. Kate's right. Get some sleep.' He patted Girish's shoulder and turned to go. Tina rose reluctantly and Kate followed, hoping that she and Hunter would go somewhere and talk. But Girish called him back. As Kate went out, she caught the beginning of their exchange.

'So it was really a good take. You are telling me the truth about that?'

Hunter reassured him. They would make a star of him yet.

With a deep sigh of satisfaction, Girish settled back against the pillows.

6

Matt's favourite part of the Umaid Bhawan Hotel in Jodhpur was the basement swimming pool. It was set in a cavernous space reached by a wide passage from the garden and roofed by a vaulted ceiling decorated with a mural depicting the signs of the zodiac (along with the odd stalactite), and had all the charm of a spa for the dying. He found it irresistible.

The rest of the hotel was cheerier but haunted by the same air of inappropriate luxury. Despite its Art Deco interiors, its squash courts, its billiard rooms and its dreamy terraces, it had a ghostly air—like an ocean liner mysteriously becalmed.

Here, on the edge of the Thar Desert, Matt felt the weight of Indian history with particular force. It was less than fifty years since the last acknowledged act of royal *sati* in Jodhpur—when the widow of a soldier prince calmly arranged her own immolation—and the walls of the great fort were proudly decorated with *satis'* handprints. Some were fakes—unnaturally shapely carvings of child-sized palms done *in memoriam*—but there were also larger, rougher and more poignant impressions in the stone, known to be the real thing.

As he headed along the corridor towards the pool, he could hear the rhythmic splashing of someone swimming laps, and when he emerged from the passage, Ward was standing at the pool's shallow end.

'A man could die in here,' he said cordially. 'Water's cold enough to freeze your nuts off.'

Matt smiled. Ward's he-man aura excited in him an adolescent urge to show off. He took off his shirt and dived smoothly into the pool. Succeeding in absorbing the cold water shock without lifting his head, he completed two quick laps punctuated by an impetuous tumble turn then leaned casually back against the wall, trying not to puff too hard.

Ward heaved himself onto the edge of the pool, a tricky movement involving a deft half-rotation of the hips. 'You know, this country scares the hell out of me.'

Yet he seemed stronger than ever. Matt suspected that Tina still aroused him but that his cynicism had reasserted itself to save him from lasting damage.

Ward moved his legs from side to side, making waves. 'Now I couldn't admit that before. Guess I'm feeling better. Gut is, anyway.' He paused to watch the waves roll across the surface of the pool and slop against the sides. 'This picture is going to be okay. You know that, don't you?'

The night before they had seen a new batch of rushes, transferred to tape and flown in from Calcutta. As promised, the fire scene had worked brilliantly and Girish was deliriously happy.

'I thought Hunter was just a flashy kid. Mind you, I still do.' Ward stood up and began towelling himself briskly. 'That business with me on the bridge with the snake . . . That's the way some of the old guys used to do it. Get their kicks trying to bluff you into things that scared the shit out of you.' He watched with malicious interest as Matt moved around cautiously in the icy water. 'These days, they've all got minds like cash registers. The schedule's everything. If they risk an actor, it's out of panic.' He grinned. 'Hunter's different. The other day with Girish. That wasn't panic. Hunter actually thinks that being scared shitless is a great help.'

'But Girish really wanted to do the stunt.'

Ward settled into a cane chair. 'Girish is a good talker. Also a dumb bastard.'

He took his time, lighting a cigarette. Matt bobbed about in the water, so interested in the conversation that he'd almost forgotten the cold. Ward went on. 'All Hunter had to do the other day was throw him a little face-saver—tell him things were going to be trickier than planned . . .'

Matt shook his head, remembering how calm Girish had looked, standing at the top of the staircase.

'Look, the kid's an actor,' said Ward. 'Not a bad one by the way. You see, it sounds fine when you're talking about it before the event. But when you're right there in the middle of it, knowing that your timing has to be right on the button or this expensive set-up is going to waste . . . well, the pressure's terrific.

'As soon as they lit up that gel, Frank Lipscombe knew it was too strong. And don't forget, Girish and Henry were standing up the top of that staircase for quite a while breathing in those fumes. Even before they started down, they were woozy. Frank could see it. What's more, he told Hunter.'

Matt was sceptical.

'Listen,' said Ward. 'I was standing close enough to damn well hear him . . . Are you a betting man?'

They discovered Frank in one of the billiard rooms, sitting in a corner, overlooked by the mounted head of a snarling leopard. He was moderately drunk and raised his glass in a raffish salute. In reply, Ward flourished a bottle brought from the bar.

Frank had been playing billiards. 'The bastards got too pissed to finish the game. Want to play?'

Matt and Ward perched at either end of a satin-covered divan.

'Maybe later. First, a question only you can answer.'

Drink had stripped Frank of his tranquil air of command and exposed his nerve endings. With his bulk and his black beard, he looked as ferocious as the trophy above his head.

'Anything,' he said. 'Ask away.'

'Just want to check on something.' Ward sloshed whisky into his glass and held it up to the light. They gazed at the glowing liquid as if at a crystal ball. 'The fire stunt . . .'

Frank's smile disappeared. 'Jake, for Christ's sake, I'm having a day off.'

'One question. That's all. Just before Girish and Henry headed down those stairs, I heard you tell Hunter that the flammable gel mixture was too strong . . .'

Frank's metamorphosis was so swift that it was almost invisible. He sat up straight in his chair, his eyes lost their bleariness and the familiar mantle of professional calm settled about his shoulders. The wild-man vanished.

'You couldn't have. Wasn't said.'

'I think it was.'

'No. The gel wasn't too strong.'

'That's not what Tina's saying.' Ward gently swilled the whisky around in his glass. The others waited and watched. 'Acorn want a report on the whole thing. She's putting it together now. I don't think you're getting an honourable mention, Frank.'

Frank stroked his beard with both hands in a distracted, face-washing motion.

'You told him, Frank. I heard you.' Ward's voice was soft, his smile conspiratorial. Its obviousness proved to be a mistake.

A slow grin spread across Frank's face. 'You like a bit of drama, don't you, Jake?'

'Don't we all? Why we're in the business.'

'Yeah, well, I can fight my own battles.' He downed the last of his whisky. 'A good drop, that. Don't drink it all at once.'

After he had gone, Jake conceded Matt the bottle of whisky that was at stake but not the victory. 'Frank's a good ol' boy.' His smile was bright with the desire for mischief. 'Hunter's lucky to have him.'

PART TWO

The fire stunt had formally put an end to Girish's and Tina's affair.

'Too much testosterone. That's his problem,' she told Matt, who had heard enough and was longing to escape the bars and lounges of the Umaid Bhawan for his own room. He had already had Girish's version, given earlier in the evening in another bar.

Girish had cared and she had let him down. 'She is a very difficult woman. From now on I am steering very clear of her. I advise you to do the same, Ajay.'

This extraneous piece of advice made Ajay smile. The most unexpected result of the fire stunt was that he and Girish had become friends. No matter how rash Girish had been in volunteering for the stunt, his steadiness under pressure had been an example of true courage. Ajay had sought him out to tell him so.

EXT. THE MEHRANGARH FORT. JODHPUR.

RAJIV and SUSIE are walking up the steep path to the fort, outlined grimly against the skyline. The scarred stone battlements rise beside them and they pause at a row of palm prints in the stone—memorials to the Jodhpur women who died as **satis**.

SUSIE touches one of the prints with her own palm.

> SUSIE: Grisly.

They continue up the path.

> RAJIV: (Hesitant) How did you and Will meet?
>
> SUSIE: You mean, what the hell are we doing together?
>
> RAJIV: (Laughing) If you like.
>
> SUSIE: The reason used to be obvious. We couldn't keep our hands off one another.
>
> RAJIV: Perhaps you should not have come to India. Perhaps Paris instead.
>
> SUSIE: Can't spend our whole lives in Paris. Anyway, Fletcher's hooked on this country now. (Sadly) It's all he talks about.

INT. THE ROYAL APARTMENTS.

SUSIE and RAJIV wander through the rooms with their latticework panels, gilt arches and walls of mirrors and mosaics.

They reach the royal bedchamber.

> SUSIE: (Glancing from a painting of one of the portly Rajput Maharajahs to the huge bed in the centre of the room) Glad it wasn't me.
>
> RAJIV: No, purdah would not have suited you.

She sighs and sits down on the bed. RAJIV looks around nervously in case the guard is watching.

    SUSIE: (Patting the bed) Come on, be a devil.

RAJIV sits beside her and she starts to cry, brushing away the tears with the back of her hand.

    RAJIV: Would you like to be on your own for a while?

She takes his hand.

    SUSIE: No, just sit there.

He strokes her hand as the tears continue to fall.

CHAPTER TWO

1

Kate dreaded the day when the picture would end. It had come to that. What she and Hunter had together could not possibly survive and the prospect was unbearable.

He comforted her, telling her she was wrong. He had actually asked her to marry him, taking her on a camel ride into the desert and timing the whole ceremony for sunset. It was supposed to be romantic. She tried to pretend, but the scene held too many ironies, some of them visible. Backlit by the sunset were rows of slender-legged memorial cenotaphs marking a Hindu cremation ground.

Now they were back in Bombay, where Hunter's other life loomed closer every day. Only that morning he had taken a call from Jess, and although she had shut herself in the bathroom as usual, she had heard enough. An unfamiliar Hunter had emerged, with an interest in house painting, school fees and junior cricket. When she came back into the room, he was sitting on the edge of the bed, staring blankly at the floor.

'She's taken him out of the school and put him in another one.'

'But that's what you wanted.'

'That's not the point. She did it without asking me. It's not the one we talked about. I've never even heard of it.'

He rarely shouted and his rising voice cracked oddly. He

sounded like an actor who hadn't yet mastered the technique. At last he recovered, taking a deep breath to signify that the old Hunter was back. He gripped her wrist, playfully shaking it in his version of an apology.

'You wanted to tell me about something. What was it?'

She'd thought he'd forgotten. For days she had put off telling him, then that morning she had woken suddenly, so full of what she had to say that she was almost choking with it. Now she found it impossible.

'We'll talk about it later.'

2

For Girish, select parts of Bombay composed a suburb of Paradise outshone only by his imagined Beverly Hills. He haunted the lobby of the Taj, chatting to the patrician beauties on duty at the tours desk, browsing through the movie magazines in the bookstore or just sitting watching the traffic go by. He was already there when Matt and Ajay arrived to share a car to the Film Factory with him. En route, he devoted himself to watching the movie posters go by, identifying faces, summarising plots and nominating those film stars he would like to see running the country.

Ajay, no fan of film star politicians, twisted around in his seat beside the driver and made a face.

Girish refused to laugh. 'I don't see why you think it's such a bad idea. For the life of me, I don't. A country such as ours needs leaders who are big enough to rise above the pettiness, the corruption and the religious differences. Heroes who can unite and inspire.' He gestured in the direction of a painted face dominating the skyline with eyes the size of fish ponds and an upper lip rising to twin mountain peaks.

Ajay shook his head in disbelief. 'Are you seriously suggesting that the M.G. Ramachandrans of this world—with all their nonsense—hold the answers to India's problems? Ramachandran . . .' He laughed. 'This was a politician who kept in touch with his constituents in the villages at election time by sending them his hat on a yellow cushion.'

'Not him perhaps, but others. They are uniquely equipped when it comes to capturing the public imagination.'

'Girish, Girish.' Ajay's laughter lit up his narrow, serious face. 'You want to make children of us.'

'No, not at all. A country like ours needs a leader who can command the love of the people. You'll back me up in this, won't you, Matt?'

The very words, 'love of the people' gave Matt the shakes. Girish was shocked at this denial of democracy.

Matt thought he must be joking. Democracy didn't come into it. 'You're talking about demagoguery.'

Girish sulked for the rest of the trip. The others, too, were quiet, subdued by the sight of the shantytowns which stretched out on either side of the highway on plains and terraces of dust and tarpaper, seeming to go on forever.

Girish cheered up again when they entered the grounds of the Film Factory. It was his first visit in twelve years. He had worked at the studio as a child actor before his fall from grace, and gazed out over its hilly, grey-green acres as if returning to an Eden regained after many trials.

'Where is the lake? I want to see the lake.'

The driver obliged, taking them to a hilltop where they could look down upon the shimmer of smoky blue across the valley. Girish sighed with pleasure.

After Girish had been to make-up and wardrobe he still wanted to explore, and he persuaded Matt and Ajay to wander through the sound stages with him before joining Hunter and the others at the location.

In a small, dingy studio used as a storeroom, they found a throne and a marriage bed left over from a celebrated television version of the *Mahabarata*. Girish's fingers lingered reverently on the gilt and plaster artefacts then, in a dusty corner, he came across the bloodied papier mâché head of a fallen hero. Picking it up, he stared soulfully into its eyes. 'Every Sunday, the whole of India stopped for this series. The power of the imagination. If that could be harnessed, just think what could be accomplished.'

Ajay laughed. 'In this particular case, we already know. Bigotry and bloodshed. There are no gods among our politicians. And no heroes either.'

Now that the Film Factory had worked its magic on him, Girish had lost interest in the argument. 'Come on, let's get out into the sunshine and see what's what.'

As the car bumped over the hilly acres, they came across a set that Matt remembered from his earlier visit. The same painted extras lolled against the same thatched huts waiting for something to happen, while the director sat smoking with the crew.

Girish greeted the sight with much excitement. 'I know that director. Can we stop?'

Mr Vaidya, the director, was again waiting for his star, but he wanted Matt to know that during the weeks since his last visit he had been busy shooting an action picture for another studio. He amiably described the plot. 'Old wine in a new bottle. Five songs, six or seven fights.'

Girish wanted to know everything. 'And who is this star who is keeping you waiting so long?'

When told, he roared with laughter. 'We went to acting classes together. Before I went back to being a juvenile delinquent.' He exuberantly nudged Mr Vaidya in the ribs. 'Now you are having to stand around waiting for Bobby while I have become the disciplined professional—always on time.' He looked at his watch. 'Oops. We must be on our way.'

He gave Mr Vaidya's hand a vigorous shake and asked him to give Bobby his regards. 'Tell him . . .' Delighted by the serendipity of it all, he started to giggle. 'Tell him how sorry I am he was running late.'

3

Perched on the edge of Charlie's desk, Kate plucked idly at the swirl of papers.

He slapped her hand. 'Don't touch anything.'

'Charlie, what's gone wrong between you and Hunter?'

'Search me.' He made a half-hearted grab for one of the papers.

'Come on, talk to me.'

He sat back and the breath went out of him in a sigh of temporary surrender.

'You want me to talk to you about Hunter? I hardly see him anymore.' He looked up at her slyly. 'You're the one who sees him.'

She was silent. He was suddenly contrite. 'What's wrong? Is the bastard making you unhappy?'

'I just can't see how it can work.'

He squeezed her hand. 'How can I help?'

'Just tell me about him.'

He leaned back with his hands behind his head. 'Well, he's very bright, but you know that. Restless sort of bright, but you know that, too. Right from the start we just seemed to get along. A lot of laughs. We both loved movies. He didn't seem to mind me not being in his class intellectually. A little bit of condescension here and there. I got used to that. I could always kid him about it. But ever since we started this picture he's been different.'

'How different?' She didn't really want to know; she didn't really want to be having the conversation. But something had to be done. One way or another, she had to make up her mind. And except for Hunter himself, Charlie was the only one who could help.

'Is this really any use?' he asked.

'I think so.'

'Okay. Well, he's always been a bad boy with budgets and schedules, but he's relied on me to tell him when to calm down. We had a kind of tug-of-war going. Competitive but basically healthy. This picture was a big risk. Huge. But we sort of figured that as long as we could keep the tug-of-war going, it would be okay.' He shook his head. 'Didn't work that way. These days, as far as I'm concerned, he's Genghis bloody Khan. If I have a question, I'm a traitor. At first I kicked like hell. And when I saw where that was getting me, I stopped. Now I just shuffle papers and keep my head down.'

His mournfulness made her laugh.

'It's true. I don't know him anymore . . . Does Jess know about you two?'

'Not yet.'

'Well, she's not going to find out from me.'

She pressed his hand with its stubby, square-tipped fingers. The nails were bitten down and made her feel sorry for him, as his gloomy words had not done.

4

Matt had bought the English newspapers from the Taj's bookshop and was sitting in the Apollo Bar over a lime and soda, trying unsuccessfully to use the problems of the wider world to escape his own. He was a great newspaper reader. Newspapers were his diversion and his refuge, his parallel reality, available for reference and refreshment. Proof of his maturity. His ability to care about life in general.

At that moment the blocks of type before him might well have been in code.

He was thinking about a scene from a batch of rushes shown the night before. Thoroughly accustomed to seeing his characters embodied in Kate, Ward and Girish, he usually found it impossible to tell much at all from the rushes. The disconnected snippets of film seemed to him to give everything equal weight. Nothing leapt out at him, nothing flowed and the presence of cast and crew in the room kept him at one remove from the events on the screen, conscious of the process that had put them there.

Last night had been different. Something had clicked. He'd been watching a scene with Girish and three Indian bit-players when he'd been struck by the way the dramatic thrust of his lines had been altered by Hunter's placement of the camera. In his view, it had falsified the whole scene, and looking back on the stream of rewrites and last-minute improvisations on

Hunter's part, he was facing up to the possibility that he might not like the finished film at all.

If he had any sense, he wouldn't let it matter. He would clear out for the day and go somewhere to remind himself that there was a world which had nothing to do with Hunter. He would ring up one of his Bombay friends and get himself invited to lunch.

Instead he brooded. He wished he could take Kate sightseeing, but he couldn't find her. He had telephoned her room several times, and got no answer. He had tried to reach Charlie as well but Charlie was busy. Everybody was busy. Wandering about the hotel, checking the coffee shop and other likely places, he had felt perilously out of touch.

Now, when he glanced up from his newspaper to be greeted by the sight of Tina coming towards him, with eyes, teeth and jewellery flashing, he didn't even flinch, grateful for the chance to be back in the picture.

She flopped into a chair, scanned the headlines of his *Sunday Times* and caught the eye of the waiter, all in one jittery movement.

'I feel like getting out of here,' she said. 'Going somewhere interesting.'

He played for time. 'Still got a bit of work to do . . . What did you have in mind?'

'You see those ferryboats over there?' She gestured towards the window and the boats moored at the Apollo Bunder. 'They go to this island . . .'

'Elephanta.'

'You've been already.'

He nodded. A chance to duck the expedition. Unaccountably he let it pass. 'A long time ago.'

'So how about it?'

The island was full of picnicking Indian families with ghettoblasters and badminton racquets. They sat on tartan blankets, juggling thermoses and plastic cups or crouched over primus stoves miraculously producing lunch for fourteen.

Matt and Tina joined a party of enthralled tourists being

led through the caves by a bossy guide who lectured them resonantly on the Shiva carvings and delivered a dissertation on the power of meditation, so efficacious in enabling all devout Hindus to remain pure amid the wickedness and filth which surrounded them. A latecomer was reprimanded for asking about a point that had already been explained adequately, and at the end, a rotund man with a singsong voice was moved to a lyrical vote of thanks for the guide's eloquence which had opened his eyes so that nothing would be quite the same from this day after.

Tina was surprisingly well-behaved. It was only when they came blinking into the sun to be met by a little girl learning to make money from tourists by parading with a brass pot balanced on her head, that she exploded. 'I mean where do these people get off? They're in there talking about karma and dharma and they're out here teaching their kids to beg.'

He suggested a drink.

At an outdoor kiosk on the hilltop overlooking the jetty, they bought warm bottles of Thums Up and sat at a table in the sun. Watching the traffic go up and down the twisting path past the vendors of coloured beads and brass elephants, she calmed down. 'What the hell, that little kid, her parents, us. We're all in the same business . . . the leisure industry. Right?'

Unaccustomed to irony from Tina, Matt took a moment to deal with the concept.

By way of assistance she gave him a burst of The Laugh and told him how talented he was. 'You and Hunter make a good team. I know he wants to work with you again.'

Matt felt better already. It didn't take much.

Tina continued. 'He didn't always feel that way. But you know all that. How he fought like hell not to have you write the script . . .

Matt said yes, he did know all that.

'Yeah, well . . . Anyway, he thought he was going to have trouble with you. That's the thing about authors—most of the time they're trouble. But you've been a doll. Letting him use your material to realise his own vision. He's very grateful for that. We all are.'

Matt's ego absorbed the backhander, converting it into a hard knot of anxiety which lodged itself behind his breastbone.

Tina's attention had already moved on. She was staring at the crowd of people on the path, all heading down towards a large queue for the boats.

'Oh, Christ. The last ferry.'

When they reached the bottom, launches were used to transfer passengers from the jetty to the ferry moored in deeper water. The launches bobbed about in the swell, causing much commotion as grandmothers and small children were handed across the rising waters.

Tina responded to the scene with elan. 'You know something. We're going to get on one of these boats.'

By the time they gained the head of the queue, the end of the jetty was underwater. Elegant women in high heels picked their way delicately across the sodden planks, their saris trailing in the shallows.

Tina took off her shoes and rolled up her Punjabi trousers to the knee, revealing alabaster-white legs and long, bony feet with scarlet toenails. As the launch pulled in, she draped her shoulder bag around her neck, hung the straps of her slingback sandals from one arm, leaving both hands free, and clambered aboard with a spidery agility that left Matt lumbering in her wake. She sat down, pink-faced and laughing.

'Your nose is going to peel.'

As she checked this disaster in her compact mirror, he asked casually: 'So where is everybody today?'

'Who's everybody?'

He put off mentioning Kate. 'Charlie. Where's Charlie?'

'How would I know?'

'Jake?'

'In his room or beside the pool. Where else?'

He felt it was safe to ask about Kate. 'I've actually been trying to ring her. There's a jeweller I know who can make a ring from a stone she's bought . . .'

'Didn't know Kate bought stones. Didn't know she bought anything.'

Tina had twisted around in her seat for a clearer view of

PART TWO

a statuesque woman in a purple and pink sari with kohl-rimmed eyes and vivid lips, who sat dominating their immediate surroundings like a resting deity.

'So have you seen her?'

Tina swung slowly round to him and looked him in the eye, making up her mind about something. Then after a long pause: 'No one's seen her.'

Out of the corner of his eye, Matt could see the Indian woman peeling an orange with pudgy, languid fingers. 'Since when?'

'Two or three days ago. The official line is that she's gone to Goa for the weekend.'

'Official line?'

'Yeah. I only saw her on Thursday night. She didn't say anything about Goa to me. But that's Charlie's story and he's sticking to it.'

'What about Hunter?'

'Hunter's in Madurai . . . There is one thing though.' She waited a tantalising beat or two. 'I happened to be passing her room early on Friday morning—we're in the same corridor—and Dr Mishra was coming out with his little black bag. He gave me kind of a sickly smile.'

Matt felt a tingling in fingers and spine. 'What did you do?'

'Knocked on her door.'

'What did she say?'

'I didn't have a chance to speak to her. Dr Mishra came back and told me to stop knocking. He said he'd just given her a sedative and she was probably half-asleep already. According to him, she'd had a bad attack of gastroenteritis and hadn't slept all night.'

'That's it then. No mystery.'

'Are you kidding? While Mishra was telling me all this he looked like he didn't believe a word he was saying. And Charlie wasn't much better.'

Tension made Matt short-tempered. 'Come on, Tina, what are you telling me?'

'Just what you're thinking already.' She fanned herself, eyes closed, head tilted towards the smudgy sky.

He reminded her irritably that more than a year had passed

since Kate's illness. 'She's made a couple of pictures since then.'

'None of them any good.'

'That's your opinion. Anyway, what's that got to do with anything?'

'Maybe she wasn't in love with the directors of those pictures.'

Matt was visited by a desire to see Tina vanish over the ferry's rail in a blur of white limbs. Pop! Like a cartoon fairy.

'Rubbish. She's been perfectly all right. Calmer than I am. And you. Much calmer than you.'

'Then where is she?'

Back at the Taj, they tried unsuccessfully to find Charlie. According to the reception desk he had been out since early morning.

They started telephoning hotels and guest-houses in Goa. None of them had Kate Conroy registered. Tina suggested she might be using another name. 'If she was after a quiet time she wouldn't have wanted anyone to know who she was.'

'She wouldn't expect to be recognised. Not in this country.'

'Oh, yeah. She's an actress, isn't she?'

He looked at his watch, wanting to believe. It was seven o'clock. This time Charlie picked up the phone. When Matt announced himself, he answered with a crisp 'yes' as if the call were part of a continuing business discussion.

'You've obviously had a long day,' said Matt. 'You deserve a drink.' He failed to mention Tina. 'I'm in the Apollo Bar.'

There was a brief pause after which Charlie said a little too fulsomely: 'Gee, I'd like to, mate. But I'm waiting for a couple of calls.'

'No problem. I'll come to you.' He hung up quickly. He made a doomed attempt to talk Tina out of joining them. 'No offence,' she said, 'but I don't trust you.'

Charlie shook his head over their foolishness and said that Tina's guess had been right. Kate wasn't using her own name in Goa. He clicked his fingers convincingly. 'Susannah? Joanna? . . . No, sorry, it won't come.'

Tina asked the name of the hotel.

He didn't know that either. 'She made the booking herself. Picked a hotel out of the guide-book.'

Matt had been feeling reassured. The prickles of apprehension returned. 'Charlie, I still don't understand. If you're in India and your gut's playing up, the best place is right here at the Taj. You don't go racing off to Goa where you're likely to eat something that will really lay you out.'

'That's what I told her but you know what Kate's like.'

Matt thought he had been starting to. 'No. I can't understand what's going on.'

'Okay.' Charlie held up both hands in jovial surrender. 'Look, she needed a rest. And she needed to get away. This thing she's been having with Hunter . . . well, it's pretty serious. And they're both doing their best to work things out.'

Tina lit a cigarette and peered hard at Charlie through the smoke. 'A rest. You're sure she's taking it in Goa and not in some classy little clinic for tired Bombay matrons? You're sure she's not lying doped up on Serepax under the care of the lovely Dr Mishra?'

Charlie's reply was ominously free of the usual bluster. 'She'll be back here late tomorrow night—ready to take the early morning flight to Madurai with us. I guarantee it.'

Early next morning Matt took off for the day, unable to bear the prospect of another twelve hours as Tina's trusted ally. He negotiated a price with one of the burly Sikhs waiting in their taxis outside the Taj, and they set out for Juhu Beach.

The man drove in the usual Sikh manner, as if the car were a dodgem with a death wish, and on the way talked Matt into a detour—a diversion into a network of pot-holed streets—where he had unexplained business. Matt gave in to the request without argument because there was no alternative. And the thought of being still for a moment had great appeal.

The driver parked the car and vanished into a nest of

shanties, leaving Matt to watch sadly over a trio of dusty, emaciated women picking methodically through a heap of rags and papers by the side of the road. He felt helpless and dispirited at the sight of them, yet as the minutes passed, pity for others was inevitably replaced by fear for himself. India, he reflected, had a way of making a person's priorities shamefully clear.

By the time the Sikh returned, he was starting to sweat, having convinced himself of his imminent abduction by bandits. He gave silent thanks as the car's engine spluttered into action again and they bounced back on to the highway where the Sikh placed his hand on the horn and kept it there all the way to Juhu.

Matt staggered out at one of the newer and smarter of the hotels along the beachfront. Its walls were only slightly discoloured by mould and the lobby had a comforting air of bustle and self-importance. He went through to the garden and sat with a beer, watching the beach traffic go by. He had no plan, wanting just to wait out the hours until dusk as peacefully as possible. But it was not long before he grew restless and left the hotel to wander along the dusty streets.

In an arcade of drab shops, he found a silk emporium full of young women and their mothers perched on stools at the counters, waiting as the shop assistants unwound bolts of cloth for their inspection. No one took any notice of him, and he stood by unselfconsciously watching the bright flags unfurl and fall in frothy piles on the counter. At first he was struck by the contrast between this ritual and the one he had seen earlier conducted by the ragpickers in the street, then gradually he began to be soothed by the play of colour and the buzz of conversation, with its absolute concentration on the merits of chiffon over georgette or cerise over citrus yellow. It helped him think.

He was puzzled by the depth of his feeling for Kate. Although it had no future, it persisted. Wherever she went once the picture was over, he would not be with her, yet he wished her well with an intensity that bewildered him. It was mysteriously important to him that she not be sick. He shrank from the idea of her being in pain over Hunter. Was this merely hurt pride? Would the fact of her pain diminish her in his eyes just because Hunter was its cause? He scrupulously examined all these possibilities and felt more confused than ever.

Back at the beachfront, Matt ordered another beer and resumed his seat in the hotel's garden. He had brought a book and tried to read, comforting himself with the thought that if it had not been for Tina, Charlie's story about Kate's whereabouts would have seemed perfectly plausible.

At dusk, he decided to walk along the beach before taking a taxi back to town. There was nothing left of the sun but a misty strip of orange, and the beach was dotted with slowly moving figures—children building sandcastles, couples sauntering along the shore, families stopping at the vendors' stalls to buy food cooked on fires flaming in the half-dark.

Matt joined the figures along the shoreline. He had gone perhaps a hundred yards when his attention was caught by a snake-charmer performing for a group of tourists looking down on the beach from the garden of one of the hotels. They had pulled chairs up to the seawall and were sitting back, feet up, watching the show. He stood looking for a while and was about to move on when he noticed a woman sitting on a chair along from the group. The fluorescent glow of a garden lamp shone on her face and it took him no more than a moment to recognise her.

At the same moment she saw him and turned away as if to get up and go. Then she seemed to think better of it and sank back in her chair, waiting for him.

He walked quickly up the beach and stopped abruptly beneath the wall, gazing up at her. A supplicant. He felt relieved, curious and faintly ridiculous.

'There's a gate over there in the wall,' Kate said flatly. 'I'll let you in.'

They ate dinner together in the hotel coffee shop, watched over by an avuncular waiter who was pleased that Kate had found a friend. 'She is reading a lot of books while she has been here,' he said. 'It is good that she has somebody to talk to.'

After the waiter had gone, he asked her why she wasn't in Goa.

'Goa would have been nice.' She smiled dreamily. 'But this place has its points.'

'We've been worried about you.'

'We?'

'Tina and I.'

'Tina worried about me? What a weird idea.'

'A professional worry.'

She burst out laughing. From his post by the kitchen door, the waiter smiled at them.

'Charlie reassured her, I hope.'

'She didn't believe him. Nor did I.'

'So where did you think I was?'

'Tina decided that you were in a fancy clinic somewhere . . .'

She gasped faintly. 'Go on.'

'She thought you were having a nervous breakdown.'

'Of course.' Behind the sarcasm, Matt heard something else. Relief?

When she spoke again, there was just the sarcasm. 'And what did you think, Matt? You haven't told me what you thought.'

He said he was too busy hoping Tina was wrong to think anything.

'More professional worrying.'

'No.' Sod it, he thought. Why bother?

The waiter brought their order. Kate sipped her iced tea. Looking for signs of exhaustion, of neurasthenia . . . of . . . it came to Matt that he didn't really know what he was looking for—except perhaps unhappiness—he noticed only that she was paler than usual.

'So will you go along with the official version? That I've been in Goa?'

The fact that she wouldn't look at him added to the insult.

'Only if you tell me the real story.'

PART TWO

She still didn't look at him. 'What else did Charlie tell you?'

'That you wanted to get away and think about your . . . whatever it is you're having with Hunter.'

The sharpness of his tone made her blink. 'Then you already know the real story.'

'So why invent the bit about Goa? Come on, you haven't been here all the time.' He looked around. 'The mould growing on the walls is enough to kill after two days.' He leaned across the table and touched her hand. 'I thought we were friends.'

At last she raised her eyes. 'All right, I'll tell you what I've been doing. There was a clinic. Tina was right about that. A smart little clinic specialising in discreet abortions. I should be there still. Convalescing. It's part of the package. This place just seemed more appealing, mildew and all.'

She turned away from his dismay. She knew he wished only to comfort her but his decency and indignation on her behalf just made her feel worse.

She had watched his figure moving along the beach, thinking idly that the walk reminded her of Matt's. Now she cursed her idleness and wished fervently that she had gone inside before he had the chance to recognise her.

She had liked being at the Oasis with the mildew and the kindly waiters. Its outlandishness suited her—lending distance and perspective and making the future possible.

With the abortion she realised that she had truly wanted a child. Natural enough, the nursing sister had said. Many patients felt that way. For a while.

It was meant to be a consoling remark, she knew, but she wasn't consoled. While the child had lived she had thought of it only as something abstract—a token promising a future to be lived with Hunter—but lying in the cool, white room at the clinic, she had begun obsessively imagining what it might have been like, considering possible permutations. Her nose, Hunter's eyes, her quietness, his poise. Like the pieces in a jigsaw, the child had danced around in her brain until she had to get out of the white room or stay in one forever.

They had not wanted her to go and Dr Mishra had been telephoned. He had arrived with Charlie and together they had tried to talk her into going back to the Taj with them. When she had insisted on Juhu Beach, they had given in. Dr Mishra had driven her to Juhu himself, taking her to the most expensive of the hotels on the beachfront. Once he was safely out of sight, she had walked out of the lobby with her overnight bag and gone to the Oasis.

She and Hunter had once fantasised about a baby. He had been more enthusiastic than she. At first she had laughed at the idea, saying that she was afraid of turning out like her own parents, mysteriously lacking the nurturing instinct. He had told her not to be silly and that she would make a good mother because she had enough of the child left in her to remember what childhood was like. The worst parents, he said, were those who had never been children. He could remember people like that from school—miniature adults serving out their time in short pants before assuming their true identities as QCs and captains of industry.

Even so, she hadn't told him when she first suspected she was pregnant. She hadn't told Mishra either. She had gone to the hotel doctor, who had found her a gynaecologist. Only after the pregnancy had been confirmed, had she tried to tell Hunter. The first time she'd failed, put off by the telephone call from Jess. Afterwards she was tempted not to tell him at all—just to go ahead and have the abortion. But the next night, she had blurted it all out.

At first he had been amazed. 'We've always used something . . .'

'Not the first time if you remember . . .'

She hadn't thought pregnancy possible. She'd had an earlier abortion with Dermott and there had been complications. When he heard this, Hunter said that she shouldn't risk a second and soon they were discussing possibilities.

Why shouldn't it work? Why shouldn't she be a good mother? Why shouldn't Hunter's marriage be ended with the minimum of damage? As she had lain beside him in bed discussing these questions, she imagined a time when the faces in the photographs of his two boys would seem familiar and affectionate, when their owners would be loving half-brothers to the unborn baby. Lying with Hunter's arms tightly around her, she had found all these things conceivable.

Hunter said he would tell Jess about them as soon as possible. 'But not before the picture's finished.'

'I know.' They had talked about this many times before.

'I just couldn't do it with a letter or a telephone call. And she can't come over. Not while we're still working.'

She nodded, as she had the other times. 'We'll wait. I'll keep the baby secret.'

He asked her if Dr Mishra knew and she told him about the hotel doctor's referral to a gynaecologist.

'Time's on our side. But what if you get morning sickness?'

'Who's to know? In India it could be anything.'

He looked suddenly doubtful. 'It's such a hard shoot. Madurai, then back to Calcutta. With the weather getting hotter all the time.'

They lay thinking about it, then he kissed her. 'Never mind,' he said. 'Whatever you do, it's going to be okay.'

'Whatever you do.' The phrase had reverberated in her head all night as she had lain trying to sleep.

By mutual consent Hunter had left her to go back to his own room and when he came back to her in the morning, she was no closer to a decision than she had been six hours before. Unconsciously, she was waiting for him to talk her into the baby. But he did not talk. He asked. How did she feel? What did she want to do? And with these questions the scenes from a harmonious future had grown increasingly dim.

She had made one attempt to get them back. 'If we want it enough . . .' She hadn't been able to finish the sentence.

He stroked her hand. 'I do want it but I'm beginning to think it might be too risky. What I don't want is for us to begin our life together with more strain than we can handle.'

She didn't press him. The scenes from the future had already receded, replaced by others in which she was alone, ineffectually patting a small, sobbing baby. In these scenes she looked remarkably like her mother.

Dr Mishra found the clinic and Hunter took her there. He couldn't stay. She hadn't expected him to. He was due in Madurai that morning so they said goodbye in the white room where he cried quite as much as she did.

As she told her story, Matt could feel her anger. Inspired by Hunter but directed at him. For caring. He went cold with resentment.

'So Hunter wasn't with you when you had the abortion?'

'I just told you. He took me to the hospital but he couldn't stay.'

He asked her when she was going back to the Taj.

'Tonight.'

'We'll share a taxi then,' he said awkwardly. 'If you want . . . I'll make sure we're not seen together, of course. I won't . . . upset anything. Or tell anyone.'

She thanked him politely.

In the taxi they said very little, but a few streets from the hotel when Matt was getting out to walk the rest of the way she turned to him: 'You don't believe this, I know, but Hunter really did want the baby.'

CHAPTER THREE

1

Their new home in the southern temple town of Madurai was a rambling, barn-like hotel with a clanging lift and gloomy, cavernous corridors arranged around a central courtyard of parched grass. The dining-room reminded Matt of the suburban hall where he had been taken to bingo games and church fellowship dances as a child. The only other guests were Baptist missionaries from the American South who gave thanks for their breakfast each morning with loud choruses of 'Hallelujah!' and 'Praise the Lord!'

The hotel had battalions of houseboys—lithe, speedy figures who emerged in swarms from the shadows at any hint of movement. There were three on lift duty—one to open the door, another to press the buttons, a third to open the door again at journey's end. When Matt arranged to send his clothes to the laundry, four houseboys arrived in his room, ready to go on arguing as long as he would let them over the finer points of labelling his laundry bag.

Even with all this attention he was lonely. He had repeatedly gone over his meeting with Kate at Juhu Beach, obsessed not with her abortion but the hostility in her voice as she had told him about it.

He'd felt it like a blow from a blunt instrument—crude, heavy and inviting retaliation. And he had retaliated, disliking the set of her mouth as she spoke, dwelling on the sallowness of her skin under the restaurant's neon light and resenting the way she had avoided his gaze. On their way back to the Taj, they had sat as far apart as possible on the back seat of the taxi, the space between them as solid and unbreachable as a brick wall.

Since arriving in Madurai he had seen her often. They all ate dinner together in the hotel dining-room and he watched her at work on the set. They treated one another with a show of good humour that should have converted the ill feeling between them into a fading memory, but he felt it there still, in her and in himself. He avoided her. Yet every time he saw her smile at someone else, it hurt.

He sat in his room writing another scene change. It was thankless work, yet it absorbed him. What pleasure he still had in the script was confined to bits and pieces of invention. He played them over to himself, creating his own movie, and when he left the room that evening on his way to show the pages to Hunter, he felt some satisfaction in his cleverness.

As usual, Hunter brought him back to earth with his automatic assumption that the words on the page were merely a spur to his own imagination. There was always something different to be done with a scene and Hunter always did it.

'What do you think if we move this line further down?' He ran a river of blue ink through the orderly blocks of prose.

Matt fought back with bantering hyperbole, saying that he'd ruined it—the whole thing shot to pieces.

Hunter was used to him. 'Listen.' He read the scene his way, altering his voice to suit each character without varying the expression on his face so that he looked like a ventriloquist or an American newsreader.

'How did it sound?' Even in the act of remorselessly having his own way, he could still make a convincing job of impersonating an attentive listener and accommodating person.

'If you'd been doing a one-man show it would have been brilliant. Since you weren't, I like my version.'

Hunter shook his head in pretended despair. They had

entered phase two of their routine. Matt, the temperamental artist, versus Hunter, the hard-head. Matt did his best, knowing it was his last chance.

'It's a question of rhythm. It's smoother my way. More natural.' He regretted 'natural' as soon as he'd said it.

'Natural? Don't you mean boring?'

'No, I don't. I mean it makes better sense.'

'But we're not making sense, we're making drama.'

Hunter had already returned to the script. His pen hovered over the page and made rapid darting motions. Soon the margins ran with blue.

Unable to watch anymore, Matt moved across to the window. A party was going on down below. Some of the technicians had dragged deckchairs onto the grass and were drinking beer while a team of waiters stood by anticipating further orders. Loud laughter enlivened the scene. Matt wished he were in it.

'I think we've got this working now.' Hunter turned the pages rapidly. The rivers of blue had multiplied, criss-crossing the clumps of type and turning the script into a map of a foreign country.

'How can you tell?'

Hunter offered to type it up and show him. Matt turned away from the window, already losing interest in the idea of joining the group in the garden. Hunter was at the computer keyboard and did not look up as he passed. 'I'll slip this under your door when I've finished.'

As he spoke there was a knock at the door. Matt opened it to find Ajay standing in the hall, a sheet of paper in his hand, a look of agitation on his face.

'I'm sorry to interrupt but I have some very bad news.'

He had had a letter from Mr Chowdhury, his boss at head office. It concerned a matter too sensitive to be entrusted to the telex machine.

Matt and Hunter passed the letter between them. Mr Chowdhury's bureaucratese was heavily embroidered but his meaning was clear. He was gravely disturbed at certain allegations which had recently come to his attention concerning Ajay's professional conduct. It was said that Ajay was being bribed by the producers of *The Indian Summer* to help conceal the fact that the film being made differed significantly from the script seen by head office. Head office had been told of these allegations by Mr Kalelkar in Jaisalmer. Kalelkar had hesitated for some time before making them known but recent events had made it impossible for him to ignore them.

'He means the fire stunt,' said Ajay. 'He was almost hysterical. I thought I had succeeded in calming him down but obviously not.'

'But where does he get this bribery story from?' Hunter passed the letter back to Ajay.

'He is an acquaintance of Singh, Joshi's right-hand man. They both come from Jodhpur originally. I think it's Singh who has been pouring this poison into his ear.'

'I see. They say they're sending somebody down here. Any idea who it could be?'

Ajay shrugged. 'Maybe Chowdhury himself. He'd enjoy strutting on a film set.'

2

The baby returned to her in a dream. It was a girl. She held her close, felt warm, petal-soft skin and woke sweating as the dream was pierced and broken. Her crying woke Hunter and he switched on the light.

'What's wrong?'

She told him and yet again he began to take her through the reasons for the abortion.

'Don't talk,' she said. 'Just sit with me for a minute.'

He did as he was told but mourning, no matter how brief, did not make sense to him. Logic was the answer. And action. As he held her hand, she could feel his impatience in the tips of his fingers.

He tried to make it up to her by day. On the set, he was over-protective. Ward watched and his anger grew.

PART TWO

They were filming in the temple. The Meenakshi Temple. She never tired of its sights. It was a wondrous place, a city unto itself, meeting the demands of body and soul with a vibrant union of faith and hucksterism. Shrines merged with market stalls; overbearing Brahmins bullied tourists into making donations; and among the families turning the act of worship into a day out were children with shaven skulls and foreheads daubed with ash in gratitude to the gods for rescue from illness or accident.

It was a propitious day for marriage and from where she sat, Kate could glimpse wedding parties parading within the network of pillared courtyards and corridors. In contrast to these flashes of colour and gaiety, grimy sleeping figures were bundled up in the darker recesses of the shrines, and ragged children wielding outsize brooms moved around them, sweeping dust into the air.

Nearby, one of the Temple's holy men was trying to talk Hunter into letting him be in the film. His fingers danced in front of Hunter's face and his brown eyes snapped and twinkled as he recited in a high-pitched, sing-song voice the story of Meenakshi and her worrisome third breast which had vanished on cue—just as the prophecy said it would—when she met and fell in love with Lord Shiva.

Kate felt as if she knew him already, this holy man. In the bookshop at the Taj, she had bought a postcard with a photo of a figure who might have been this one's twin. He was sitting on a low stone wall smiling winningly at the camera, his brown beard fluffed up around impossibly white teeth, his long hair caught up on top of his head in a smoothly combed ponytail. Like this one, he wore a short white tunic, anklet and necklaces, and he had been leaning back on the wall, arms and body taut, legs crossed daintily at the ankles. He reminded her of a Betty Grable pin-up.

Ajay watched him in amusement: 'Impressive old fraud, isn't he? I hope Hunter's not susceptible because he won't rest if he thinks he's got a chance of getting his face before the camera.'

Ward ambled across to view the performance in close-up.

'I've got an idea . . .' they heard him say. The holy man capered about flirtatiously in front of him.

Kate could see what was coming.

'Go on. Quickly,' said Ajay. 'Don't let him get away with it.'

Ward glared at Kate as she approached the group. The morning sun highlighted the angles and hollows in his face, giving him a tense, wolfish look. All morning he had been fussing with his costume. Three belts and one pair of shoes had been returned to wardrobe.

Kate treated him to a sunny smile which came quite naturally, for his abrasiveness did more to keep her going than Hunter's anxiety. She looked forward to her fights with him.

'Not another change, Jake. Please.'

'I'm talking to Hunter. If you don't mind.' He gave her a mock bow and turned back to Hunter. 'Listen, how about Fletcher and this guy have a little set-to . . .'

Again she interrupted. 'It's a great scene as it is. You'll wreck the rhythm if you change it now.'

She meant it. It was one of the few scenes unaltered from the book. She wanted it left alone for Matt's sake as well as her own. Once again she was feeling guilty about Matt, whose only sin had been to be in the wrong place at the wrong time.

The holy man scrutinised her with loathing as Hunter reread the scene. When he declared there would be no change, Ward pulled a face and walked off.

Girish had been watching from the sidelines. 'You are absolutely right. It would interfere with the mood of the scene. And for no good reason. Jake is just flexing his muscles, isn't he? I'm now learning to see the difference between his genuine insights and the tricks he uses in the hope of enhancing his own role. Very instructive, I must say.'

3

Matt arrived in time for the main set-up of the day. It was a love scene and he was curious to see how it would go.

PART TWO

Curious and uncertain. Love scenes were not his specialty, yet Hunter had made few changes to the script on the page and had made a point of saying how well it worked.

It was to take place inside the tallest of the temple's *gopurams*, a great lacy pyramid rising in terraces hundreds of feet into the air. Hunter and Charlie had wrangled about the difficulties of getting the equipment up the tower's narrow spiral staircase, and Hunter had prevailed. Teams of grips had spent the morning heaving up lights and two cameras and wedging them into the small stone square in which they were to work.

The script had Susie run from a row between Fletcher and Rajiv in the temple below. Fletcher was to chase her up the staircase and for the first time say he loved her. They would both be out of breath from the climb and Fletcher would gasp out his words of love as if they were to be his last. Susie would cry but remain sure of her love for Rajiv, and by the end of the scene, Fletcher would be crying with her.

Matt felt anxious just thinking about the task of simulating these emotional extremes. He made the long climb and found a corner on the landing out of camera range. The walls and the stone floor were encrusted with bat droppings, and faint squeaks issued from the darkness above. He watched them film Kate running up the stairs. She arrived breathing hard, then it was Ward's turn.

After arguing in a desultory way about the lighting, Ward asked for a run-through. Hunter refused him. 'I want you to keep it for the camera.'

About to protest, Ward changed his mind. 'Okay. Let's see . . .' He peered into the stairwell. 'Let's say, I go down to the end of that second spiral . . .'

Hunter shook his head. 'All the way to the bottom.' His words drew shufflings and murmurings from the crew. He ignored them.

Ward grinned. 'You're kidding.'

Hunter grinned back. 'No, I'm not.'

Ward treated his audience to a nonchalant shrug and turned back to Hunter. 'Okay, you're the boss.' Giving a cheery wave, he disappeared into the stairwell.

All were silent on the landing as the sound man recorded Ward's footsteps climbing the stairs, light and rapid at first, then slowing dramatically as he neared the top. When he appeared his chest was heaving and his shirt clung damply around his shoulders.

'Susie . . . please . . .' He launched into his lines, gasping authentically between the words.

'Cut,' said Hunter.

Ward turned to him in amazement.

'Emphasis.' Hunter repeated Fletcher's last line of dialogue with a barely discernible change of inflection.

'Christ,' said Ward. 'It makes no goddamned difference.'

'It makes all the difference in the world.'

Ward considered, concluded. His expression hardened. 'As I said, you're the boss.'

When he next appeared, he had to pause in the doorway, bracing his hands against the frame as he caught his breath. When he spoke, his voice had a break in it and when he came across to embrace Kate he stumbled against her.

'You can't be in love with him,' he gasped resonantly, exhaustion adroitly transformed into passion.

She gazed into his face, which had lost its bluff arrogance and become strained and humbled.

'I'm so sorry, but I am.'

'I love you.' He spoke as if he had just made this discovery and the wonder of it still alarmed him. 'I should have told you.' His voice dropped to a husky whisper. Matt was enchanted by the effect of his own words. 'Now you won't believe me,' Ward said.

On cue—miraculously, it seemed to Matt—Kate started to cry. 'But I do believe you.' To Matt's ear, she managed to make the words sound both sad and angry; Susie resenting the assault on her sense of certainty.

Ward gazed at her silently and touched her face. A single tear welled up in his eye and rolled down his pink cheek.

'And you're telling me that . . .'

'Cut.'

The actors turned to Hunter slowly, swimmers in a dream.

'Are you all right, Jake?'

PART TWO

Still under Fletcher's spell, Ward took a moment to come round.

'All right? What do you mean, all right?'

'You're looking terrible.'

Above the rafters, a bat squeaked in its sleep. Otherwise there was silence while the dozen people crowded together in the dank, ill-ventilated space translated the word 'terrible' in their heads. Matt knew that these translations would correspond more or less—that they included the words, 'old' and 'exhausted', adjectives that each of them had used of Ward in private but would never even think of hinting at in his presence, because they respected his vanity as an aspect of his talent, as valuable in its way as strength or intelligence. Now Hunter had violated it.

'Take a break, everyone.' Then, spying Melanie, who refused to meet his eye: 'Make-up. We need you.'

Head down, Matt weaved his way through the crush and quickly descended the stairs. The irony of it, he thought. That the thing to turn him against Hunter—to harness finally and for all his gathering resentments—should have been Hunter's treatment of Ward. Not the script, not Kate, not Girish and the fire stunt, but the sight of Ward's pink, flustered face absorbing Hunter's assault on his pride.

Ward's earlier embarrassments at Hunter's hands had been different—endured for the good of the work. Ward had been goaded into delivering—he had realised what was happening and consented to the process. But today, after he had achieved his best, Hunter, with premeditated brutality, had decided to sacrifice it for the pleasure of performing a particularly thorough act of public humiliation.

Until that moment, Matt had been ruefully resigned to the probability that Kate would be happy with Hunter; now he no longer believed that Hunter was interested in happiness.

Kate, too, had been apprehensive about the love scene, fearful that she had jeopardised it in winning the battle over the holy man. Yet when the time finally came, the jostling for the camera's eye had ceased and she and Ward had put aside their ill feeling and become direct and generous with one another. Thought was left behind, reflex took over and Fletcher was there, inviting her response with an intensity that dispelled inhibition and brought her own feelings lightly to the surface. When Hunter had aborted this exchange, her resentment had left her breathless.

'Why did you do it?' she asked him that night.

He regarded her with astonishment. 'He was getting too cocky. You of all people should know what he's like when that happens. For God's sake, I thought you'd be pleased to have me pull him into line.'

'But it was a great take.' The one they had eventually printed had not been nearly as good, spoilt by anger and weariness.

'No, it wasn't.' She realised, with horror, that he meant it; that he had never seen the magic. His eagerness to teach Ward a lesson had blinded him to it all.

4

'You must prove to me that there's absolutely no substance to any of it.'

Chowdhury was a small, spry figure with the expected air of self-importance. He was wearing a safari suit in grey cotton drill and his sharp-nosed features, framed by silvery waves and grizzled sideburns, gave him the appearance of an angry eaglet cheated of its dinner.

'You know that none of it's true.' Charlie bristled convincingly. Chowdhury had restored some of his old verve. 'We haven't been unfair, inaccurate or offensive . . .' He gave the phrase a satirical spin, 'It's rubbish.'

'After all,' said Matt, 'you've read the script.'

'Which keeps changing.'

'And all the changes are passed on to you.'

Chowdhury flourished his letter from Kalelkar which related in full the story of Girish's accident. 'So many changes that there is complete and utter confusion. A jigsaw of changes.' He glared at Ajay. 'Things should never have been allowed to reach this point.'

Charlie suddenly seemed weary of the whole business. 'What exactly do you want us to do?'

'I am not going back to Calcutta until I'm absolutely certain that we can approve the work you've done so far.'

And so Chowdhury became the means by which Matt was at last shown the shape of the film in progress.

Hunter ushered them into a large, bare room, tucked away at the end of one of the hotel's echoing corridors, where a projector and screen had been installed. Chowdhury was greeted with a persuasive display of charm. Hunter was pleased to have the chance to bring him up to date with their progress, grateful to have the involvement of his office, looking forward to having his opinion.

Chowdhury allowed himself to be steered towards a battered armchair in the centre of the room. Charlie and Matt settled either side of him with Ajay next to Matt. In front of Matt's chair was an ashtray on a tarnished brass stand. It contained three cigarette butts stained with orange lipstick.

Hunter took his place behind the projector. 'Now the film begins with footage we have yet to shoot, so let me just explain how our main characters meet and what brings them to India . . .'

As Hunter fondly conjured Susie and Fletcher into being, using some of Matt's words, some of his own, Matt started to soften. It's going to work, he thought to himself, and that's all that matters. Ward doesn't need me to feel wounded on his behalf. Kate will be all right. I'll be all right. The rest is bruised ego. What matters is that we're doing what we came for.

The screen lit up. Matt felt a sudden, intense delight in the fact that the glowing images floating there in the dark would not have existed without him. Hunter adopted them, he thought, but I gave birth to them. He settled down, a willing subject for seduction.

He was wooed first of all by the skill of the actors. Ward,

Kate and Girish might not have been his fantasies come to life, but once again he found them wholly convincing alternatives. Ward was always himself yet so open to the camera that his failure to achieve transformation never mattered. Instead, he offered surrender. Even of vanity. Often he seemed aged and tired; at other times wonderfully renewed, vigorous and in his prime.

Kate did succeed in transforming herself. The alterations wrought by hair-style and make-up were complemented by changes of voice and walk and body language. It was consciously done—a methodical compilation of mannerisms and inflections married to an intelligent reading of motivation and temperament, but not dull. To Matt it seemed to dance and glitter, lit with intuition and the insouciance of someone having fun. Because of it, the mischievousness of Girish's Rajiv was happily accommodated.

Matt was so entertained by their skill that it took time for other impressions to impinge. When they did, he resisted them, not wanting to see, blaming his own prejudices and resentments, his reluctance to abandon control of the plot to Hunter. It was Ajay who alerted him—Ajay's quick, anxious glances towards him, perceived out of the corner of his eye.

Hunter's India was the problem. The snake-charmer, the Tollygunge Club, the Maharajah's train. And other things. It was Matt's India, too. He had written many of the scenes that grated and jarred. Written but never visualised them as they were on the screen: instruments used to burlesque and lampoon.

Matt had written them with affection. True, he had wanted people to laugh, just as he had wanted them to laugh at Fletcher and Susie, but he wanted the laughter to arise from a conspiracy between characters and audience. His India had been knowingly and wittily aware of its own absurdities and anachronisms. His India had moved him with its daily demonstrations of the force of human personality. The ability of its people to resist absorption into this greatest of all crowds. Against all odds, to remain themselves. He had wanted to celebrate individuality, as he had in the book. It was what

Ajay had seen there; what they had both hoped to see in the film.

Instead, Hunter had condescended. Coldly. He had opened a yawning gap between screen and audience. Distanced them with harsh lighting and distorting camera angles. He had invited those watching to be sardonic and judgmental. Even worse, he had interpolated moments of cloying sentiment and overbearing pomposity.

There was dialogue Matt had never heard before—given to Rajiv and to Fletcher. Lines which offset the coldness and the condescension with earnest and abstract assertions about India's greatness, its history, the richness of its culture, its prospects and its politics. They were bombastic and overheated and had clearly gone down well with Chowdhury, who nodded sagely when the lights went up and announced himself reassured.

'We'll have to keep closely in touch, of course, from here on. There are slight matters of emphasis . . .' His eyelids flickered momentarily while these were considered. 'But on the whole, I think I can tell Kalelkar that he has nothing to worry about. That your hearts are in the right place.'

As they walked back along the winding corridor, he mused on one of Fletcher's speeches. 'He is right, of course. Everybody wants power but no one is willing to take responsibility. Since Mrs Gandhi's death, we are sorely in need of leaders who do not recoil from the hard decisions . . .'

'Absolutely,' said Hunter.

INT. THE MEENAKSHI TEMPLE

FLETCHER is leaning against a pillar, breathing hard and close to tears.

RAJIV comes out of the shadows and approaches him tentatively.

FLETCHER looks up. RAJIV lays a hand on his shoulder.

> RAJIV: Are you all right?

FLETCHER shakes him off, stands back and stares hard at him.

> You're so bloody young.

He pauses and comes closer to RAJIV, staring into his face . . .

> And smooth. Christ, your skin's as smooth as hers. (A bitter smile) It's a wonder you could get a grip on one another.
>
> RAJIV: (Miserable) I wanted to tell you. We both did.
>
> FLETCHER (Sarcastically) But you didn't want to kill the golden goose. Right?
>
> RAJIV: No, it wasn't like that.
>
> FLETCHER: I think it was.
>
> RAJIV: (Emptying his pockets) Take your bloody money then.

When FLETCHER makes no move to take the notes, he flings them at him and walks off.

PART TWO

5

Kate came out of the make-up trailer and headed towards the *gopuram*, pressing through crowds of extras, taking care not to trip on the cables snaking through the dust, and finally reached the cool, grey temple gloom where she was treated to the sight of Hunter and Charlie swept up in a rare moment of shared satisfaction.

They were standing together beside the camera on a raised platform, looking down on a milling crowd of make-believe worshippers gathered around a gated shrine. Inside was a golden carriage. She knew its age, the details of its workmanship and exactly how much it cost. The Golden Car was Charlie's pride. He talked about it as if he'd built it himself.

'Hunter wouldn't have even known it existed without me,' he had told her. 'Then I had to put up with all that crap from the powers-that-be before they'd let us use it. God, what it's done to the budget.'

He and Hunter stood gazing over what they had made together. Looking at them, she could see their friendship as it must have been before . . . before what? She still found it impossible to understand the collapse of something which had been so firm for so long.

She had tried to talk to Hunter about it. 'Why are you making him so miserable?'

'Look, Charlie's his own worst enemy. I have to protect myself. And the picture. If I let him, Charlie will limit me.'

'I think you're doing him an injustice. He wants to make it work just as much as you do.'

'He may want to, but he's lacking in imagination. He thinks small. He always has and he always will.'

'You could at least get Tina to lay off him.'

He smiled. 'Tina's a barbarian, but she's got a lot of guts. She'll always go the extra mile.'

'All right, then. For friendship's sake. Don't you worry about him at all?'

He kissed her. 'Yes, I do. There'll be plenty of time for friendship after the picture's finished.'

She wondered. Even as she watched, the space between them widened. Hunter was already turning away to speak to someone else and Charlie hovered, lost in mid-sentence. Then he raised his arms in a half-hearted gesture, both hopeless and offhand, scrambled down from the platform and disappeared in the crowd.

It was dusk. The Car was trundled through the gates of the shrine ready to be taken on a circuit of the temple, followed by the crowd. Everybody was barefoot. Playing a Western tourist among the extras, Matt flexed his toes against the warm stones, afraid of being trodden on.

As the Car moved forward, the crowd went with it—so suddenly that Matt was almost swept off his feet—then spaces opened, the pace slowed and the crowd became a holiday crowd, relaxed and exultant.

A child tugged at his sleeve and gave him a frangipani plucked from a garland. Up ahead, the progress of the Golden Car was being assisted by a generator on a handcart tended by two Brahmins, while an elephant preceded them and two camels loped along behind. More Brahmins brought up the rear, banging drums and playing horns and pipes, and two trucks with mounted cameras crept alongside, while a third cameraman on foot darted amid the crowd.

After the circuit was completed, the Golden Car was returned to the gated shrine and Shiva's effigy brought in a small palanquin to lie beside Meenakshi in her own shrine which sat in a pool of lemony light. The audience was poised on its rim, packed tightly—a craning, murmuring mass concentrated on the figures of two Brahmins who lifted Shiva from the palanquin and gently, but briskly, with a practical, parental air, prepared the statue for bed. One set of clothes was exchanged for another and the Brahmins, like elderly children with a favourite doll, placed Shiva at Meenakshi's side.

Matt watched uneasily. It was all very picturesque—and spiritually sustaining to those so inclined—but it was also dangerously cute. He was afraid of what Hunter was doing with it. Although he felt that both the film and Fletcher were irretrievable, he couldn't let go. How was Fletcher being prompted into responding? Matt suspected that he was turning misty-eyed and paternalistic. Fletcher was going soft. No doubt about it. Matt had made up his mind to say so, even knowing that it was hopeless, but now that the rewrites were finished, Hunter was elusive. Since the screening of the assembled footage, Matt had hardly seen him.

When all was done, he went looking for Ajay. He knew that Chowdhury would be making him miserable, having brought with him the drab life that waited back in Calcutta.

'It beats me how you can bear to work for such a person,' Girish had said with more sympathy than tact, and Ajay had flushed and snapped at him: 'Simple, isn't it? I have no choice.' Then he had let loose, raging at all the circumstances which had conspired to make him a bureaucrat.

The temple was emptying fast but there was no sign of him, and when the extras had dispersed there were only the grips, packing away the lights and cables. Feeling edgy and frustrated, Matt wandered off into the darkness in search of a taxi.

On his way to the gates, he cut across one of the pillared courtyards. The crowd of extras had disappeared with surprising speed and all that could be heard was a faint traffic hum. At the sound of voices, he stopped, startled at their closeness.

Then he realised that the sound had drifted some forty metres. The voices belonged to two figures leaning against a pillar diagonally across from him. It took a moment to distinguish their outlines, then he had them. A man and a woman, embracing. Their laughter carried on the still air.

Her laugh especially. Unmistakably. The Laugh. At first he assumed the obvious—that the man with her was Ward. He listened again and, to make sure, peered hard at the man's silhouette, noting its slimness, its tallness, and the hand which brushed back the floppy hair.

As he continued to watch, the two heads came together in a long kiss.

PART THREE

CHAPTER ONE

1

They were back in Calcutta. Ajay had put away his crew T-shirt and reverted to his city uniform of white shirt and dark trousers, and the proximity of Mr Chowdhury weighed heavily on him. Over breakfast in the Grand Hotel, Kate tried to cheer him up. 'Maybe he'll get promoted out of your life.'

Ajay grinned in spite of himself. 'You'll have him running the country next.' He poured milk into his coffee, watching the creamy whorls spread and vanish. 'Not long now. What will you do when the picture is finished?'

'I don't know. My agent has sent a couple of scripts. Nothing very exciting.' On impulse, trying out the idea, she said, 'Maybe I'll have a holiday . . . but I'll be back here for the premiere.'

'I'll look forward to it.'

'How about we go together? Unless, of course, you're in love by then. In that case, you're excused.'

He laughed. 'In love or not, it's a date.'

Charlie had arrived. He slid into the booth beside her and nodded at Ajay. 'You two plotting something?'

'Nothing you need know about,' she said.

'Story of my life at the moment.'

He signalled to the waiter. She observed him sadly. His pessimism was now habitual. She longed for the old, jokey Charlie.

'The guys from Acorn got in yesterday. Dennis Meyer and this cowboy I've never met before called Milton. He's been following me around like a bloody sniffer dog.'

Ajay grinned at Kate. 'Thank you for breakfast. I'd better go to work.'

'A nice kid,' said Charlie, looking after him. 'Sensitive.' The word set him sighing again.

'So what's happening?'

'I wish I knew. Hunter was shut up with Tina and Dennis Meyer for the whole evening. Something's up.'

2

She saw nothing of Hunter until the next day. Then he sought her out in her dressing-room at the studios in Tollygunge, saying that he had something to show her.

He led her along to the room where the rushes were screened. The only person present was the projectionist. They sat down before the screen.

It took a moment for Kate to work out what she was looking at. Then she identified the narrow street bordering the gardens of the Peacock Palace and glimpsed her own figure and those of Ward and Girish, weaving through the crowd of extras. The film had been shot from above. She wondered idly about this then forgot everything as the crowd's rhythm—an orderly bustle—was eerily transformed by the unexpected. The process was not sudden, as she remembered it. It began as a ripple at the edge of the frame. A shout went up and before she had realised what was happening, the bustle was no longer orderly but jagged and unruly. People crashed into one another, tripped and fell over others. And as the ripple grew into a wave engulfing the whole scene, the camera's eye became selective, focusing on herself, Ward and Girish.

It recorded Ward's reaction to the stone which struck the point of his shoulder, then honed in on Girish as he went down from the blow to his ankle, and stayed close as she struggled to help him up. As the clubs rose and fell on the backs and shoulders of those around them it was still there, searching out her face and recording her panic and helplessness. It was with her when help came and it followed her frantic dash with Girish across the street and out of range, tracking her with a remorseless intrusiveness, determined to catch every aspect of her distress, every panting breath, every wince and grimace.

Not until the screen went blank did she grasp the full implication of what she had just seen—that the eye guiding the camera had been Hunter's.

He was calmly asking the projectionist the running time.

She was silent, realising something else—that he was going to find a way to use the images.

'I know what you're thinking,' he said.

How could he? She didn't know what to think.

'The police . . .' she said numbly. 'The police should have this.'

'Why? They'd only have impounded it. We'd never have seen it again.'

'But those thugs . . . their faces are visible. They could have charged them.'

'Joshi would only have bribed somebody and got them off. Anyway, I wasn't absolutely sure of what I'd got. Not until we'd had it processed. The lab took a long time with it. Then I didn't know if we could cut it together properly. I'd almost put it out of my mind.'

'It was you, wasn't it? You shot it yourself.'

'Yes, I did. I'd gone upstairs. Just playing around. To see if I could get another angle on the scene.'

'You were standing there panning and zooming while . . .'

'Kate . . . I was terrified. But there was nothing I could do from up there. I think I even forgot I had the camera. It could have been my own eye. That's the way it felt.'

He leaned across and tried to take her hand. She brushed him off.

'I know it's upsetting.'

'It's eerie. It makes me feel . . .' She stopped, distracted by all the questions buzzing around in her head.

His shoulders slumped. He seemed . . . how did he seem? Contrite? Guilty? Neither. As she looked into his face, she saw that he would not have understood any of her questions even if she'd found the words. His eyes glittered with excitement, with dazzlement. She looked into them and saw only the reflected power of the images from the screen.

He took her hand and raised it to his lips, as if bestowing a precious gift.

3

Hunter planned to kill Fletcher off. His word processor sat on his desk waiting to take down the details. Struggling to absorb the news, Matt couldn't take his eyes off it. When he asked if it were Acorn's idea, Hunter didn't bother to lie. 'No, it was mine.'

'It's terrible,' Matt said inadequately.

Hunter hadn't expected him to like it. He was regretful and sympathetic, spoiling the effect with a sudden, gleeful smile. 'It'll work, though.'

It was then that Matt was told about the riot footage and Hunter's plans for it, a melding of fact and fiction that seemed so strange, so arbitrary, that he had trouble at first in seeing past the mechanics of it.

Hunter explained patiently. 'There are several ways we can do it. Of course they all involve reshooting some of the stuff at the Peacock Palace.'

'You want to go back there?'

'It can't be avoided.'

Matt asked about Joshi.

'He's not to know the footage exists. We make up a story.' Naturally, he had it all worked out. Joshi would be told that some of the original stuff had been ruined by the lab. Since most of the new sequences would be shot inside the palace, the filming would be quite simple.

When Matt brought up Chowdhury and the Ministry,

Hunter said comfortably that they wouldn't have to know. Nor would Ajay.

'He'll have to find out,' protested Matt. 'He'll be on the set.'

Hunter shook his head. They would keep the scenes inside the palace until last. They would involve only a few people. 'He may not even have to know they're being done.'

Matt said that he'd know later when he lost his job.

'Come on, Matt.' Hunter had the decency to look exasperated. 'By the time the film comes out they won't care what's in it. For God's sake, we've spent enough money in this country. That's all they're really interested in.'

Matt was still struggling. 'You're telling me that Fletcher is killed in the riot and Susie and Rajiv go off into the sunset together. Finis.'

Hunter sought to comfort him. 'Fletcher gets a good death scene. Ward'll be very happy with it.' He spoke firmly and calmly. At the thought of Ward's vanity, he smiled in amusement. Right is on my side, his serenity said. I don't need to be vulgar about it.

'So they stay on in India?' Matt was caught between a desire to have done with it all and wanting to know the worst.

'Of course they don't. They leave. To live in America.'

Matt was appalled. Rajiv wouldn't know what to do in America. 'It's India he's interested in.' He was struck by the sound of his own voice, a squawk, verging on hysterical. 'He'd always be wandering about, thinking he ought to be here.'

Hunter had no answer to this. He just went on looking expectant, as if waiting for Matt's mood to change. Belatedly, it began to occur to Matt that he was being asked to collaborate in his characters' downfall and he wistfully recalled the days when they used to talk about preserving the spirit of the book. He said he supposed Hunter hadn't meant any of that. It had just been a ploy to keep him happy on the job.

Hunter considered the accusation courteously. 'No, I did mean it. The book got me started. But I was going to take off sooner or later. That's what being a film-maker is.'

From their opposite vantage points they contemplated the impasse.

'It's probably better if I don't hang around,' said Matt insincerely. To leave and go home would be the sensible thing to do but good sense now seemed out of his range.

Hunter said he should stay. 'Definitely. You must stay.' He was warming to the idea. Was it malice? Matt preferred to think the worst, although the expression on Hunter's face was infuriatingly benign. 'You've come this far,' he said. 'See it out. I'd like you to.'

4

Matt took Ajay to a noisy cafe and, over a cup of milky tea, told him about the riot footage.

As Ajay listened, his lean, serious features took on an expression so perilously close to resignation that Matt wanted to shake him. 'Such an ending makes nonsense of everything, but it's hardly surprising given what we've seen already of Hunter's work.'

'Ajay, is this going to lose you your job?'

Ajay glumly admitted the possibility. 'Chowdhury will enjoy consigning me to some backwater. And there's Joshi. Who knows what influence he has and with whom?'

Matt leant across the table, trying to compete with the surrounding din. 'You have to warn Chowdhury. Tell him everything. About the footage, Hunter's changes, everything.'

Ajay drew back—in swift retreat from such a thought. 'No, it would be toadying. It could stop the film being finished.'

'No question of that. It'll be finished whatever happens. Go on. If not for yourself, for Fletcher.'

Matt didn't mean it. He had abandoned all hope for Fletcher, as he had for the film. Real life was important now. Unlike Fletcher, Ajay was not a lost cause.

PART THREE

5

Matt and Kate sat in the garden of the hotel, trying to find a path through the thickets of ambiguity and inhibition that had obstructed all their conversations since Juhu Beach.

Matt was bursting with information that he had no way of disclosing. Kate should be told about the kiss between Hunter and Tina but the news should not come from him. Charlie, who would have been the perfect go-between, would neither answer Matt's telephone calls nor respond when he knocked on his door.

Kate broke an uncomfortable silence. 'I'm sorry about this idea of Hunter's . . . what he's doing to the script,' she said. 'Something gets into directors . . .'

She smiled uncertainly, craving indulgence for Hunter, the perverse genius. He smiled back, politely going along with it. It seemed to him that neither of them had much invested in the words being spoken; that a much truer conversation was being conducted in their stumblings and silences. In this subterranean exchange, Kate was saying, I know you hate him. I'm not sure I like him either, but it's too late now. I've gone too far. I'm committed.

'I'm trying to tell myself it doesn't matter anymore,' he said, 'but it does.'

There was another silence, ended by the approach of Tina, thoroughly Indianised in pale pink raw silk and embroidered slippers.

'Tea. Great.' Catching the eye of a passing waiter, she called for an extra cup and lounged back in a chair, contentedly fanning herself. She had just come back from Joshi's house, petitioning for right-of-way for their return to the Peacock Palace. 'It worked like a fucking dream. The old creep bought the whole story. We paid, of course. More truckloads of rupees but it's going to be worth every one.'

Noticing their lack of enthusiasm, she fixed on Kate. 'What the hell's bugging you. Believe me, you should be over the moon about this. It's a very punchy scene. It adds a whole new dimension to your performance.'

'Genuine fear,' murmured Matt. 'It works every time.'

Tina chose not to hear him. 'So it's all set,' she said.

PART THREE

INT. HOTEL ROOM. NIGHT.

FLETCHER is at the mini-bar. He curses under his breath as the bottle of beer in his hand opens in a rush and sprays froth on the carpet.

SUSIE brings a towel from the bathroom and starts to mop up.

> SUSIE: Rajiv isn't to blame. You and I were all wrong together.

FLETCHER sits watching dazed as she scrubs at the carpet.

> SUSIE: We're too different . . .

She stops scrubbing and sits back on her heels, looking wistful.

> . . . which was fun for a while.

> FLETCHER: I thought so.

> SUSIE: But I couldn't keep you interested.

> FLETCHER: Not true.

> SUSIE: I don't know enough.

> FLETCHER: (surprised) About what?

> SUSIE: The right things. And I talk too much.

> FLETCHER: The last bit's true. But I like it. I like your talk.

He leans forward and grabs both her hands.

> FLETCHER: It could still work.

> SUSIE: Do you think so?

6

Fletcher's final resting place had been marked out in chalk on the floor of one of the palace's museum-like rooms. To add atmosphere, some of the marble busts and sombre Victorian portraits had been brought from the room at the top of the stairs and looked down dolefully on the scene.

Ward circled the chalk marks warily, checking camera angles. 'This better work,' he said gruffly to Hunter.

'It will.' Hunter's smile was radiant. Kate had never seen him look happier. The night before he had proposed to her again. He had changed his mind and was ready to ask Jess for a divorce now, before the film was completed. He was certain that she would be civilised about it and agree that their feelings for one another were exhausted. Little Pete might even be happier once they had made the break. After all, sensitive children were inevitably affected by the tension in a household, no matter how well suppressed.

Ward was staring at the chalk marks, still uncertain. 'What if it doesn't work?'

'You know what'll happen if it doesn't work,' said Hunter. 'We'll use one of the other endings.'

The night before, taking care to keep their activities quiet, they had dressed a studio to look like the airport terminal and shot two alternative endings. In one, Susie and Fletcher flew off together leaving Rajiv regretful but basically relieved; in the other, Rajiv and Susie left arm in arm, after seeing Fletcher's corpse on to the same flight.

Kate had gone through the process without making up her mind about any of the outcomes, which were only abstractions now that the script was so changed. She supposed that she would rather have Fletcher live. The other alternative was too sudden, random, uncalled for—a bit too much like life itself.

Watching Ward prowl around the chalked figure on the floor, Girish muttered discontentedly to himself. He preferred the scene in which he saw off the other two. He liked the idea that Rajiv's should be the last face that the audience saw.

PART THREE

Ward was saying very little, perhaps weighing up the pathos of his death scene against the indignity of going out in a body bag.

He prepared for his big moment. The chalk marks were wiped away and the special effects people checked the wound they had attached to the back of his head. There was comparatively little blood—just a rivulet running from nape to throat and a smear on his shirt. The medical details were hazy, but he would move in and out of consciousness while waiting for the ambulance to arrive, and die while the paramedics were lifting him on to a stretcher.

Hunter took them through several rehearsals, being unusually gentle with Ward, who responded with the old professionalism. All trace of doubt had disappeared; his voice came through in a cracked whisper which reached magically to every corner of the room; his head moved restlessly from side to side; his eyes squinted with the effort of focusing on Kate's face, then Girish's, and he croaked out a blessing on them both. He also urged them to stay together if this was really what they wanted.

The 'if' clause was Ward's idea. Fletcher would not give in that easily, he argued. Even on his death-bed there would be some fight left in him.

Matt and Ajay were watching from the doorway, out of sight of Hunter but with a clear view of the action. Although Ajay had refused to warn Chowdhury of Hunter's plans, he had agreed to go to the palace with Matt and confront Hunter, who thought him safely on the other side of the city with the second unit. They would watch the shoot and when it was all over, Ajay would take Chowdhury a report of all that he had seen, covering himself by saying he had found out what was happening only at the last minute.

Matt reacted to Fletcher's last words with an intensity that surprised him. He didn't believe what he was seeing for a moment, yet he felt moved by it. From this he gathered that the transfer was complete. In his mind, Ward, to whom he had once objected so strongly, had become Fletcher. With his solid, three-dimensional self, he had overpowered and destroyed the shadowy creature of Matt's imaginings. Matt mourned the passing of both Fletchers with each sad, husky sound that Ward uttered.

When it was over, a small group, led by Hunter, gathered around the actors, slapping backs and offering muted words of congratulation. As Hunter spied Matt and Ajay, his face lost its broad smile and went blank. Matt had expected anger but saw only surprise.

He came straight over to them, wiping the sweat from his face with a yellow bandanna. Close up, he looked nervy, animated, every movement charged with self-satisfaction. His body language said, nothing can touch me now; his words were bland. 'When did you arrive?'

'We've been here for quite a while. I met Ajay at the hotel—told him what was happening.'

'Last-minute arrangement,' said Hunter to Ajay. 'We didn't have time to let you know.'

Ajay shook his head. 'I know the whole story. No need to play games with me anymore.'

'Have you told anyone else?'

'Not yet.'

'Which means?'

Matt was relieved to see that somewhere in the course of things, Ajay had become invigorated by anger. 'Which means I shall have to, of course.'

'I see. Well, in that case, I've one last favour to ask.' Hunter still showed no resentment. Matt cast around fruitlessly for a way to make him mad. He wanted them all to get mad. He wanted a free-for-all. His very own riot—something to release the tension that he felt pulsing in the close, humid air. Instead they calmly took their cue from Hunter's unnatural politeness.

'We have a couple more set-ups to do . . .' He asked Ajay if he could delay his visit to Chowdhury until they were done. 'Tell him the truth—that I misled you.'

He ushered them out into the garden to explain the first of the scenes. He planned a long tracking shot running part-way through the garden and into the street. Matt had noticed the camera tracks on the way in—laid across the grass and the potholed bitumen outside the gate. The street had been cordoned off as before, but the people of the neighbourhood continued to slip under the cordon, becoming indistinguishable from the milling crowd of extras.

Hunter explained that Susie and Rajiv were to walk behind the shrouded body of Fletcher as it was borne into the lane. Matt immediately imagined Joshi's men arriving in the middle of it but Hunter, of course, had a contingency plan. There were dummy pages of script in which Fletcher had died naturally of a heart attack.

Morning became afternoon and as it grew hotter, Matt and Ajay retreated to the shelter of the palace terrace while final preparations were made. Hunter darted about in the sun, wearing his planter's hat, his denim shirt stained with dark patches of sweat, his energy undiminished.

Matt watched his progress moodily. Hunter had described the alternative endings to him with the air of a conjurer deciding whether to produce a flock of doves or a silk handkerchief. What he most wanted now, he had said with a sensuous movement of arms and shoulders, was to be in the editing room in Sydney pondering his artistic choices.

Out on the lawn and in the street, the confusion was abating. The street had been cleared of everybody but crew and extras; Kate was emerging from her trailer, Girish was waking up from his doze on a banana-chair. At the gate, Matt could see Tina approaching with Milton and Dennis Meyer. At the sight of Ajay she abruptly changed direction, going over to speak to Hunter. The other two continued towards Matt.

Matt already knew Milton, who had a puppyish manner and bounded about on light, springy feet in brand new Nikes. Milton had engaged him in a long talk about 'potential properties', his phrase for books he had read lately. 'Hi, Matt.' He nodded at Matt and Ajay, then turned to introduce Dennis Meyer, whose name Matt had come across in his recent reading on corporate Hollywood. Dennis was on the rise. 'Ah, the writer,' he said. 'I was wondering when I was going to meet you.'

Matt stood up to receive a firm handshake from Dennis who was untouched by Calcutta's grime in poplin trousers and a shirt of white Indian cotton tailored somewhere far away like Paris or London. Everything about him was measured and deliberate, as if he were a visitor from another planet carefully mimicking earthling manners and customs. In the face of what looked like his complete lack of humour, even Tina seemed intimidated and could often be seen biting her lip in an agony of self-censorship, although she had failed to do anything about The Laugh, which escaped at unlikely moments, soaring towards a startling new set of top notes inspired by high anxiety.

Dennis took a chair next to Matt, regarding him with unabashed interest. 'Unlike the rest of the creative community in Los Angeles, I actually admire writers.'

While suspecting that Dennis's intensity could be directed at will towards anyone who crossed his path, Matt was flattered, then worried. Moments spent in the company of a receptive Dennis had the power to change his life forever. He should have prepared. He should have been bursting with ideas, weaving plots and sub-plots, hypothesising like crazy.

'So this is it.' Milton broke the silence. He couldn't sit still and was standing in front of them, rocking back on his heels. He looked at his watch. 'Not long now till we have a wrap. Then the real work starts. The selling.' Dennis gave Matt a rueful smile, acknowledging the harsh commercial realities. 'Hey!' barked Milton. 'Looks like they're all set.'

Hunter was directing a rehearsal. The camera was mounted on the dolly tracks and Andy McCaffrey and his camera operator were conferring over the image in the lens.

Tina squatted next to Ajay's chair. Matt could just catch her words which were sharp and sarcastic. As she walked away, Ajay looked after her miserably.

'Don't worry about her,' said Matt. 'She's not worth it.'

'She's right. I will be running off to Chowdhury. The thought of it . . . the thought of going back there to that office where he rules the roost . . . The thing that I worry about most is that one day I may find myself becoming like him.'

'That's rubbish.' Matt laid a hand on his shoulder. 'Come on, let's go and see the show.'

Ajay refused to be distracted. 'You know, the way things are set up in the office the system positively encourages you to make things hard for your colleagues—to protect your little bit of territory.'

'All bureaucrats are like that.'

'Here it's much worse . . . I'm sorry. I shouldn't be going on about it. The thing is that I've had the experience of working with you and Kate and the others. That's what matters.'

'You've done a lot for me, Ajay.' Matt patted his shoulder awkwardly, hoping that his words didn't seem perfunctory. Without Ajay he might have become completely lost in Hunter's cinema of infinite possibilities.

7

They had finished rehearsing and were preparing for a take. The camera commenced its gliding progress across the grass. Girish put his arm around Kate and they followed the stretcher which bore the sheeted figure of Ward's stand-in. Once again, Matt marvelled at the actors' skill. Both were convincingly stricken. Girish's eyes blinked rapidly, luminous with unshed tears, and Kate had used the time spent alone in her trailer to achieve a mood in which weeping seemed to come easily. In the sunlight, before hundreds of people, tears coursed down her cheeks and her lower lip trembled as she gave in to the moment with a voluptuousness that Matt couldn't begin to comprehend.

When they reached the gates, their pace slowed and Girish tried to comfort her, drawing her close. This moment was Tina's idea—insurance in case Ward got his way and Hunter decided that it was to be the final scene. On no account was the audience to be left with an image of unadulterated grief, so Girish coaxed from Kate the hint of a smile with its reminder of life's comforts and continuities. Matt could see the point.

They moved through the gates and out into the street. On cue, the crowd fell back, letting them through. The extras streamed into the lane.

Matt was with the others out of camera range and awkwardly moving backwards when he felt Ajay tug at his sleeve.

'Look!' He was pointing above at one of the overhanging balconies of the houses which bordered the lane.

As Matt watched, there was a blur of movement, a contorted face and an upraised arm, then a flash of orange followed by a smoky hiss. Something came hurtling through the air, trailing vapour, and as it hit the ground it exploded. People scattered in all directions, colliding in a milling confusion of bodies.

A stone landed at Matt's feet, kicking up dust. It was followed by another, then another. One struck the head of the camera with a crunch of plastic and glass, and through the press of people Matt glimpsed Hunter's face, eyes squeezed shut, lips shaping a circle of disbelief. He had gambled on lightning not striking twice. Matt saw him lunge towards the camera, but ahead of him, men were spilling out of the side streets and crashing through the cordon into the crowd. Men with clubs. Matt saw Hunter falter at the sight before he regained his balance and went rushing on.

The men with clubs were everywhere, picking their targets at random. A man beside Matt went down, the air leaving his lungs in a soft, guttural sigh. Ajay was ahead, pulling Matt along by the sleeve. Then he stopped and suddenly changed direction.

Matt followed as the crowd parted for an instant to show Kate on the ground, a bright trickle of red striping the side of her face. Ajay crouched beside her. People went cannoning past. Matt's path was blocked.

A threshing arm caught him a stinging blow on the cheek, making his eyes water. He pushed hard, the tide of people turned and he was swept past Ajay and Kate.

He twisted around and was trying to force his way back

when just ahead of him he caught sight of one of the thugs. He had noticed the man before. Dressed in a brown T-shirt and grubby white jeans, he was laying about him with a dogged ferocity that marked him out from the surrounding mayhem. He chose then he struck—an eerily methodical figure. As Matt watched, he lit on Ajay and Kate. Gleefully. Changing pace in mid-stride, he veered towards them, hitting out at those in his way.

Panic made Matt careless of those around him. He charged forward, using elbows, knees, shoving, kicking, determined to get through.

They arrived at the same moment, he and the man. Matt elbowed someone aside and there, in front of him, Ajay was bent over Kate, who knelt, dazed, a hand to her head.

Matt shouted then wished he hadn't, for his voice was only a distraction. They turned towards him and he cried out again, pointing to warn them of the danger at their backs, but before they could move the man was on them.

He went for Ajay, bringing the club down heavily across his shoulders. Ajay turned, tried to grapple with him then staggered as the man's arm was raised once more.

Matt pushed on, unable to plan or even to think. He threw himself at the man, grabbing him around the knees and bringing him down. He toppled with a thump—a sound as solid and conclusive as a closing door. Matt felt his body sag in relief, then the man's foot lashed out and kicked him away with a blow that made his stomach heave and his vision blur.

When he could see again, the man was beating Ajay on the back, his arm ranging back and forth in long, brutal arcs. Kate was pulling at him but he disregarded her; all his dull ferocity was concentrated on Ajay, who had managed to grasp his legs and, as Matt watched, tripped him up again. The two wrestled as Matt tried to reach them, then suddenly the man sprang up and was off, lost in the crowd, leaving Ajay stretched out on the ground, his shirt stained with blood.

Kate got to him before Matt. 'I saw it,' she said. 'A knife. He had a knife.'

The crowd parted, help arrived. Somehow Ajay was carried to the room where Ward had lain only hours before.

Matt and Kate crouched beside him. Blankets had been brought from the dressing-rooms and spread over him in an effort to drive out the chill that Matt could feel as he took his hand.

Someone was saying that he should not have been moved. Someone else was saying that it was too dangerous to leave him within range of the throwers of stones and petrol bombs. Matt tried to warm his hand in his own. Kate took his other hand in an effort to do the same.

His face looked ghastly. There was dried blood around his nostrils and his eyes slipped in and out of focus without seeing. He tried to talk but the words became a cough and a trickle of blood showed on his lip.

Kate called out. 'For God's sake, where's Mishra?'

Breathlessly, Dr Mishra pushed through the crowd and sank to his knees at Ajay's side. Matt got up to give him room and at that moment it happened. There was a gasp from the person standing next to him and Matt looked down to see Ajay's chest heaving, his mouth bloody.

There were no final words, no easy drifting between waking and unconsciousness. Ajay died with cruel inappropriateness, choking on his own blood.

CHAPTER 2

1

The smoggy sunshine was starting to burn away the early morning coolness and the daily parade across the Howrah Bridge was gathering pace and volume.

Unable to sleep, Matt had risen at first light and walked through the streets to the flower market, hoping for distraction in the colour and bustle, and for a few minutes he had found some ease in standing at the end of the bridge looking down on the skeins of orange and gold, white and crimson, spilling over the edges of the traders' great cane baskets. But now, walking back across the bridge, as his nostrils filled with acrid traffic fumes, he was taken back to the day, only weeks before, when they had filmed Ward and the snake-charmer, and the recollection led him inevitably to the memory of Ajay lying on the marble floor of the Peacock Palace.

He found himself obsessed by questions of cause and effect. His mind kept probing for places where the path of events might have diverged if circumstances had been different. If, on their first visit, Hunter had not taken a camera to the palace's upper floor; if Chowdhury had been warned of the decision to return to the riot scene; and, worst of all, if Matt had not talked Ajay out of going off as bidden to spend the day on the other side of the city.

All these thoughts were still rattling around in his head when, later in the morning, he knocked at Charlie's door, ready to meet Ajay's father, who had come to Calcutta to claim his body.

Mr Gupta proved to be a dry stick of a man whose chief visible emotion was bafflement at his son's involvement with people from the film industry.

Charlie had come out of seclusion to meet him and both Matt and Kate had asked to be present. Girish, too, had insisted on being included. Over tea in Charlie's suite, they did their best to describe the circumstances of Ajay's death.

'You see, he was trying to save me.' Kate's voice strained in an attempt to make an impression on Mr Gupta's stern bewilderment.

'He was very brave. And good. A good person,' said Matt. 'We all liked and admired him very much.'

An exasperated Girish chipped in, trying to fracture the formality and get to the essence of things. 'To be honest, Mr Gupta, in the beginning I was thinking your son was a prig. But I was wrong. It was simply that he took his time in making up his mind about people. We became firm friends.'

Mr Gupta's gaze took in Girish's pale green silk shirt open far enough to show a hint of curling chest hair, the white jeans and black and silver Nike trainers, and his narrow face creased with the effort of understanding.

'I wanted him to be a teacher,' he said finally, 'but it was politics that interested him.' He repeated the word in disgust. 'Politics. He had all sorts of ideas. We had many arguments . . .' The sternness returned and he looked about him, giving up on understanding and resorting to politeness. 'You are all being very kind. I must go now. There is so much to do.'

Matt pursued him to the door, seeking one last chance to explain Ajay to his father—a presumptuous act as he realised when Mr Gupta turned large, sad eyes on him. 'My son and I had just begun to write to one another again. I'm not yet sure whether that makes his death easier to bear or not.'

PART THREE

2

She woke at three. The green figures on the dial were the first things she saw as she moved from sleep into a panic which pitched her back into the crowd in front of the Peacock Palace to witness all over again the killing of Ajay.

When he had reached her, she had been drowning in the crowd—so dizzy she had been on the verge of fainting. He'd come swimming out of the mass of bodies, bobbing and ducking at such a rate that he caught her as she fell. He'd grabbed her hand, and she'd felt borne up, as if they might take off and float to safety.

But his strength, his lightness of spirit had not been enough. Out of nowhere had come the man with the club, his arm swinging to a rhythm so regular and unalterable that it seemed to have been set in some place far beyond ordinary human impulse. She had looked right into his face and all she could understand was the intensity of his rage.

Then she saw that she and Ajay were not alone in the crowd—that Matt was with them. And the rest was a blank until the moment when Ajay was set down on the floor of the palace and his blood was everywhere. Red, that brash, gaudy, good-time colour. She would never see it again without remembering its slick brightness against the pale marble.

All his strength was gone, all his hope, and he seemed so absurdly young that it was all she could do not to turn away. The terror and sadness of his eyes had been too much, but she hung on and she and Matt hovered over him, patting and stroking like grieving parents.

The moment of his death had been more terrible than anything. The contorted face, the struggle for breath and the final rattling sigh of pain and defeat.

Matt told her to come round straight away. He was waiting for her in the corridor. Struggling into his bathrobe, only half-awake. As soon as she saw him, she started to cry.

'Hey, it's all right. Come on.' He drew her inside. 'You're shivering. I'll get you a blanket.'

He tried to lead her to a chair but she didn't want to sit down. Involuntarily, ridiculously, she followed him to the cupboard, standing close by while he took down the blanket. When he wrapped it around her, she held on to him and couldn't let go.

'It's shock,' he murmured. 'Delayed shock.'

He told her what she wanted to hear—that they had done all they could for Ajay; that no one could have done more; that it was fate, rotten bloody fate.

When the shivering continued, he started pulling more blankets out of the cupboard and spreading them on the bed. 'Lie down and I'll take the armchair.'

Obediently, she got into bed and let him tuck the blankets around her, but it did no good. Her whole body shook—even her teeth, chattering so comically that she felt herself overcome by laughter.

He said it was hysteria. 'I think I should get the doctor.' She calmed herself long enough to tell him he mustn't.

'I can stop. See.' To prove it, she sat up and the blankets fell away, making the shivering worse.

Matt looked stricken, as if he thought she might die.

She tried a reassuring smile. From the look on his face, its effect must have been fearsome.

'I'll ring for more blankets.'

'No, just sit here with me.'

He made her lie down again and perched on the edge of the bed. She grasped his hand and watched him anxiously, afraid of falling asleep in case he moved off to sit in the armchair. Any prospect of peace seemed mysteriously linked to his presence.

'You know, in spite of everything, Ajay was still a Hindu,' he said. 'He believed in karma. At the end, he would have felt . . .' The sentence dissolved. He made another effort to finish it. 'I mean, there would have been some . . .'

'It's all right. We don't have to talk.' The chattering teeth made her stutter. 'You lie down too. Then we can sleep.'

They lay demurely, separated by a layer of blankets, his body no more than a consoling pressure felt against her back.

'I liked Ajay so much,' she said, as they drifted off to sleep. 'I hope he knew.'

'He knew.'

Matt had expected her to disappear before dawn, and to wake thinking he had dreamt the whole thing. But she was still there, sitting wrapped in the blanket in the armchair by the window.

'I'm sorry,' she said. 'You must have thought I was mad.'

'No, really. How are you feeling?'

He might have been asking her if her cold was better. Hunter would have known how to break through, he thought bitterly. If Hunter had been there, the mood would have been precisely as Hunter wanted it.

He hated Hunter. Lethal hatred. And since killing was out of the question, he wanted to do the next best thing and tell Kate all about Hunter kissing Tina in the grounds of the Meenakshi Temple.

'Kate,' he said, then stopped. How to go about it? I think there is something you should know. For your own good? How po-faced. For my own good. That's what he would really mean. For my future happiness I want you to forget Hunter and love me.

'Yes?' She was waiting for him to go on, with a grateful, sweet-natured look on her face that made his heart break.

'Last night—I'm glad you thought of me. I . . .' He stopped again. She was already rising from the chair, escaping his embarrassment.

Trailing her blanket, she came across, bent down and kissed him lightly on the cheek. The kind of kiss which proclaimed him a good, reliable friend. They were pals. The thought made him want to throw up. Hopelessly, he watched her leave.

3

Charlie found the spiciest dishes on the menu and, after a long consultation with the waiter, announced that he was feeling a little better. He doubted the wisdom of telling Kate about the kiss between Tina and Hunter. After all, it might have been a one-night stand. It was a sexy place, the Meenakshi Temple. In its own way.

Matt felt the familiar weight of the old, debilitating pessimism, then he threw it off. 'No,' he said, stubbornness renewed. 'I want her to know. She should know.'

Charlie sipped his beer. 'Tina's not his type . . . at least . . . Hell, how do I know what his type is?'

'You've known him all your life.'

'He's changed.'

The night before, Charlie had been up late having discussions with Milton and Dennis, who had been about to fly back to Los Angeles. During the attack that killed Ajay, crucial footage had been exposed, and even the magazine containing the film of Fletcher's death scene had been smashed. Appalled by the violence, Dennis had wanted to abandon all plans for incorporating Hunter's riot scenes into the film. To the amazement of all but Tina, Hunter would not give up the idea.

'The thing is, Hunter's got the knack of putting the nasty bits out of his mind,' said Charlie. 'That's where I come in. Came in. I took care of them.'

Depressed by the restaurant's staid, sombre atmosphere, Matt recklessly poured more beer, although he had been drinking for hours. Charlie's willingness to do Hunter's dirty work mystified him.

'I liked the bastard, believe it or not,' said Charlie. 'And I'm a good organiser. I'm proud of that. I like having a million things on the boil at once.'

Matt, the obsessive, one-task-at-a-time man, shook his head in distaste as Charlie plunged on: how he had loved setting up this picture. Okay, so India was a producer's nightmare. To him, that was a great incentive. He liked the place. And now he knew it. Really knew it. His voice dropped. Matt had

PART THREE

to listen hard. 'Hunter doesn't. To Hunter, it's still a frigging fairyland. It shows. It shows in the picture.'

'I know, but I didn't think you did.'

Charlie admitted that he'd done his best to keep his opinion to himself. 'But Hunter twigged. Anyway, Tina was in there white-anting me. She's as wild as he is. No nerves. No scruples. As hard as nails.' Smiling grimly, he admitted his hatred. 'Never felt that before. Bloody scary.'

Matt was so pleased by Charlie's confessions that he felt an uncharacteristic desire to be rational about Hunter. He tried to sum up a host of contradictory impressions. Hunter always seemed so detached, even reasonable. He reconsidered. 'It's just camouflage, isn't it?'

Charlie briskly dismissed these meanderings. Hunter did what Hunter wanted. That was all you had to know about him. There was only one way to stop him—come up with something he'd want to do more.

Matt brought them back to the subject of Kate. Did Hunter really love her?

Charlie found a cigarette in his shirt pocket, thought about lighting it with a match from the book on the table, then changed his mind and tore it in half, littering the table-cloth with shreds of tobacco. 'Hard to believe,' he said.

Matt's head cleared and it suddenly seemed very important that Charlie should talk to Kate. Not tomorrow or the next day, but there and then. 'A proper talk, Charlie. You owe it to her.'

Charlie got no answer when he telephoned Kate's room, nor when he tried again half an hour later. He and Matt were crossing the garden courtyard in search of her when a familiar figure came out of the darkness.

Matt was the first to recognise him. 'Mr Singh?'

Before Matt could draw back, Singh had grasped his fingers in an eager handshake. 'Mr Matthews, Mr Wells. We are just leaving. What a pity. Mr Joshi and I have been having a meeting with Mr Hunter and Miss Epstein. Miss Conroy was also with us but she developed a headache and has gone upstairs to rest.'

This time when they called Kate's room, she answered instantly. A few minutes later, she joined them in Charlie's room, sweeping in with such rapid, angry steps that to Matt the air around her seemed to hiss and ripple.

She wore a small square of sticking plaster over the cut near her hairline, and without make-up her features seemed ill-defined, except for her eyes, which shone with a fixed brightness.

'What's happening downstairs?' Charlie had been stimulated by her mood and moved about the room with some of his old energy.

'I couldn't bear it. I had to come away.' She said that Joshi was blaming an anti-government group for the riot. 'The same one that he invented before, I think. He knows about the film Hunter took of the first riot . . .'

'How?'

She glanced at Matt without really seeing him. 'He claims the word had got round, the rioters heard and that's what brought them back.'

To Matt it now seemed bizarre that they had ever imagined outsmarting Joshi. From the outset, he would have regarded the production as heaven-sent—a plaything available for manipulation and exploitation as long as it was in his vicinity. He would long ago have planted a man among the Indian crew members.

Charlie was still doubtful. There was a chance they could be wrong.

'No. It was Joshi.' Conviction made Kate's voice sound harsh and strange. 'The man who killed Ajay . . . I thought I'd seen him before. And tonight, just before I came in here, I remembered. He was in the front garden of Joshi's house the day we went to lunch.'

Hunter had given her a spare key to his room, and she waited for him in an armchair by the window, hands in lap, mind in neutral. She felt grateful for this detachment, a relief from the obsessive imaginings of the past hours.

She gazed around the room—at Hunter's cardigan draped over a chair; at the neat stack of CDs; the book beside the bed. These familiar objects, which had endeared themselves to her as intrinsic parts of his portable world, were no longer symbols of stability, only self-containment. She shuddered.

At the sound of his key in the lock, she drew herself up stiffly in the chair, and as he came through the door, wearing his usual uniform of well-washed denim, she observed him dispassionately as if compiling impressions of a stranger.

He was humming to himself—a barely audible buzz of elation that animated his movements and transformed long-legged grace into bustling self-satisfaction. The humming stopped when he saw her.

'Are you okay?' He knelt by her chair, gazing up at her, anxious to please. 'I was worried about you.'

'Were you?'

He apologised for the presence of Joshi and Singh. 'I tried to phone your room to warn you, but you were already on your way down.'

'How did it end?'

In deference to her mood, he had subdued his excitement. 'We came to an arrangement.'

She supposed Ajay hadn't been mentioned. He grasped her hand in both of his. She felt part of a tableau: The Marriage Proposal. Perhaps the same thought occurred to him, for he rose and began striding about the room in a pantomime of earnest self-examination.

'We've been through this a million times. I know how you feel about me at the moment. I don't blame you for that. But this is it for me. My big chance. There won't be another one. For you either. And if getting it right means dealing with a crook like Joshi . . . well, the prospect's repellent, I know . . . but there it is.'

Kate continued to be surprised by her own calmness—the heavy nervelessness of arms and legs, the unchanged rhythm of her breathing. 'I've got more to tell the police,' she said.

'I've remembered something . . .' She still had hopes of shaking him with her certainty.

As she went on, Hunter stopped pacing and, with startling swiftness, his expression was transformed. Excitement dissolved into hostility. 'You can't.'

'Hunter, I have to. You know I do. What about Ajay's father? What about the things you said to him?'

In the end it had been Hunter who had managed to make Mr Gupta understand something of Ajay's life with the production. Hunter's grave face as he had talked about the responsibility he felt as a foreign artist trying to depict India's complexity; how Ajay had helped; how much they had all relied upon him. 'We admired your son very much. He did a lot to help us understand. He was a good and serious man.'

They had all talked of Ajay's goodness, but no one had thought to mention his seriousness. The one word that Mr Gupta had wanted to hear. His sad face seemed to lighten at the sound of it. At last someone was speaking of the son he knew. 'We will do everything we can,' Hunter had said, 'to help find the man who killed him.'

Once again he dropped to his knees, but this time did not take her hand. 'Listen to me, what were you doing before you got this part? You were making a mess of your life. That's what you were doing. Miss Vague and Highly Sensitive pissing it all away. Hopeless unless directed otherwise. Well, now you've got a director. Me. And I'm telling you to keep away from the damn police and anybody else you feel like confiding in until I get this picture finished.'

He grasped her elbow and pulled her to her feet. His face was flushed with anger. 'Now be a good girl and go to your room because I need sleep and so do you.'

4

Girish had been watching television in his room and, after showing them in, threw himself back on the sofa and sulkily grasped the remote control to call up an anaesthetising montage of video images. Kate removed the device from his grasp and switched off the set. He looked at her resentfully.

She spoke without hesitation, noticing Matt's flash of curiosity at the cold, flat, uninflected tone with which she pronounced Hunter's name. She had told no one about the throbbing sense of outrage she felt. She didn't want to talk about it. She wanted to act on it.

When she had finished telling Girish what she wanted him to do, he sighed so heavily that his swelling chest strained the buttons of his shirt. 'Such confusion. I'm such a great admirer of Hunter's judgment. He's the director, after all. He and Tina set great store in this new ending.'

'Girish,' said Kate. 'There's no guarantee that there won't be more trouble. If we go back to the palace, someone else could be killed.'

Girish turned mournful eyes on her, insisting he thought of nothing else but wondering if he were merely afraid for himself.

Kate smiled. 'There is one more thing. I want you to come with me while I explain how I feel to Tina.'

He took another deep breath, acknowledging this prospect as an even greater challenge than the one under consideration.

5

How to persuade Ward? Matt said Kate should leave it to him. 'Things have gone too far between you two. He won't listen.'

She was reluctant to give in. There were things she wanted to say to Ward. She wished to find words to acknowledge the world they shared before the cameras; to tell him how badly she had felt when Hunter had spoilt their scene together in the Meenakshi Temple. But Matt was right. It was too late.

Ward was having a late breakfast in his room after a visit to the hotel's health club. He looked pink-faced and pleased with himself. Mopping at his face with the white towel draped around his neck, he waved Matt to a chair and sat down in front of a plate of bacon and eggs.

Matt glanced around the room, which was very neat except for a clutter of papers by the telephone. Beside Ward's beloved fax machine was a photograph of a pretty girl with a brilliant Californian smile.

'My daughter.' Ward's tone was indulgent but dignified. 'Grew up with her mother. Now she's talking about wanting to live with me. *Kids*. Anyway . . .' His eyebrows twitched in slight puzzlement at what he was about to confess. 'It'll be good to get back to her.'

So Ward had a life—something more than the consolations of vanity. A serious life. Matt thought this could be helpful.

Ward was daintily removing rind from his bacon.

'Kate's decided not to do any more work on the picture,' said Matt.

Suddenly attentive, Ward asked about her contract.

Matt told him the truth—that she had conferred with her agent and been told that she'd already fulfilled the terms of employment.

Ward chewed steadily, considering. 'I didn't think she and Hunter would last.'

Achieving a careless shrug, Matt went on to reveal their suspicions about Joshi and the riot. 'She thinks we should be telling the police instead of throwing more money at him.'

Ward was silent. Matt fancied that he could follow the progress of his thoughts. He imagined him comparing the film's old ending with the new ones forming in Hunter's head, reviewing his feelings towards Tina; looking forward to the comforts of home.

'I was never as crazy about the new ending—excuse me, endings—as Tina is,' he said finally. 'She thinks the sun shines out of Hunter's asshole. But I don't know, those guys from Acorn seem pretty convinced.'

'Who says?'

'Tina.'

'Does she?' Matt was seized with an authorial urge to regain control of the plot. 'Well, they're not.' He retailed the news of Acorn's disapproval, tossing Dennis's name around with all the brio of a Hollywood insider. Dennis wasn't sold on Fletcher's demise, and he, personally, agreed. 'The audience has been led to expect an upbeat ending. If Fletcher croaks they're going to feel cheated—as if somebody's switched plots on them.'

Ward was amused, saying he'd been wondering when Matt was going to start sounding like a writer. 'I've been thinking to myself, this guy isn't human. Hunter's throwing all sorts of shit at him and he's still coming back for more.'

'Enough's enough.'

Ward continued to smile. 'In my experience, a writer's judgment is not all that great when it comes to his own script.'

Matt steered the conversation away from fiction and back to the real-life dangers of a return to the Peacock Palace, then, risking a final touch of melodrama, let his gaze drift across to the photograph of Ward's daughter and settle there.

6

Charlie surprised them by volunteering to join the party, persuading Ward to be present, even telephoning Tina to arrange the meeting. When she came on the line, Charlie gleefully held the receiver away from his ear. Her voice could be heard all over the room.

'She's been missing me.'

'What did you say?' shouted the voice.

'I said we're coming straight round.'

As soon as Kate saw her, she realised how much she was looking forward to what she was about to do. Tina was using an office in the studios they had hired in Tollygunge. She had a cigarette clamped between her teeth and was about to make a telephone call but dropped the receiver back into its cradle as soon as they entered the room.

'For Christ's sake, Charlie. Where have you been?' She

glanced at Matt but avoided Kate. Since their return to Calcutta, there had been no more bantering conversations, no more girl talk.

'What is this?' Tina had just taken in the fact that Ward and Girish were also squeezing into the tiny office.

There was brief hiatus as they all looked for somewhere to sit. Ward and Kate were given chairs; Charlie perched on the edge of Tina's desk, obviously amused that she had to raise her eyes to speak to him. Hemmed in, Tina reached for the telephone again. 'I think Hunter should be here for this.'

He came straight round from his office along the corridor and did a mock double-take at the door. 'What's this?'

Tina shrugged. 'Ask them.'

Kate seized her moment, beginning with her refusal to return to the palace and ending with her intention to go to the police. Tina's interruptions made it easier for her to avoid Hunter's eye. He stood against the wall behind Tina's desk with his arms folded.

'You won't work again,' said Tina, her voice rising. 'Everybody in the business is going to know you're trouble.'

In the corridor, eavesdroppers hovered, their reflected outlines visible through grimy bubble glass, their murmured words drifting over the plywood partition.

Hunter asked Tina if she'd finished. His blunt tone made her blink. 'I'd like to say something.'

As Tina subsided, he turned towards Kate, pitching his voice so low that they might have been the only people in the room. 'We're doing the reshoot first thing in the morning. We work all tonight if necessary, setting up. We'll be there, with or without you, no matter who you talk to or what you do . . . And Tina's right incidentally. We'll let people know about your lack of professionalism.'

He addressed the room. 'Now I think we should all disperse and get on with it.'

'Hang on,' said Matt. 'Jake has something to say.'

Ward had his head down, studying his fingernails. Kate had been conscious of him beside her, withholding judgment. At the sound of his name, he looked up, startled.

Before he could answer, Girish interrupted, asking how they could possibly reshoot without Kate.

'You'd be surprised,' said Hunter.

Girish persevered. 'But how exactly?'

Looking bored, Hunter explained that not all the palace footage had been destroyed. 'We already have some scenes with her. And there are always stand-ins, Girish. I don't have to show her fully—just suggest her presence. It's Fletcher's death scene we're interested in. We can do without the rest. We can fake it.' As he talked about the sleight-of-hand involved, he ceased to look bored and became increasingly absorbed by the intricacies of the tricks he was about to perform.

Kate understood. It was the irony of the situation that excited him. She felt it, too. Rage brought tears to her eyes. She blinked them back and saw that Hunter's maddening composure camouflaged a sense of betrayal as fierce as her own. They glared at one another. Love had been turned on its head.

Matt and Charlie pursued Ward back to his hotel room. Charlie was still high on the scene in Tina's office, but it was Matt who kept the pressure up.

'Just tell me why.' He dragged his chair across to Ward's so that they were almost knee to knee.

'I'll tell you one thing.' Ward's dry laugh had a revealing note of self-congratulation. 'It's not because of Tina.'

'What then?'

Ward invoked the old reason—professionalism. To Matt, there seemed something religious in his refusal to look beyond it. For him, Hunter and professionalism seemed to have merged. His own personal godhead. No matter how many times Matt went over it all, Ward doggedly returned to the fact that Hunter was still the director. Finally, he shook his head, leaned back against the chair and closed his eyes.

Charlie, who had lit a forbidden cigarette, batted at the smoke guiltily. Matt continued to stare into Ward's impassive features. In frustration, he made a face—rolled his eyes, twisted his mouth out of shape, gave Ward the finger, willed him to open his eyes and look.

Charlie started to laugh, then to giggle uncontrollably. At last, he managed to splutter, 'Let's go and have a drink.' Ward's eyes opened instantly.

'You go down. I'll join you,' said Matt.

As the door closed behind them, he picked up the phone and asked for Frank Lipscombe's room.

7

Early next morning, Matt took a taxi to the Peacock Palace. A small crowd was already beginning to gather, but the only sign of the production unit was a trailer parked in the garden. Eventually, he found Hunter inside the building with Andy McCaffrey and a small group of grips and technicians, standing in a circle of light on the spot where Ajay had died. The marble had been scrubbed clean and the chalk marks had been redrawn in readiness for Fletcher's scene.

Matt couldn't stop staring at the chalk marks. Their clear, sweeping outlines were a denial and an affront. He was tempted to dash across the room and try to smudge them out of existence.

For some time, he remained ignored on the darkened edge of the room, then, during a lull in the action, Hunter came over. Once again, he was frustratingly good-humoured and conciliatory. 'No hard feelings, I hope.'

'Oh, Hunter, you are so full of shit.'

'Look.' Hunter led him onto the terrace. 'Matt, you're a good writer, but you're never going to be really good because you don't value your talent. Artists are not nice people. Not the great ones. How could they be? When they're up against the wire, they have to keep remembering that the work's the only thing that really matters. It has to be that way. Why try otherwise? There's no point in being mediocre—although . . .'

Hunter had been regarding Matt with amiable arrogance, the lecturer on sure ground. Now his mouth drooped at the

PART THREE

corners. He looked slightly sorrowful, but only slightly. 'Admittedly, I have found you have to pay quite a high price. The work does rob life of some of its flavour . . .' Again he faltered.

Matt decided to help him out. Despite Hunter's view of his limitations, he was not entirely innocent of sins committed in the name of art. 'You mean it has a way of turning you into an audience at your own performance.'

Hunter had the grace to look a bit sheepish. 'Exactly. Everything at one remove.' He brightened up. 'But you do have the consolation of knowing that no matter how bad things get, nothing is wasted. It can all be used eventually. It makes it so much easier to take risks . . .'

'And so much easier to exploit people.'

'If you like. As I said, the best artists are not nice. They don't have to be.'

The conviction behind his smile made Matt feel chilly just looking at it. There was no more to be said. He reverted to practicalities.

'Where are your actors?'

'Kate's stand-in is in wardrobe.'

'And Girish?'

Hunter's expression changed. He looked annoyed. 'He's late.'

'What about Ward?'

'He'll be here.'

Matt nodded calmly. Inside, he was anything but calm. He wanted to jump up and down chanting, 'I win, I win.' He wanted to give in completely to ignoble, childish joy at Hunter's imminent frustration. Dignity prevented him—and he didn't yet quite believe it. Something could still go wrong. A lifetime of pessimism told him so.

The night before he had hoped that Frank Lipscombe would finally feel free to set his loyalty aside and say what he really thought about Hunter and his plans—hoped but not really expected. He had made his phone call on impulse as a last resort.

Frank was already drunk—much drunker than he'd been at the Umaid Bhawan when alcohol had produced only morose irritation. This time he was really angry. Yes, he'd be delighted to join the group downstairs in the bar, he told Matt. He was just in the mood for a talk.

And once he started, they couldn't have stopped him if they'd wanted to.

There were many causes of his rage and Hunter was at the root of them all. Frank began with Girish's accident and, as he talked, Hunter's errors of judgment multiplied along with other instances of his stubborn disregard for the safety of those working for him. It was a tale so densely packed with technical refinements, with such a complex chain of cause and effect, that Matt had lost his way in it. But Ward hadn't. As Frank talked, weaving patterns of emphasis in the air with his big, meaty hands, Ward had sat for hours taking it all in.

'The business with Girish was the start of it,' said Frank. 'I've worked with Hunter before. We've never had any trouble. Charlie knows that. You could talk to him. But not this time. So I'm telling you, Jake. The last place I'd be tomorrow morning is that bloody palace.'

Ward had been absolved. Hunter was no longer somebody to be feared; somebody with a knowledge of all his faultlines and an ability to turn him into a better, braver person. Hunter was a phoney. With his good ol' boy integrity, Frank had effectively stripped him of his power.

Once he was sure of the outcome, Matt telephoned Kate's room to give her the news. He did not tell her what Frank had said about Hunter. It would have been a graceless thing to do, he decided reluctantly; too much like gloating. He dwelt instead on the existence of Ward's daughter, reason enough for him to accept Frank's warning about returning to the palace.

'We should celebrate,' she said. She had been in bed and still sounded sleepy.

'Definitely. When?'

'What's wrong with now? Come and have a drink with me.'

She greeted him in her dressing-gown with a hug, and as he

breathed in her flowery perfume mingled with the muskiness of sleep, he was aroused with a joyful sensuality that left him light-headed.

While she poured drinks, they talked over all that had happened. Or almost all. Both avoided the question of Hunter and his motives, and after the first intoxicating moments he began to loom between them, an invisible presence, poisoning everything. As always.

Instead of talking about him, they discussed Ward. 'He is gutsy,' said Kate. 'I haven't got his sort of guts. He was right about that.'

Matt wanted to reach out and touch her. He could think of nothing else and for the first time since he came into the room, they fell silent. Finally, she was the one to make a move, crossing the room to sit beside him on the sofa, but when he leaned over to kiss her, she turned her head away.

'I'm sorry. I though I could,' she said. 'I felt so happy when you came in.'

'I know. So did I.'

Once again he assumed his customary role, Mr Nice, The Man Who Understands. 'It's too soon,' he said.

'Maybe.' She attempted a reassuring smile so unconvincing that he rose at once. But at the door, she did kiss him. His cheek burned all the way to the lift.

Back in the bar, Ward was eager to give Hunter the news of his decision straightaway. He wanted to wake him up and quarrel with him. He wanted to make a party of it. Matt wouldn't let him. He had a better idea.

A taxi pulled up at the palace gate, and a moment later Tina emerged and came running across the grass towards them. She lost a sandal on the way and stooped to retrieve it, but was in too much of a hurry to step into it again. She covered the last few yards at a limping trot, waving the sandal like a baton.

Hunter followed her progress, looking blank.

'It's Jake,' she said, coming to a sudden stop. 'The asshole's gone. He flew back to LA an hour ago.'

8

In the flare-lit gardens of the Tollygunge Club, Matt told Kate about his call from Dennis Meyer, turning it into a performance, putting care into his imitation of Dennis's monotone, getting the syntax right, inserting all the pauses and paying special attention to Dennis's well-mannered preliminaries which, on the line from Los Angeles, seemed even more like the learned responses of a friendly alien. In his circumspect way, he had been very upbeat. He wanted Matt to know that he remembered the details of their talk at the Peacock Palace and that he'd meant what he said. Writers were his kind of people. 'As I told you, it's not exactly a popular view in this town.' And he had laughed.

Matt liked the laugh. The laugh was a surprise—a gravelly gurgle with a touch of dryness in its bottom register, which suggested that he had a working knowledge of earthling absurdities, after all.

Another surprise was that he had read Matt's book twice. 'Impressive,' was his judgment. He cleared his throat, signalling that he was about to venture on to delicate ground. 'On the whole, I think things worked out for the best. With the ending, I mean. Hunter's a bright boy. Who knows? We might have taken the new ending to a sneak and the preview audience might have loved it.' This time his laughter had a wholly surprising manic note. 'And I might get struck by lightning standing in front of my office window. No, don't tell Hunter, but I kind of like the picture as it is.' There was talk about release patterns and marketing strategies, then he made the offer.

'Not a firm offer,' Matt told Kate, aware of sounding as if he had swallowed Dennis whole, book reading and all. 'I mean, I know what it'll be like. I'll get over there and he'll

PART THREE

show me something impossible and that'll be the end of it. But what the hell, it'll be interesting to have a look.'

She asked him if he would go straight on to Los Angeles from India.

'Yes.'

'Good.' She was thinking how well action suited him. He had stopped looking like a man marooned and was no longer straining to please. His face was smoother, his smiles went all the way to his eyes.

'We can keep one another company.'

'I don't think so.' His expression was so solemn that she felt a wicked urge to laugh.

'I'm sorry,' she said quickly, trying to cover up, but he wasn't fooled. 'What the hell.' He surprised her by suggesting they dance.

The portable dance floor set up on the lawn was filled with unlikely combinations of people welded together in loving embraces. Girish had his arms wrapped around Melanie, whose head was buried in his shoulder; George was doing a sprightly quickstep with one of the Indian technicians; and several couples had crept away to the dark places under the trees, where all that could be seen of them was the glow of their cigarettes.

Kate had been to the police to tell them about Ajay's murderer. Charlie and Matt had gone with her and waited while she went through the photo file of convicted criminals. The police had promised to interview Joshi about the man, and she had promised to return to Calcutta if they came up with a suspect. Sadly, there was nothing more to be done.

She had not seen Hunter since the meeting in Tina's office and wished she could say that she didn't want to. But she wanted to know more. She wanted to know how she could have been so wrong; wanted to know, but shrank from the anxiety of finding out.

She also wondered about Tina. Could Hunter be in love with her? Possible, and at the same time unimaginable. For one thing, they moved at different speeds, their physical rhythms so out of kilter that their coming together would be less an act of love than a collision between grossly unequal objects. Who would sustain the most damage?

While she had been preoccupied with these thoughts, she and Matt, like everyone else on the dance floor, fell naturally into an embrace. Influenced by the atmosphere. Was this the only reason? Now that they had ceased to talk, she felt detached from him, despite the thickness of his shoulder under her hand and the clasp of his fingers with their pale Irish skin and the fuzz of black hair above the knuckles. The contrast with Hunter's honey-toned smoothness brought on a treacherous stab of physical regret.

'What's wrong?' asked Matt, not so detached from her, after all.

'Let's go for a walk. Over there where it's quiet.'

She took his arm and felt a rush of gratitude and affection. How nice it would be to love him. He was a man who ought to be loved. She felt sad for him. She leant lightly on his arm, its hard muscularity transformed in her mind to something fragile and easily hurt. They walked to the furthest reaches of the garden.

'Tell me, is it really all over between you and Hunter?'

Once again, the reminder that he took her as seriously as she herself did, brought out the worst in her. She laughed, no longer protective, and said distantly that she didn't feel like talking about it.

'Okay, okay. It's not a proposal, or even a proposition. It would simply be nice to know if we could see one another from time to time without me having to put up with the knowledge that you're languishing over bloody Hunter.'

Perversely, she found his annoyance much more acceptable than his sympathy. 'Yes, I want to see you in Los Angeles. I thought I just said so.'

'All right.' He took her hand. 'Let's go back to dancing. It's safer.'

As they returned to the party, Tina and Hunter, close to the edge of the dance floor, stopped dancing and came towards them. Ignoring Matt, Hunter walked straight up to Kate and, without a word, took her hand and led her onto the floor,

PART THREE

leaving Tina looking after them and Matt experiencing an intense attack of déjà vu.

'Come over here and sit down,' said Tina, 'before you throw up.' They found a stone bench under a banyan tree.

'I'm too much of a bitch for him. His nerves can't stand me.'

'His own words?' Matt asked dully.

'Oh, he didn't have to tell me.' Tina hacked at the Tollygunge Club's carpet of emerald turf with a three-inch heel. 'I worked it all out for myself. It wasn't hard.' She sighed. 'Hunter's such a WASP—heart, brains, balls and cock. He's so goddamned calm. You know, I wanted to take Jake apart for dropping us in the shit like that. I was ready to get on a plane and go straight after him. But Hunter just shrugs his shoulders and says, you win some, you lose some. On to the next.' She made another gash in the lawn. 'A noisy Jewish princess like me doesn't have a hope in hell up against an attitude like that.'

'You looked as if you were getting on pretty well to me.'

'Oh, we did it a couple of times, but if you want the truth, it wasn't sensational. No . . .' She cocked her head at him, measuring the distance between them. 'It's Kate he wants. Miss Ladylike. Take a look.' Her gesturing hand shot past his face, just missing his cheekbone, and his gaze swung back reluctantly to the dance floor.

Hunter was reminding Kate of their night on the train when they had wandered out across the stony Rajasthani ground and sat on the boulder under the stars to talk about the films they would make together.

Looking at him now, she saw that he had meant it. The glint in his eye, the quivering tautness of the arm that drew her to him—everything about him told her that he had been as romantic about the prospect as she herself.

In her mind, she had accused him of many things. At her angriest, she decided it was all a lie. The talk of love, marriage, children. The love-making itself. All a lie acted out just to get her through the picture. Now she understood that he did love her; and that he saw a future for them together.

She remembered them sitting together in the grounds of the Victoria Memorial; how she had held up her hands in the shape of the camera lens; how he'd followed her with the lens through the rioting crowd. Perhaps it was then that he'd fallen in love with her. She knew, too, that he would see nothing strange in this; that to him, love and work were indivisible. In his own way, he loved her and he believed that this way was hers, too. In his mind, they were a match. He stood waiting patiently for her to decide.

Tina was giving Matt gratuitous advice. An amusement for her, torture for him.

'Kate's not your type. You'd depress the hell out of one another and she knows it. Has she told you yet?'

'I haven't given her the opportunity.'

This admission brought on The Laugh. It rose in the air, flushing out startled couples from their hiding places under the trees.

Matt thought that he would like something very bad to happen to Tina, something that would silence The Laugh forever. He imagined her struck dumb—sentenced to a lifetime of sign language. He worked on this idea for a moment, cancelling the sign language by adding arthritic fingers.

She had grown bored with his silence and turned her attention back to Hunter and Kate. 'You know, they look kind of right together. Give them a few years and they'll have these nasty little kids who have violin lessons and perfect bone structure.'

Matt had been thinking the same thing. 'Are you ever wrong?'

'My God, the man bites.' She surprised him with a doleful sigh. 'I was wrong about Hunter. I thought he was like me. Wrong, wrong.'

Hunter had gently grasped Kate's arms and held her in a loose embrace as they continued to talk.

'Look at her,' said Tina. 'She's hooked.'

PART THREE

Matt stared at the figures on the dance floor, willing them apart. It was palpable, this effort of will. He was convinced he could see it, shooting out across the grass, laser-like, fantastic, a pure beam of will, his very own special effect. As it reached Kate, his mind's eye enveloped her in it, a pulsing beam of light so dazzling that he wondered why it wasn't lighting up the sky. Then it faded and Kate moved out of the circle of Hunter's arms, crossed the dance floor and walked across the lawn towards the bench under the banyan tree.

EPILOGUE

They had filled the pool at the Oasis Hotel. It glittered in the morning sun, giving off potent fumes which mingled exotically with the smells from the kitchen.

Kate was still looking for film stars. All she could see were a couple of sleek Englishwomen from the rag trade, talking business while fending off the attentions of a portly Tamil in a sarong, who wanted to tell them about his Bombay holiday. Otherwise she had the garden to herself.

After a while, she went to sit on the seawall. The scene was much the same as it had been all those months ago when she had first come to Juhu. The snake-charmer was cursing some fleeing tourists and the boys were swimming their horses in the flat grey waters.

There were no Russians. Instead, Matt was standing on the shore, in close communion with her old friend, the boy with the bent-back finger. As she watched, the pair of them crouched on their haunches and Matt started drawing patterns in the sand. The boy seemed hypnotised by the symbols, whatever they were. Matt could have been confiding the secret of eternal life.

They had arrived at the Oasis the night before from Los Angeles for the film's Indian premiere. Matt had wanted to go straight to the Taj but she had insisted on the pilgrimage to Juhu. She didn't really know why it seemed important and he didn't press her.

They had finished shooting the film six months earlier, and for the past four, she and Matt had been living together.

EPILOGUE

The world's most tentative lovers. To go to bed together for the first time they'd had to get drunk. Then more weeks went by before she had asked him to stay the night. Next came a weekend; and after another cautious interval, a week in New York. Finally, full of promises that he'd leave at the first hint of things going sour, he moved out of his apartment and into her house in the hills.

He came with just two suitcases and three boxes full of books and CDs. The taxi-driver helped him unload them. Two months in Los Angeles and he still hadn't bought a car.

'This is it?' she asked in disbelief, staring down at the scuffed canvas hold-alls and tatty bundles of cardboard and string dumped on her doorstep.

'It was a furnished apartment. I didn't need much,' he said stiffly, as if she were passing judgment on his whole life. He unpacked in silence, stowing everything so expertly that she could hardly tell it was there. He was like someone who had spent years in prison.

Gradually, she encouraged him to spread, seeing it as a challenge. She cleared out a room and took him shopping for a word processor he said he didn't need but wanted desperately as soon as he saw it. He wrote at night, coming to bed in the early hours of the morning.

She often thought of Hunter—memories which still held their glamour, shimmering with a sexual regret divorced from everything else she felt about him. On another level, she regarded him as a bad accident from which she had been lucky to escape with her sanity. She didn't like to think what might have happened if Matt hadn't been there.

Their life together yielded up odd, endearing discoveries. She learned that some of his fears were even sillier than her own. He believed everything ever written about the dangers of living in Los Angeles, and if she were fifteen minutes late getting home, greeted her like someone back from the dead. He worried about muggers and earthquakes, and the sound of the branches scraping against the roof at night got into his dreams, transformed into the creaking timbers of ghost ships and haunted houses.

Happily, he enjoyed being laughed out of these fears, and she enjoyed being the comforter for a change.

He was working for Dennis Meyer. Uncle Dennis, as they referred to him in a wary, jocular tone, reminding themselves that there was still plenty of time for him to prove too good to be true. But for the moment, Dennis had them firmly under his wing. Every morning Matt went off to working sessions in Dennis's garden—the only one in the neighbourhood without a pool—where they were busy on a script designed to become the first step in Dennis's grand plan to bring back the cinema of literate dialogue. Kate had a stake in it too, for she was to play the lead—a svelte, cosmopolitan type without a worry in the world and a wardrobe worth keeping at the end of the picture.

Neither she nor Matt was sure about the future that Dennis was mapping out for them—they just knew that he was giving them necessary breathing space. At night when Matt stayed up writing, he was not working for Dennis but himself. Making notes for a new novel, which he jubilantly showed her each day.

She, on the other hand, was learning how to be happy when not working.

Early next morning, they checked out of the Oasis and took a taxi into the city.

The roadside *bustees* looked like bomb-sites, little more than dust and ashes, but as they got closer to the city, people began to emerge miraculously from what seemed like nothingness. People in clean white cotton and rainbow colours, some with papers and briefcases, all with a look of purpose, going about their business.

At the Taj, Girish was waiting. He had woken early to welcome them and, as soon as they got through the doors, was ready with handshakes and embraces. 'So much to talk about. Quickly, check in. Then you must let me buy you breakfast. I have rung Charlie's room.' His smile gleamed, still vibrant with the urge for mischief. 'You know what he's like in the morning. But he'll be here.'

Charlie arrived in time for eggs and coffee, managing to look grumpy and pleased at the same time. 'So here they are at last. The lovebirds.'

They all cast appraising glances at one another. Girish remarked that Matt's pallor had been coloured by the beginnings of a West Coast tan, that Charlie was not smoking and had lost weight, and that Kate's hair, which was back to its old length, suited her so much better than Susie's lacquered spikes.

'You are quite transformed. Although you're looking marvellous in the film, of course. I've already seen it by the way. They put on a special screening for me in Calcutta.'

'And?' asked Charlie.

Girish's eyes shone. Kate observed his new sophistication. His shirt was fine white cotton instead of coloured silk and only one button was undone instead of three. Even so, he had retained his feral look. Streetwise as ever, he darted quick, covert glances around the room as he talked, checking on passing traffic.

'Oh, I couldn't be more pleased. It's done me no end of good already. The word has been out for weeks. I am getting so much work you'd be amazed.'

After breakfast he said he had something to show them. He would say no more and directed their taxi-driver along Marine Drive towards Chowpatty Beach. Just before they reached the top of Malabar Hill, they veered right and plunged down a steep hill towards an intersection choked with traffic spilling from half a dozen different directions.

It took Kate a moment to life her gaze from the honking tumult around them and another moment to recognise Girish's face in the huge painted profile suspended above. The black hair was flecked with gold, the wheatish complexion daubed with patches of light and shade to make nostrils flare and cheekbones jut. He wore gold earrings and his bicep swelled above a carved armband hanging with gold chains.

The flesh and blood Girish laughed in delight at the collective shout of recognition. 'What do you think? Not bad for a Bengali boy, is it?'

The driver looked up at the hoarding, glanced at Girish, and as he made the connection, the taxi slid into the car in front of them and came to a clattering, tinkling halt as bumper bars buckled and headlights shattered. Doors slammed and the two Sikh drivers advanced on one another, fists raised.

'Oh, oh,' said Girish, and went after them.

A crowd was already gathering, but as Girish reached the quarrelling men, their driver dropped his fists, laid one hand on Girish's shoulder and with the other pointed up at the giant profile.

Heads turned, there were smiles and nods, and for a moment, it seemed to Kate, the world stopped as everybody contemplated the god-like image suspended in the murky air.

BEYOND BERLIN
Penelope Nelson

'swift-moving and energetic . . . Nelson is behind her stage and in control.'
Sydney Morning Herald

For Libby Milroy, 1970 is a year of political protest, sexual obsession and self-discovery. Arriving in Berlin at the height of the international student rebellion, she is intoxicated by the excitement that the city seems to promise. So much so that she ignores the warning signs as people close to her move from street protests to the politics of terrorism.

Twenty years later, she is asked to confront the loyalties and dilemmas of her youth and be ready to make some tough decisions about the future.

1 86373 847 9

SWIMMING IN SILK
Darren Williams

Winner of the *Australian*/Vogel Literary Award

'Highly evocative . . . what captivates is the landscape.'
Jill Kitson

'The writing is an absolute pleasure, creating an atmosphere that draws the reader in.'
Marele Day

Brilliant skies, sudden storms, black nights and a ramshackle house that is disintegrating into the rainforest. Sheltering from their pasts, Cliff, Susan, Daniel and Jade experience a few oddly idyllic days and nights together in the small coastal town two of them call home and to which the others have returned.

Swimming in Silk is an extraordinarily evocative and sensual novel about the mysterious and intricate relationship between people, the elements, and the land in which they live.

1 86373 849 5

BRACELET HONEYMYRTLE
Judith Fox

Shortlisted in the *Australian*/Vogel Literary Award

'Wonderfully sustained . . . the sense of fulfilment achieved in simple reflection is marvellous.'

Jill Kitson

'A splendid, moving book.'

Andrew Reimer

Annie Grace is an old woman. She tends her garden, and cares for a baby, her great great-niece, Kimberley. It is a quiet life.

Born into a strict Christian family in Sydney at the start of the century, Annie contends with an overbearing mother and a harsh religion. Yet something stirs under the starch of faith. Annie finds a friend late in life and discovers a passion for living to equal her passion for gardening. In her sixties, Annie confronts her mother.

This is the story of one woman's struggle to lay claim to her own life. And within the seemingly narrow contours of family and church and garden, Annie discovers that it is, after all, a big life.

1 86373 850 9

A MORTALITY TALE
Jay Verney

Shortlisted in the *Australian*/Vogel Literary Award

'Like flood, heat, age and guilt this book creeps up on you—forcing you to take notice.'

Jennifer Rowe

One rainy night Vincent Cusack appears, briefly, lit up for one final, fatal moment in the headlights of Carmen Molloy's car. Carmen is unquestionably an honourable woman, yet is able to drive on home and to be apparently shocked and saddened by news the next day of Vincent's untimely death.

In an exceptionally witty, perceptive and challenging literary debut, Jay Verney teases readers with fascinating 'What if?' questions as Carmen hosts Vincent's wake, avoids police questioning, battles a chorus of internal voices—and promises herself she can get away with the most disturbing of crimes.

1 86373 669 7